HALL OF INFAMY

by

AMANITA VIROSA

Published by **CHIMERA** (aka the **BEAST**)
ISBN 9781780806679

A WELCOME AND A FAREWELL

'Oh, look, Amelia, the hawthorn is in bloom!'

The hedgerows that sped by the carriage window were dusted with white blossom, but Amelia gave them only a cursory glance. She regarded Clara through heavy-lidded eyes and gave a bored yawn. 'Really, Clara, I do wish you would stop bouncing up and down. One would think you had never been to Hatherby before!'

The fact was that the countryside, the rolling hills, the thickly wooded hollows and neat hedgerows exhilarated her, too, with its magical aura and half-forgotten familiarity. But the Honourable Amelia Colinbrooke was a dignified young lady of nineteen, educated and extremely conscious of her position. She most emphatically was not a giddy girl to be over-excited by the prospect of release from finishing school. Therefore she shook her head pityingly at Clara, reminded herself that her cousin was only just eighteen, and turned her attention back to her novel, leaving the younger girl to press her face to the glass of the window and exclaim excitedly over the commonplace country sights.

Cousin Clara was a pretty, slender girl with innocent blue eyes and rosebud lips so sweet that Amelia sometimes felt the urge... but they were not at finishing school now. The time for those girlish passions was past, along with the disciplinary regime of Madame Chavaroff's Academy.

Amelia had found it very hard at first, but in the final year she had progressed to prefect status, and the opportunity to wield the rod herself had reconciled her to the strictness of the institution. She had ended up a staunch supporter of corporal correction, and watching Clara fidget made her regret that the opportunity for its infliction was now past. Amelia had only infrequently had the opportunity to make her cousin strip and bend before her prefectorial cane, but she could still see Clara's plump bottom and slender thighs...

Amelia shifted on her seat, regretting that she had laced her stays so tightly. The May sun was brilliant and it was getting uncomfortably hot in the carriage. She took a lace-trimmed handkerchief from her purse and wiped her brow, turning her gaze from Clara's tiny satin-encased waist to the window, and hastily resolving to think about something else.

The view was changing now, the pastures and hedgerows giving way to thicker woodland, until the train was passing through a deep forest. Suddenly, Amelia felt apprehensive, and even Clara became quiet. It was as if the woods evoked some long-buried memory, as if something sinister and ancient lurked in this remote part of the country. Clara's big blue eyes blinked at her anxiously, the pretty lips forming a questioning 'O'. Then the forest opened up again, giving way to sun-flooded fields, and the feeling passed, leaving Amelia smiling wanly at her own foolishness.

'Do you think Jamie will be at Hope Hall too, this summer?'

Clara's transparent attempt to ask this with an air of indifference provoked a derisive snort from Amelia. 'I have no idea. I hope not!'

The last time that the cousins had visited Hope Hall, Clara had developed a serious crush on Jamie Fanshawe, a distant relative. Amelia, on the other hand, had detested the slightly older boy's lack of respect for her, and she had bridled at the liberties he had attempted. Even though they were related, she had decided, Master Fanshawe was very ill bred. The dreamy expression that settled on Clara's countenance at the mention of his name irritated Amelia. The image of Clara's bottom came to her mind again unbidden. By Isis, Amelia thought grimly, I'd put Jamie Fanshawe out of your mind, if I had the opportunity!

To Amelia's relief, she did not know the boy who waited for them with the carriage at the tiny station. If Jamie had been at the Hall, Lady Alicia would most likely have sent him to greet the girls. Instead a burly, tongue-tied boy - a stable-lad, Amelia supposed - collected their trunks from the guard's van and hefted them onto the carriage, before giving his hand to Clara, who blushed foolishly as she allowed him to help her climb into the carriage.

'I can manage, thank you, boy!' Amelia said sharply, noting with a certain satisfaction that the lad flushed a deeper shade of red. Content that she had put him in his place, she settled herself comfortably next to Clara for the short drive from the railway station to the great estate of Hope Hall.

She had forgotten. It had been two years. She had forgotten the awesome aspect of the great walls that encircled the grounds, ancient and encrusted with ivy. She remembered once asking Alex - also her cousin, but much older than her, so she always called him 'uncle' - what the imposing walls had been built for.

Alex had laughed disconcertingly. 'Cattle. They are for keeping in white cattle, I believe.' Why this should cause him such amusement had remained a mystery, like his use of the present tense. There were certainly no wild cattle in the estate any more, if indeed there ever had been.

The hoarse croaks of rooks circling the stately elms beyond the gates brought back memories of the mysteries that seemed to cloak the hall: strange cries in the night, strange looks between the servants, odd clothes and odder objects. Questions answered by infuriating chuckles and, 'All in good time, when you are older,' and sly smiles from her aunt. As the great iron gates were unlocked and opened and the carriage swept on in, Amelia felt goose-pimples rise on her nape and Clara grabbed her hand.

'Amelia... what do you think... will happen?'

Amelia forced a sneer. 'What do you mean, you silly girl?' The gate clanged shut behind them as they sped up the gravel drive, the sound coldly ominous in Amelia's ears. 'We are to stay with Alicia and Alex for the summer. I expect there will be garden parties, hunt balls and fetes.' She took a deep breath, banishing the ridiculous feeling of apprehension with a laugh. 'Yes, I expect there will be lots of village fetes!'

'Really, Mrs Pritchard, I am sure there is some mistake. If I could just speak to my aunt?' Amelia was furious.

The housekeeper, a black-garbed woman in her forties, of ramrod carriage and flinty eye, was unmoved.

'Lord and Lady Feversham are visiting the Hatherby Reformatory. Their instructions were quite explicit. I'm to put you girls in the nursery.'

Miss Pritchard was unsmiling, but something about her demeanour made Amelia suspect that she was enjoying this bitter humiliation of her betters.

'Please follow me. Betsy is drawing baths for you. I expect you will want to change.'

The housekeeper turned, and Clara looked at Amelia. 'Come on Amelia, there's no point in making a fuss. It's probably just a mistake. We can sort it out when Aunt Alicia gets back.'

Miss Pritchard stopped and looked back with what Amelia could have sworn was a smirk. Clara pleaded with her eyes. The stable-lad who held her trunk was looking away, but Amelia was sure the brute was grinning.

Amelia picked up her purse from the carriage seat. 'Oh, very well. I shall come with you now as I do need to change, but let this be clear: I shall not stay in the nursery and I will not be treated as a child!'

The bath had gone some way to soothing Amelia's ruffled composure. She might be too mature to be relegated to the nursery but she had to concede that the half-dozen airy rooms in Hope Hall's fine east wing were comfortably appointed. She even had the bigger bathroom to herself.

This was actually a little disappointing. Amelia would not have objected to an opportunity to reacquaint herself with Clara's slender charms. But at least she was able to luxuriate in the scented water, and she let the fatigue of the long journey dissolve away. As she did so, Amelia soaped her legs, and let her fingers caress the insides of her thighs. She thought of Clara, naked, in the adjoining bathroom, as her fingers reached the lips between her legs. So lost was she that even when she heard the maid enter with her clean clothes, she continued to caress herself lazily, eyes closed, dreamily remembering how her pretty cousin had flinched and whimpered beneath her disciplinary cane.

'Frigging yourself again, Amelia? I see you haven't changed!' The voice was amused and, to Amelia's utter horror, male. Startled from her reverie, she let out a startled shriek and sat up in the bath, clasping her arms in front of herself to cover her full breasts.

'Jamie, get out, get out this instant! This is indecent! Get out, before I tell Aunt Alicia.'

The young man leant against the doorway and smiled insolently. 'Tell Aunt Alicia? Tell your cousin? Tell her what exactly?' he sneered. 'That I caught you busily engaged in self-abuse?'

Amelia felt her cheeks flame even more brightly as Jamie sauntered over to the bath.

'Anyway, it does not matter. Lady Alicia and Lord Alex have put me in charge of the nursery. It is felt that you and Clara need some discipline - you especially. I'm to take you down a peg or two, Amelia!' He bent and caressed her slender neck. 'This summer, I have complete authority here. It is my most welcome task to teach you a little humility.' He kissed her nape.

Amelia quivered in outrage but could not prevent this liberty without exposing her breasts, so she simply hissed, 'Don't touch me.'

Jamie just laughed, and Amelia felt his fingers grasp a fistful of her luxuriant auburn curls. 'Ow!' she shrieked as he hauled her by the hair. The young man heaved her out of the bath and propelled her across the room and through the door, straight into the adjoining parlour, before releasing his grip. Amelia stood naked and dripping, trying to cover both her breasts and sex, blinking back tears of pain and furious outrage.

Clara was standing staring at her, with her eyes wide and cheeks bright red, dressed in a quite extraordinary costume: a little smock of cream silk so thin that Amelia could clearly see her cousin's nipples pressed against the fabric. The frock had only puffy little quarter-sleeves and was so short that its hem barely reached to Clara's crotch, and failed to cover her frilly girlish knickers. In their turn, these were all but legless, and exposed a great deal of slender thigh above the tops of white silk stockings which were gartered just above the knee.

Despite the shamefully revealing nature of the costume, Clara did not emulate Amelia's attempts to cover herself. Instead, the younger girl kept her hands clasped behind her neck as she stood there.

'Where are my clothes?' Amelia demanded, looking from her cousin to the sneering young man. 'I demand to be given my clothes!'

He spread his hands. Amelia had to concede that he was handsome, with his aquiline nose and long, fair, swept-back hair. Jamie was lithely built and turned out in what she supposed was the latest fashion among public school bloods, with an immaculate cravat of blue and silver and a fine black velvet waistcoat. The worst thing was his air of self-assurance. He seemed perfectly relaxed.

Finally, he deigned to answer her. 'Amelia, Amelia,' Jamie sighed. 'Your wish is my command!' He bowed ironically and tugged the bell-pull. Seconds later, a buxom maid bustled in carrying a few flimsy scraps of fabric. Amelia recognised a set of garments identical to Clara's humiliating outfit.

'Never!' she hissed, although her mouth had gone dry, and she could not resist another appalled glance at Clara. 'I am not a child!' She blinked back tears of sheer indignation. 'I will not wear little girl's clothes. I won't! I won't! I won't!'

She had given in, of course; she had had no choice. She had rushed around in a fit of fury but there were no clothes in the nursery. She could hardly have searched the rest of the house, naked as she was - she might have run into servants, even guests, and the thought had been too appalling. It had been bad enough, being naked in the nursery.

Betsy, the nursery-maid, a big buxom girl in a neat grey uniform, had stood waiting impassively. Her pretty, plump face had been close to expressionless but Amelia had understood the twinkle in those brown eyes only too well.

Amelia had sworn revenge but in the end she had allowed Betsy to help her into the flimsy garments. However, she had refused to stand with her hands clasped behind her neck in line with Clara, as Jamie ordered. Instead she had stood, scowling sullenly in the corner, covering her breasts as best she could.

'Amelia, Amelia,' Jamie sighed, but seemed amused rather than exasperated. 'Why can't you be more like your little cousin?'

He opened a tall fitted cupboard to reveal a heart-stoppingly comprehensive selection of whips, straps and sticks. Amelia felt her knees go weak as he thoughtfully selected a four-foot length of yellow cane.

'Kooboo.' Jamie smiled and flexed it experimentally, then slashed the implement through the air. The familiar whooshing sound brought goose-pimples to Amelia's arms. 'I expect you used to employ it at Madame Chavaroff's academy. I believe she has the reputation of using the best materials. No doubt it's been some time since one was used on you.' He turned to the maid. 'The trestle, Betsy.'

The girl hastened to obey, hefting a heavy wooden trestle out of an anteroom and hauling it into the centre of the parlour. The device was topped with a well-worn leather pommel. Amelia regarded the apparatus with horror, knowing all too well the purpose of the thing.

'Now, Amelia, I'd like you to drop your knickers and bend over the trestle for me, if you please.'

Amelia glared at him, her eyes locked onto his in a furious defiant stare. 'Never!' she spat.

Jamie chuckled. 'Never is a long time, my pet. Betsy, go to the stables and ask Mr Blackstock to come and bring a couple of stable-lads. We may need a bit of muscle, and they will enjoy the show.'

The blood drained from Amelia's cheeks. She maintained her glare a little longer. Surely he was bluffing? He would not, could not dare... But she saw no hesitation in his hazel eyes and suddenly she realised that he was perfectly capable of carrying out the threat. Her shoulders drooped and she hung her head, defeated. 'No. Please don't,' she mumbled as a tear rolled down her cheek. 'I'll do what you say.'

'What a pretty arse your cousin has, Clara. Kneel down there - closer, I want you to watch this. You will take her place if you look away. Betsy, hold Amelia's hands; she seems a little skittish. Now, Amelia, I'm going to give you six for cheek and six for disobedience.'

Amelia gave a little gasp as the cane was laid across her bottom-cheeks.

'You don't know how long I've waited for this moment, Amelia, or frigged myself off imagining this scene.' Jamie chuckled, and the cane was lifted. Amelia gave a little whimper of pure terror as the tension mounted. Everybody in the room held their breath but the mantel clock ticked inexorably on.

Whoosh... Thwack!

Amelia tried to fight the shriek but the pain was just too great. It seared across her bottom, forcing a cry from between her gritted teeth. Oh, God, it was worse - much worse - than she had imagined. She could not stand another eleven strokes like that!

Whoosh... Thwack!

Again the blaze of pain.

'Stop wriggling, girl, and keep your legs straight.'

'Ooh! Ooh! Aah!' Amelia sobbed as the pain coursed through her in waves. Blinking away tears, she looked back through her own legs to see Clara kneeling to face her bottom, so close that the cane must have only just missed her face. Clara had a glazed expression, part terror and perhaps part something else, and her eyes were brimming with tears.

Jamie grabbed Amelia's hair, and wrenched her head back until she had to look into his eyes. 'Welcome back, my dear Amelia. Welcome to Hope Hall.'

'Rather thin pickings today, Mrs Fraser.' Lady Alicia peered through her lorgnette at the line of girls who stood trembling and barefoot on the stone flags, wearing nothing but thin cotton shifts. The glasses made her look formidable, but they could not disguise her striking beauty. Lady Alicia Feversham, the Marchioness of Hatherby, wore a long bustled skirt of purple velvet and a matching tightly tailored tunic, adorned with military-style piping. A miniature top hat in purple satin with a ribbon and bow completed the outfit. Emma Swift would have felt abashed in so splendid a presence, even had she been allowed her clothes.

'Well, Alex,' the grand lady continued, lowering her lorgnette again, 'what do you think?'

Her husband lit his cigar, leant back in his chair and swept his gaze along the file of candidates. The Marquis was a big man, handsome and possessed of a splendid set of whiskers. Emma had never seen a man so immaculately dressed before. His Lordship wore a dove-grey morning suit with a silk top hat and matching gloves. His waistcoat was gold and richly embroidered, his cravat a similar hue. Even the yellow horn handle of the riding-whip he toyed with seemed to match. If she had not been too timid and fearful of the consequences, she would have probably just stood and stared.

Seats had been brought and set out for the grand couple in the exercise yard, a cheerless square surrounded on four sides by the grey stone buildings of the reformatory. Furtively, Emma glanced up at the little windows in the wall she was facing, above the visitors' heads. She could just make out the faces pressed against the bars of every dormitory and cell. For the girls incarcerated in the Hatherby and District Reformatory for Females, this was a rare diversion from the usual grim regime.

'They're all good workers, ma'am.' The directress of the reformatory glared fiercely at the dozen young women, and Emma dropped her gaze back to the ground. 'Stand up straight, girls!' She pinched the plump upper arm of a buxom girl with sandy hair. 'Maisie is as strong as an ox, ideal for kitchen work. I understand that that is what you're wanting.'

Lady Alicia gave the woman a slightly disdainful glance. 'Indeed, we do need a kitchen-maid, but I like to give my staff the opportunity for elevation. I want a girl who might be trained as a lady's-maid, eventually.' She raised her lorgnette again to peer at Emma, who stood blushing furiously and kneading her shift in nervous hands. She dropped her eyes, but could feel Lady Alicia's gaze on her breasts, the shape of which the thin shift could not quite conceal, and sense the woman's predatory interest. 'What is that one called?'

'Emma Swift. A pretty little chit, but not the sturdiest we have.'

'How old is she?'

Emma tried to swallow but found her mouth had gone quite dry.

'Just eighteen, ma'am. We've had her about two months.'

'Have you thrashed her much?' The relish in the Lady Alicia's voice made a cold shiver run down Emma's spine.

'Not particularly, ma'am. She gets the birch now and then, as they all do. But she is not particularly wilful or wicked.'

'I see.'

Emma sensed disappointment in her tone, and for a moment thought that she was not going to be chosen. She could not have said if this were more a cause for relief or for disappointment. The chance to leave the grim reformatory was appealing, and the opportunity to get a good position did not come often to girls in her situation. Yet something about Lord and Lady Feversham made her feel a deep sense of foreboding, and she had heard the rumours, dark rumours whispered by the girls in the dormitories at night, about the things that happened at Hope Hall.

'Alex, do you see anything that might suit you or shall we look elsewhere?'

Lord Alex stood and strode over to his wife's side. He studied the girl standing next to Emma, a tall and leggy beauty with a mane of long dark hair.

'This is the girl I wrote of, sir.' The directress hovered eagerly. 'Polly Thomas.'

'Yes, well,' the Marquis said, 'fortunately that is no matter to change. Certainly this is the only filly that might be any use.' His voice was a bored, disdainful drawl. 'She is certainly quite a height.'

'Six foot, near as dammit. She is twenty years of age,' the directress put in.

'Twenty, eh? Hold this!' He handed his crop to Mrs Fraser and removed his grey silk gloves. Seizing the tall girl's upper and lower lips, he forced her mouth wide open and peered inside, to the accompaniment of a startled gurgle. 'Good strong teeth, anyway,' he conceded after a thorough examination. He pulled his gloves back on and took back his crop.

Emma heard a stifled gasp and, glancing sideways, saw that his Lordship was now raising the girl's shift with the handle of his whip, perusing her revealed thighs with an air of weary scepticism.

'Mrs Fraser, I hope you feed your livestock properly. These fetlocks are really rather lean!'

'Polly is fresh off the train, your lordship. We have only had her for three days. I sent word as soon as she arrived, being as you had asked for a long-shanked girl. I do assure you, Lord Alexander—' the directress spluttered on.

'Yes, yes,' Lord Alex interrupted. 'I'm sure, I'm sure... Anyway, I'll take her. She has the length of leg I'm looking for and she looks strong. There should be time to feed and train her up before the Cup. Do you want this little chit as well, Alicia?'

Emma swallowed as the man's riding-crop lifted her chin.

'I rather think so. Lift your shift, girl, let us see what we are getting for our money!'

With cheeks aflame, Emma tentatively lifted the hem of her chemise, mortified that she was revealing naked legs, not only to the grand couple but to the massed ranks of inmates peering down from their cells, yet not daring to disobey the order of so formidable a lady. Even so, part of Emma felt outraged at the order. This usage seemed to her more suited to that of a concubine, displayed on some eastern slave block, than the proper scrutiny of a maid by her prospective employers. Still, she did as she was told, and she did not protest. For one thing, Emma had no wish to renew her acquaintance with the reformatory birch. For another, something told her that Lady Alicia was the sort of lady who would enjoy dealing with rebellion.

'Higher, girl! Right up. I want to take a look at your titties.'

Almost swooning with the shame, Emma hoisted up her garment. She buried her beetroot cheeks in the folds of the shift, and tried vainly to close her ears to the conversation.

'Also a bit skinny, perhaps, but I think she will fill out nicely. What do you say, Alex?'

'Nice high titties, round and firm as peaches. Neat little nipples, shapely legs, trim waist. Should clean up quite a pretty little chit.'

'I believe so. She can start out in the kitchens, helping cook. Since Lucy's elevation, she is always complaining about being short-staffed.'

'We're sadly short of staff all round since we lost Daisy and Grace, of course,' Lord Alex said a little mournfully.

'Yes, well, darling,' his wife said, perhaps a little tartly, 'if you will play cards with blackguards like Jack Campion...' She paused and a fonder note entered her voice. 'I wonder when he's coming back?'

'When he wants, if he hasn't got his head chopped off by some foreign potentate!' Lord Alex said, laughing as he turned to the directress again. 'Very well, Mrs Fraser, how much for the pair?'

'The usual fee for Polly, plus ten guineas for the paperwork. Emma comes a little steeper, I'm afraid.'

'But you said a minute ago that she was not so sturdy,' Lord Alex's deep voice broke in.

'Your lordship, I was not so keen to get rid of her. She is particularly pretty and Justice Ormorund expressed an interest when he sent her down.'

'Oh, he did, did he?' Lady Alicia's rich voice was full of merriment. 'That old lecher goes through maidservants like a fox through a hen-house! Well, I want the girl. The old sot shan't have her - at least, not until he comes to tea. What do you want, then, Mrs Fraser? Name your price.'

'Twenty would compensate for the Justice's displeasure. I think I could interest him in some of the others. She is the prettiest, but he does tend to like them more robust.'

Laughter echoed around the yard: Mrs Fraser's ugly cackle, Lady Alicia's high peal of merriment and her husband's throaty chuckle. Emma kept her face buried in the folds of cotton in her hands and smothered a sob.

'Very well.'

Lord Alexander did not seem too put out at the price, but the cold clink of golden guineas sent a shiver through Emma's soul.

'When can you let us have them?'

'Not till after Sunday. I can't give them their farewells before then. I'd suggest Thursday. Then they won't have to kneel in the carriage the whole way!' The directress guffawed heartily.

Emma felt as if she had been struck. She had thought - at least she had hoped most fervently - that this unlooked-for parole would have spared her the dreaded 'farewell'. A sigh from her side told her that Polly had just seen similar hopes cruelly dashed.

As a minor first-time offender, Emma had been spared the full rigour of the reformatory 'welcome' and 'farewell'; whippings which were administered pitilessly with a stretched bull's pizzle. Even so, her 'gentle welcome', bestowed with a moistened cord cat, had been quite enough to ensure that she slept on her stomach for two nights in a row.

No one had told Emma that she might drop her chemise but the attention of the gentry seemed to have shifted, and so she took the chance to let go of the hem and cover her nakedness again. Fortunately no one took any notice. It was as if she and Polly were insects, peered at briefly by these grand visitors before being relegated once again to utter invisibility.

Mrs Sykes, the wardress, barked an order and Emma turned on her heel in obedience, finding herself looking at the base of Polly's neck. It was, she realised for the first time, a particularly shapely nape, long and elegant with flawless golden skin that contrasted both with the plain white collar of the big girl's chemise and with her tightly bound black hair. A wisp of this had escaped from the bun, and the strands of fine dark hair curling around a single mole on that shapely back seemed strangely sad to Emma.

Yet more poignant, however, was the paler ring of skin encircling the base of her nape. There was no mistaking the mark of a neck-iron, worn by a poor captive trudging, or perhaps labouring, under the hot sun. Well, Polly, Emma thought as the order barked out and they moved off in single file, perhaps life will be kinder to us both from now on!

The file of girls was made to pause at the door of the north wing and stand aside. Solemn young women, clad in the grey uniform of the reformatory, were bringing out equipment. Four girls grunted with effort as they hauled out a heavy birching bench. Other young women trotted glumly past with burdens, birch rods, in their arms. Emma waited with mounting impatience as a second bench was taken out and set down in front of the visitors' chairs. The directress is putting on a show for them, she realised. A pretty girl from Humility Block hurried past, carrying a pail of brine and another full of sponges. The expression on her face, and those of the other grey-clad girls, left no room for doubt who the stars of the imminent performance were about to be.

It was a long way to her dormitory, a journey involving many stairs, and the unlocking and locking of numerous iron gates and doors. Emma fairly itched to get going, but there was nothing she could do but stand and wait. Finally they were told to file back into the building. Emma hurried up the stairway after Polly and the others, hoping she would get back to the dormitory in time, anxious to find a place at one of the barred windows, so that she could see. She could not have explained it if asked. The prospect of a whipping always seemed to have this effect on her. Emma was both appalled and furiously excited. Most of all she was consumed by an almost compulsive sense of curiosity.

'Do you know, I believe we shall get along very well here for the summer, Betsy.' Jamie leant back in his chair and put his hands behind his head with a satisfied smile.

Betsy knew better than to answer him and carried on with her work, tidying away the things that Master Jamie had taken out to use on the young ladies. She hoped his taste for flogging had been sated by the evening's activities. First he had caned Miss Amelia which, Betsy had to admit, she had much enjoyed watching. Then he had spanked Miss Clara, afterward giving her a mere four light strokes with the cane, a count which seemed scarcely adequate to the nursery-maid. He had stayed a long time in Clara's little room, though, and Betsy had heard girlish moans through the door. Surely he must be satisfied for the night?

She picked up the cane and took it to the cupboard.

'No - leave that! We shall want it in a minute. Run down to the drawing room and fetch me a brandy. I shall see to you when you get back.'

Oh, Lord, Betsy thought, her heart pounding as she hurried down the stairs and along the corridor. She was plainly going to be served a portion of rod soup tonight, after all. There was no denying that Jamie was a demon for dishing out the cane, and he seemed to like Betsy's big and all-too-tender bottom particularly as a target. She just hoped she could get the brandy without incident. Swallowing anxiously, she knocked on the drawing room door.

'Enter.' The languid tones of Lord Alexander summonsed her into the room.

Betsy sighed. She had hoped that the Marquis and Marchioness would not yet be back from their visit to the reformatory. She took a deep breath and stepped inside.

'Well, girl, what is it?' Lord Alex was sprawled in a leather-upholstered chesterfield, a balloon of brandy in one hand and a fat cigar in the other. Kneeling before him, and difficult to ignore, was a girl. It was not hard to recognise Lucy, his chambermaid. The girl's brown ringlets and plump bottom were distinctive even from the rear. The latter was quite bare, Lucy having stripped to her white corset and black silk stockings, and her head was bobbing busily about his crotch.

Lady Alicia, resplendent in a gown of crimson silk, was lounging on a couch, a little to one side, idly fingering a long and very slender dressage whip. Several welts, narrow but deep red, already graced the creamy flesh of Lucy's bottom. Betsy knew quite well whence the livid stripes had originated. She studiously avoided Lady Alicia's eyes. Something like this was what she had been afraid of.

'Master Jamie, sir, asked me to fetch him a brandy.'

Lord Alex gave a distracted grunt before waving his cigar towards the decanters. 'Well, get on with it, girl, and be sure to pour the lad a decent measure.'

Betsy hurried over to the cabinet that held the glasses and took a balloon over to the side table that supported the flasks of drink.

'By God, that's it. Good! Yes! Oh, yes!' Lord Alex groaned again.

Betsy tried to ignore the slurping noises.

Pffft!

Her hand trembled at the sound of the whip cutting through the air and into Lucy's bottom but she managed not to spill any brandy.

'Damn! The little bitch nearly nipped me,' Lord Alex barked.

'Tsk, tsk, she must be flogged.'

'Yes, dear, of course - but let's just allow the baggage to finish... Yes, that's it!'

Betsy escaped while their attention was still on Lucy. Once out of the drawing room, she leant back against the wall and gave a big sigh of relief. The nursery-maid knew, from bitter experience, that had Lord Alex and Lady Alicia delayed her, then Master Jamie would have blamed her rather than the culprits, and would have punished her accordingly. Fairness never seemed to interfere with flogging matters at Hope Hall.

'What are you doing, girl, lounging around chewing cud like a heifer?'

Betsy could not quite prevent a startled squeak escaping. Mrs Pritchard emerged, quite silently, from a doorway opposite.

'Oh, sorry, Mrs Pritchard, I was sent, I was just—'

'Just idling is what you were doing, girl! You are a lazy good-for-nothing. Get on with your duties instantly.'

Betsy turned and trotted down the corridor as quickly as she could, but it was not fast enough. Mrs Pritchard's harsh voice called after her. 'Oh, and put two black marks against your name in the big book. You should know by now what happens to idle trollops at Hope Hall.'

Betsy climbed the east wing stairway disconsolately. Twenty minutes earlier she had been hoping that she might get to bed unscathed. Now she had Master Jamie's cane to look forward to, and the black marks would mean at least two dozen with the birch, come Sunday. She had not liked the way Lady Alicia had looked at her, either. Like most maids at the hall, Betsy felt the best way to be looked at by the imperious Lady Alicia was, generally, not at all.

'You took your time!'

Betsy knew better than to protest. 'Sorry, sir,' she said anxiously, but he smiled indulgently as she handed him the glass.

'Oh, that's all right, Betsy,' he said, taking a sip, 'I am in a good mood tonight. Take off your dress. I'm going to thrash you - but don't worry, I'm not cross with you.' He grinned and put the brandy glass down on the low table beside him, picking up and flexing the kooboo cane in its stead. 'No, I'm going to flog you now strictly for my pleasure.'

Thank you, Master Jamie, that makes all the difference. Betsy could not quite suppress the flash of sarcasm as she pulled off her grey nursery uniform. She did not dare articulate the thought, but her cheeks went a little pink and she felt suddenly afraid that he might read her mind.

'That's better. Now I can see you. Should we get you a "tutu" like the chambermaids, instead of that grey sack?'

Betsy said nothing. Lucy and Kitty spent a good deal of their lives in abbreviated mockeries of proper maids' uniforms. The very idea of spending her days dressed like that filled Betsy with horror. Her own outfit was perfectly respectable, if a little dull. Still, she knew her opinion was not really being sought.

'Hm.' Jamie sipped his brandy thoughtfully, keeping the cane in his other hand. He used it to tap a suspender clip where it clasped the top of her black woollen stocking. 'I think we will have the skirts taken up to here, anyway. It is just too much of a business getting them out of the way every time I want to give you a quick freshener.'

Betsy tried to stop her bottom lip from trembling.

'Of course,' he sighed, using the cane to stroke the side of her leg, over the woollen stocking, 'these will have to go. I'll order some silk hose for you. Won't that be fine?'

This was a direct question and so she had to answer. 'Yes, sir,' she said, trying to sound appropriately grateful.

In truth, fine silk stockings were the last thing that she wanted. The things laddered if you looked at them too hard. Betsy had seen the chambermaids bent over far too often, as they were made to atone for sins that they had been adjudged to have committed against expensive silk.

'Drawers now, Betsy.' Jamie's voice was low and even-toned, but there was no doubt that it was an order. Her fingers fumbled at the knot as she wondered if he would order these replaced as well. The old-fashioned drawers could be opened easily enough at the back for purposes of punishment, but they would look ridiculous with a shortened skirt.

Betsy's face was crimson as she resumed her position. It seemed she would never get used to this: standing in nothing but her long black corset and her stockings, breasts bulging out of the top and private parts entirely bare to the young man's scrutiny. Her fingers fluttered at her sides, desperate to cover her nakedness - but the cane, languidly waving in Jamie's hand, kept them trembling in their place.

'By God, you really are a great piece, Betsy.' Jamie chuckled appreciatively and took a swig of brandy. 'I don't know when I've seen bigger titties. Unhook your front and get them out for me.'

Betsy had always been big. Some might have called her fat, although she had a waist even without the benefits of corseting. The tight-laced beast she struggled with now could not quite force her plumpness into a fashionable hourglass, but it certainly emphasised her curves. It was back-laced and hooked at the front so, theoretically, it should have been simple to undo, but the pressure exerted by the merciless lacing meant she had a real struggle to unhook it at the top. Finally she got the first metal fastening open.

'No, don't take it off. Just get those titties out!'

Betsy had hoped she would have escaped the thing, at least for the duration of her punishment. The long corset always made bending over such a trial. She did as she was bidden; having loosened the top she was able to pull her breasts out and over the top of the corset's front.

'Hands on your head.'

Scarlet-faced and totally exposed, Betsy did as she was ordered. Her breasts were relatively firm and shapely, considering their size, and the action pulled them up so that they jutted out before her.

'What's this?' There was a sharp and displeased note to his voice. She felt the tip of his cane poke at her pudenda.

Betsy had no idea. She looked down but all she could see was the white expanse of her breasts, blotting out anything below.

'I - I don't know, sir,' she said hoarsely.

'I do. It's stubble. This is poor grooming, Betsy, do you not agree?'

Betsy tried to blink back her tears. 'Yes, sir. Sorry, sir,' she managed.

'Never mind. Put yourself a black mark in the big book, get yourself sheared first thing, and we'll say no more about it. Now, come here. No, closer.'

Hesitantly, she stepped closer, until she was right at his side. Jamie put the brandy balloon down, though he retained the cane. Betsy closed her eyes and tried to control her breathing as he ran his hand up her thigh and over the big mounds of her bottom. He rested it there for a moment, using his fingers to caress her left buttock gently.

'Wonderfully firm. You really are quite magnificent, you know.'

Betsy bit her lip. If you like my arse so much, Master Jamie, she thought suddenly, what do you see in that skinny little bitch Clara? She was surprised at the vehemence of the emotion. Surely she was not feeling jealous? Cross with herself for being foolish, she pushed the thought away.

'I've changed my mind. I'm not going to cane you. You can put this away.'

Betsy took the cane and scurried over to the big cupboard, trying not to let hope into her heart. It stole in all the same.

'Oh,' Jamie said as she put the cane in its place, 'and bring me a two-tailed tawse.'

'Lower, come on, touch your toes!

The corset creaked in protest as Betsy tried to comply. If she had been allowed to unhook it altogether, she might have had a chance, but with the stiff whalebone resisting every inch it was quite hopeless. She was red-faced from exertion as much as humiliation now, and the effort was making her pant and her breasts heave. All the time, as she struggled, Master Jamie stood at perfect ease beside her, sipping his brandy, and letting the thick tawse swing languidly from side to side in his right hand.

'Come on, you can do better. You must!'

Again, Betsy tried to bend further, fighting against resilient whalebone. 'I'm sorry, sir, I can't.'

'In my school—' the young man took a final swig and set the glass down on an occasional table '—there was a master, Mr Whitstable by name. He always used to tell us that there is no such word as "can't".'

Betsy tried to stifle a little wail as she sensed him move into position at her side, and just a little to the rear.

'Quite absurd, of course,' Master Jamie continued conversationally. 'After all, how could he have said the word himself, if it did not exist?'

Betsy knew it was coming now, at last. She tensed herself and gripped her own legs as low down as she could manage, which was just above the knees.

'What he meant, of course...' Jamie murmured thoughtfully. There was a sickening hiss, followed by a loud retort and white fire shot through Betsy's upper thighs, making her grunt as she desperately fought the need to cry out in pain. '...was not that "can't" does not exist...'

There was another hiss. Another even more explosive crack, and a stripe of flesh across the middle of Betsy's buttocks was on fire. The pain made her gasp for breath and desperately knead the fleshy thighs above her knees.

'...but that it was forbidden.'

Betsy let out a long and heartfelt sigh as the blaze of pain started to subside.

'Now, bend over further, Betsy.'

She managed to fight the corset enough to let her grab her shins just below her knees.

'A little better, I suppose,' Jamie said grudgingly. Betsy gritted her teeth as she sensed him raise the strap once again.

'Ooh, ooh, aah!'

'Stop whimpering, you silly girl.' Jamie's words were stern but his tone was tolerant, even fond.

After the belting, he had let her take the corset off and she now wore nothing but her woollen stockings. Betsy lay, sniffling, across her master's lap, as he sat on the chaise longue and applied cold cream liberally to her throbbing hindquarters.

She was usually less conscious of her behind than she was of her breasts but, right now, it was the other way round. The tawsing had not been the worst beating she had taken, but Betsy had an especial dislike for the split-tailed belt. It had been a new one, fresh from Mr Kimblewick the saddler in Hatherby. The strap was as thick as a finger, yet the leather was so flexible it felt like a whip. Betsy did not know how many strokes Master Jamie had given her, just that it had been too many. Her young master had taken his time, for time was his to take. The thrashing had been for his pleasure and he had made sure that he had taken it at his leisure. Betsy's part was but to bend over obediently and endure.

Still, there was pleasure for her in his touch now, and her sobs were sobs of relief more than of pain. There was something indescribably delicious about the feeling of the cold ointment as it soothed her scalded skin and, though she had made little sound through the belting, she could not stop some gasps escaping as he stroked.

'Don't tell Miss Amelia about this, Betsy,' Jamie said with a chuckle. 'Or that haughty little baggage will start expecting such privileges, too.'

'Ooh.' A louder gasp escaped her lips as his fingers started to probe between her thighs. She had been expecting that. Though thankful that the tawse had been put down, she was not yet relaxed. Betsy could feel his hardness pressing into her belly, and it told her that he had not entirely slaked his lust with Miss Clara. Her work was not yet finished for the night. The only question was what form it would take.

'Well, what a surprise!'

Although he could not see her face, she hung her head as if to hide her furious blush.

'You are dripping, girl. Betsy, I declare you really are the most perverse little slut. One only has to lift a hand to you and you start gushing like spring.'

Betsy yelped as he withdrew his probing hand and gave her still-sore bottom a resounding slap.

'Right, get down on the floor. I'll have you on all fours. I was thinking of buggering you, but it seems a pity to waste such lubrication.'

Betsy scrambled, eager to obey, kneeling on the floor. She dared a furtive glance towards him and caught a glimpse of his hands unbuttoning his flies, then her heart fluttered as he took out his member, stiff as a soldier and with a resplendently crimson head.

'And anyway, I'm sure Miss Clara has the sweetest little virginal rose-hole, just waiting to be ringed!'

Betsy had been secretly relieved and pleased to hear that she was to be screwed rather than buggered. The tone of eager anticipation in her master's voice replaced relief with a hot surge of jealousy. But she was given no time to dwell on the subject.

'Get your legs wider apart, girl,' he grunted as he got into position. Betsy complied and grabbed handfuls of the carpet. She gave a low groan as he eased himself into her, then a sharper cry as his well-muscled belly and thighs rammed into the tenderised flesh of her rear. Then he reached round and took a breast in each hand.

'That's it. Good girl - let me right up.' He slid deep inside her. Betsy's groans turned to high-pitched squeals. With every thrust, she felt herself driven deeper towards complete delirium.

The relentless squeezing of her breasts wrung frantic cries from her lips, and even Betsy could not have said if they were screams of pain or pleasure. The only thing she still knew was that she had a problem. She could feel Jamie's climax coming, sense it building as his pelvic thrusts became less controlled. Unfortunately, the position in which he was taking her did not provide contact where she needed it the most. She was moaning with desire now, half-insane with pleasure-pain, but she needed something more to trigger her orgasm. She had received no permission to touch herself, and the thought of doing what she had to do unbidden was dreadfully daunting. But then, that fear just cranked up her arousal to an even higher pitch.

Finally as Jamie began to groan, she took the chance, lifting one hand from the floor and ramming the heel of her hand over her clitoris. It did not take much, which was just as well, because she did not have much time. Master Jamie was gasping. The orgasm seemed to come from somewhere deep inside her, spreading out in ripples of electrifying pleasure, wiping everything and everybody from her consciousness.

She came back to earth on the floor to find Jamie still entwined about her. His strong arms around her felt wonderful, and the gentle way he kissed her neck made the plump maid purr with pleasure.

'Very nice.' He stroked her cheek gently. 'You fuck like butter, Betsy. Only—' Betsy stiffened at the word, her warm glow dispersing, '—I was wondering. When, exactly, did I give you leave to frig yourself?'

15

A Stable Relationship

'Oh dear, oh dear, Amelia. What are we going to do with you?' Jamie sighed theatrically. 'Mr Catchpole has come all the way from Hatherby to perform his office, and Mrs Pritchard tells me that all the servant girls have already been done. Yet you persist in this obstinate refusal. Tsk, tsk - you really do seem determined to make life difficult for yourself!'

Amelia glared at the young man, who had emerged from his room as immaculately dressed as ever, this morning sporting an emerald cravat and an embroidered silk waistcoat of gold thread on dark green. She and Clara had been roused a full two hours earlier by Betsy. Once again dressed in the costume of the previous evening, they had been set various demeaning tasks while he idled in his bed. It was not boot-cleaning that had provoked Amelia's rebellion, however.

'I won't, I won't, I simply won't let that man—' she shook her head vigorously, as if unable to say the word, '—do *that* to my...' Again, her words tailed off.

'Amelia, do be careful. Your face has gone quite purple.' Jamie turned to the housekeeper, who was standing stiffly at the door. 'Mrs Pritchard, would you mind explaining what happens to the maids on those occasions they miss the barber's visits?' he said pleasantly.

'I - am - not - a - servant!' Amelia said through gritted teeth. All the same, something about his calm tone chilled her. She glanced at the housekeeper and was mortified to see her sour smile.

'Why, in that case they have to be sent into Hatherby, Master Jamie. To be shorn in Mr Catchpole's special barber's chair. He has straps and what have you, so that uncooperative "customers" can be secured, for their own safety. He says the razors are too sharp to work on anyone who might thrash around.'

'Good lord,' said Jamie, 'and is that expedient often resorted to?'

'Oh, no, sir. The maids all try to avoid it most diligently. The barber's shop is on the high street and, well, when a girl is being shaved... Well, some of the commoner people tend to congregate and stare.'

'Oh yes, he has a fine shop front window, I recall, but what about the blinds?'

'Mr Catchpole says he can't draw them, for want of light, sir. That's why, when he comes to us, he works in the Whippery—'

'All right, all right,' Amelia broke in bitterly, her resolve having been dissolved by this discussion. 'If I must endure this outrage, I suppose I must. What purpose this indecent procedure serves eludes me, but I will not be gawked at by the collected labourers of Hatherby.'

'I'm so glad you have changed your mind, Amelia. Mrs Pritchard, would you be so kind as to escort Amelia and Clara to the Whippery? Perhaps you might explain to them why we have to have the lower orders shaved this way.'

'With pleasure, sir.' Mrs Pritchard gave Jamie a brief nod and opened the door for the cousins. Amelia followed Clara out of the parlour miserably.

'We shave our girls strictly for hygienic reasons,' the black-clad woman said as the two girls preceded her down the nursery stairs. Amelia clenched her fists in impotent fury as the woman continued conversationally, 'It's particularly efficacious in preventing pubic lice, which can be a problem amongst the commoner sort of girl, you see.'

Amelia did not know the long high-ceilinged corridor that Mrs Pritchard ushered them down. Nor did she know to which far part of the hall it led. Even so, a feeling of dread crept over her as the girls' high heels clacked on the parquet flooring. For one thing, there was something ominously gloomy about the passage. For another, there was the word "whippery", which hardly boded well.

'The Whippery was built by the twelfth Marquis of Hatherby, nearly two hundred years ago.' The usually dour Mrs Pritchard became more loquacious with every step. 'All the maids hate this walk,' she said with obvious satisfaction. 'You girls will learn to fear it as much before too long, I expect.'

There were carved marble friezes on the walls now and Amelia glanced at them as they passed. To her horror, she realised that they skilfully depicted numerous figures, mostly rather plump-looking young women being bound to posts and benches. Some were being tied and stripped. Others were evidently about to be flagellated. Further down the passage, others were depicted actually being whipped. Amelia looked away again.

'These bas-reliefs were commissioned at the same time as the Whippery was built.' It seemed the sharp-eyed Mrs Pritchard had noticed her interest. 'There's nothing like them in the three counties. The twelfth Marquis was a man truly dedicated to the rod.'

There was a tone of outright admiration in her voice. Amelia glanced again at the reliefs and shivered. At the further end of the series girls were being taken down from their whipping posts and... Hurriedly, she looked away again.

'In those days, the Lords of Hatherby could do pretty much exactly as they pleased.' Mrs Pritchard sounded regretful that such days had passed, even a little sad. 'And the estates were vast. That's why the Whippery had to be so large.'

They were past the friezes now but shelves of massive black books lined the rest of the corridor.

'These are the big books of Hope Hall. They go back nearly two centuries,' the housekeeper continued informatively. 'You will see that they used to flog staffs of forty or more maids at a time. Not to mention footmen and stable-boys... Ah, me!' Amelia had never seen the woman so excited and enthusiastic. 'How these walls must have echoed with their squeals!'

At the far end of the corridor there was a sort of lectern containing a huge open book. Mrs Pritchard paused to show them the names inscribed there. Amelia suppressed a smile as she saw the name of Betsy among those of the maids. Then her pleasure curdled for, at the end of the list of names, she saw her own and Clara's.

'This is the current big book and this page represents the present week. When you are told to add a black mark you will do so, like this.' Mrs Pritchard took a pen from an inkwell which was set into the stand, and carefully drew a black cross next to Amelia's name. 'The usual tariff is one dozen of the birch for each black mark, paid off after church on Sunday.'

'But...' Amelia looked at the mark, then up at the still-poised pen, with horror.

'That is for this morning's little tantrum,' Mrs Pritchard said with satisfaction. 'Normally, you will be sent down here to inscribe your own fate. The contemplation engendered by this walk is considered salutary.'

Before Amelia could protest further, she turned to the side and threw open a set of large double-doors. Amelia and Clara stepped into the Whippery and both stood looking around in awe. What struck Amelia most was the elegance of the chamber. After Mrs Pritchard's commentary, she had expected the room to be larger. Not that it was small. The Whippery was circular and divided into two halves. One half had several semi-circular banks of seats of reddish oak with crimson velvet cushions.

'Seating for seventy people altogether,' Mrs Pritchard said smugly. 'Not that it needs to very often, these days.'

The second half of the room was made up of a small stage flanked by two tiers of more basic wooden benches, arching off at either side, and cut off from the platform by a door on either side. The whole of the Whippery was as light as a conservatory, despite the quantities of woodwork. More than three-quarters of the circular building was composed of tall glass windows, which started just above the level of the highest row of seats. Above these was a small wall, then another row of lights, this time sloping inward, to meet the base of a glass and ironwork cupola high above.

'The stage faces south, to get the best of the light,' Mrs Pritchard said reverently.

Amelia was already looking at the stage. Affixed to its back wall was a great St Andrew's cross, and at either side were ranged several dismal-looking whipping-blocks and trestles. However it was none of these that held the young woman's appalled attention, but a portly man of about fifty, sitting calmly reading a newspaper. Beside him was a simple narrow table, topped with white enamel, and placed in the centre of the stage.

'Ah, excellent. These must be the new ones. Lovely, lovely!' The little balding man jumped up and peered at the cousins through round glasses, and rubbed his hands together delightedly. Amelia gave him her most disdainful stare, which had no apparent effect whatsoever.

'Have you sufficient hot water, Mr Catchpole?' Mrs Pritchard asked.

'Oh yes, thank you.' He indicated a steaming bucket. 'Betsy just brought me some more down. Now, young ladies.' He turned to Amelia and Clara and smiled. 'I'm afraid I shall have to ask you to take those knickers off.'

Amelia was in such a hurry to get the ordeal over with that she found she had pulled her own frilly pantaloons off before Clara, who was no doubt struggling with shyness, had got hers halfway down. Thus she felt the little man's surprisingly firm grip on her arm as he steered her to the table first.

'Sit up here for me, dear.' Amelia took a deep breath, told herself that this was better than the barber's shop, and did as she was told. The enamel was wet, and so cold on her naked bottom that she gave a little gasp.

'That's it. Good girl. Now I want you just to lie back for me - yes, yes, that's lovely.' She felt the silk of her smock turn wet and clammy from the water on the table, and almost wished she had taken the damned thing off. It had ridden up to her waist in any case, and she could see her own pubic curls as she anxiously raised her head. Mr Catchpole bent and took her wrists, then guided her hands until her arms were extended down two of the legs of the table.

'That's it. Now grip the legs really, really hard.'

'Oh, what...?' By the time Amelia felt the straps deftly pulled tight around her wrists it was too late. She gave a gasp of surprised protest. She had not seen any restraints around the table legs. With a surge of outrage, she realised that Mr Catchpole must have had them secreted in his pocket.

The barber stood up, smiling down at her. He placed a plump hand on her bare belly where the smock had ridden up and patted her consolingly.

'There, there. I just need to make sure you do not wriggle about. I'd hate to nick such lovely—' Amelia ground her teeth as he caressed her belly longingly, '—lovely skin.'

Mr Catchpole bent and produced another two straps from his capacious pockets, and Amelia, realising that it was futile to fight, let him secure her ankles to the other two table legs. With her legs strapped apart and her smock pushed up, she was all too aware of her exposed sex. Mr Catchpole went over to a bag at the side of the stage and produced another strap. This he passed under the table and over her belly, tightening it until Amelia gave a little squeak. She was close to immobile now, but the barber was not finished. More straps secured her legs to those of the table, just above the knee.

'There now.' He patted her on her bare belly again.

'Oh, please...' Amelia squirmed as his hand moved inexorably towards her pussy. She bit her lip as he tugged the dark pubic curls professionally.

'Ah, lovely,' he said again, patting her furred mons.

At that moment, Amelia very nearly unleashed a torrent of invective. However, he did something which stopped her uttering a word. With one surprisingly deft movement, he produced a cutthroat razor from his waistcoat pocket and opened it. It transformed him from irritating to terrifying in an instant. Amelia froze. With his free hand, Mr Catchpole continued to fondle her pubic bush, then she felt a pinprick of pain.

'Ooh!'

'Sorry, dearie.' He smiled down at her. 'Just need to test the blade.' He held up the pubic hair he had plucked out and did something with the razor that Amelia couldn't see.

'Hm. Better give it a quick hone, anyway.' He walked over to the St Andrew's cross. Following him with panic-stricken eyes, Amelia noticed for the first time a razor strop hanging from the top of one of the arms of the cross.

Fwist, fwist, fwist. The regular rhythmic sound of the stropping razor cranked up Amelia's already stretched nerves.

'You, dear,' the portly barber restored the razor to his pocket and crooked a finger at Clara. 'Come here, please.'

He had the blonde girl stand close to Amelia's pelvis, and then Amelia swapped a panicked look with her cousin. Clara's rosebud lower lip was trembling, and there was real fear in her wide blue eyes.

Whistling to himself, Mr Catchpole started to lather up a shaving brush. Amelia gasped when the creamy froth was smeared over her sex. It felt most peculiar: wet, warm and sticky. 'Oh, ah, what, what are you doing?' she asked.

'Don't be impertinent, girl!'

'Oh, that's all right, Mrs Pritchard,' the portly barber said soothingly. 'I don't mind explaining to the young lady. You see dear, to get a really good shave it is necessary to engorge the pudenda. As the area swells up, it tautens the skin, and considerably improves the result.'

Amelia was unable to continue the conversation, by now being occupied in fighting helplessly against her bonds. Her pelvis tried to writhe of its own volition, in response to the circling of his shaving brush, and Amelia could hear her own voice making odd mewling sounds.

At last, the barber gave the soap and brush to Clara, and then produced his razor again. Amelia stopped squirming; she was almost too terrified to breathe.

Scritch, scritch, scritch. He shaved her in deft strokes which were almost as rhythmic as the stropping. Amelia relaxed a fraction as her last protection against complete nudity was briskly stripped away. The feeling of the razor on her tender tissues was indescribable. Frightening, for the blade was so sharp: yet oddly comforting, too, for she could not move at all, and there was something reassuring about being completely in Mr Catchpole's professional hands. He might be a dirty old man, she told herself between whimpers, but he was not about to nick a customer. Or even, Amelia thought bitterly, considering the reality of her present status, damage a customer's goods.

As she lay back on the cold enamel, Amelia did all she could to think about something else. She looked at the empty banks of seats, grateful at least that there was no audience for her humiliation. She looked at Clara, holding the soap cup and shaving brush obediently. She could not look into Clara's eyes for long, though, because the fear in the blonde girl's face enhanced her own. Mrs Pritchard's contempt was even worse. In the end she looked at the blue sky through the glass of the cupola, and watched the clouds scud by.

At last he paused and went to re-strop his razor. Amelia lifted her head and saw her own pussy quite shaven. It made her feel incredibly naked and exposed, having her legs strapped helplessly apart and quim devoid of hair. At least, she thought, the ordeal must be over. However, Mr Catchpole returned to his station and took the brush from Clara once again.

'But - but it's done. Ooh!' she said as the brush stroked her again.

'Just a little stubble to clear up, my dear,' he said, pausing to beam down at her, 'in the region of the clitoral hood.'

The table creaked as Amelia bucked helplessly against her bonds. The cold metal touch spiralled in, as the brush had, and the world seemed to spiral along with it. Amelia heard a girl moaning and shrieking, but it seemed to be someone far away.

'That will do, I think,' a man's voice said; she heard the snap of the razor being closed.

'No... please... don't stop. I mean... I need...!' She heard her own voice protesting as she fought the bonds with ever-increasing frenzy.

'Listen to the little slut!' Mrs Pritchard spat contemptuously.

Mr Catchpole chuckled, however, and said, 'Just wait a minute now, dearie.'

A rough towel was placed on her shaven mons and, as the bound girl shrieked in response, the little man rubbed it vigorously. Then, as she squealed and squirmed, he slid a finger into her wet sex, with his other hand stroking the part that drove her wild. The little man efficiently manipulated her to and past the point of no return, all the while whistling professionally.

He was still whistling the jolly music-hall tune when Amelia's body exploded into ecstasy.

The clouds had gathered as the day progressed and, by late afternoon, passing showers had left the cobbles of the courtyard slick and wet. Twice Kitty nearly went over, as her impossibly high heels skeetered on the treacherous surface, and she only regained her balance at the last minute. The reluctance with which the blonde maid approached the stable-block was, however, by no means solely due to the difficulty involved in negotiating the terrain.

Something about Lady Alicia's manner at teatime had made her nervous, and anxiety had translated to clumsiness. Kitty's hand had trembled as she poured afternoon tea and a few drops spilt into the saucer. Naturally, her mistress had regarded this as deliberate. Kitty had quailed before Lady Alicia's wrath, as the Marchioness made it abundantly clear to the maid that she regarded the small spillage as an act of deliberate insubordination.

Standing with her head bowed, enduring the torrent of invective, Kitty had awaited the inevitable order to bend and lift her skirts. Her gaze had been transfixed by Lady Alicia's dressage-whip, which she slashed viciously through the air for emphasis while listing Kitty's failings in detail. However, the dreaded order had not come. It turned out that Lady Alicia had something worse than her riding-crop in store for the maid today.

'Clearly, I have been too lenient with you, recently. It is time you were reminded of your place, my girl. Later this afternoon, after you have served tea, I want you to go to the stables and ask Mr Blackstock to give you a damned good belting. Wear your "tutu". I won't have you trailing mud and dung into the house on your hems, and don't bother with drawers or knickers. You won't be needing them this evening.'

Kitty tried vainly to tug the hem of her dress down. The flouncing skirt of her "tutu" was buoyed up by half a dozen little petticoats and she could feel the breeze on her bare flesh, exposed above her stocking-tops. It really was unfair! The maid's full uniforms were old-fashioned, and their billowing skirts could be a sore trial, yet they would have been quite respectable had they not been so low-cut at the front. Cruelly, this modesty was a privilege allowed mostly inside the hall.

Kitty's heels slid again and she struggled to right herself, having to bend forward to regain her balance as she did so, and all too aware that she was treating anyone watching from the hall behind her to a good view of her naked bottom. The logic of not dragging those long-hemmed gowns through mud and worse was unassailable, yet Kitty could not see why the uniform's skirt had to be so short. Hemlines below the knee would have been both practical and modest. Above the stocking-tops looked indecent and absurd.

'Yes, what is it, girl? What do you want?' Kitty coloured under Mr Blackstock's cold appraising gaze as he dropped it from her full breasts to her silk-sheathed legs. The head groom was balding and had a definite paunch, but his arms were powerfully muscled and his strength legendary. Blackstock wore only a much-stained leather apron on his upper body, and his arms were beaded with sweat.

The maid swallowed hard. 'Please, sir, I... I've been sent...'

Mr Blackstock raised his gaze again to the full breasts proffered by the half-cups of her bodice, in a way that made Kitty's stomach churn with anxiety. 'Well, I can see that, you silly little bitch!' he growled. 'The question is, what have you been sent for?'

Kitty hung her head. 'For a b-belting sir,' she whispered.

'For a what? Speak up, you little trollop! What do you want?'

'I, er, want a belting, sir,' Kitty mumbled unconvincingly.

'A belting, eh?' he bellowed. 'You want me to give you a leathering, do you?'

'Y-yes, sir,' Kitty sniffled, tears welling in her eyes.

Blackstock strolled over to the trembling maid. He grasped a handful of her golden curls and forced the hapless girl's head back, forcing her to look into his glittering green gaze. Kitty felt herself impaled by his predatory stare, assailed by his stench. Kitty, used to the delicate perfumes of Lady Alicia's boudoir, felt her senses overwhelmed by the rank odours of horse-sweat, human perspiration, leather and manure.

Her bodice was low-cut, and Mr Blackstock had only to flip her nipple with his thumb to free it from the film of lace that veiled it. Taking the nub of flesh between finger and thumb, he squeezed and twisted until Kitty moaned in pain.

'Don't you say "please" in the big house, you cheeky little bitch?' he hissed into her ear.

'Ow, ooh, please... sir... ow...'

'Please what?'

'Puh... please... ooh... please can... ow, may I... ooh, have a b-belting... sir... Ow...!'

'You see.' He let go of her nipple but retained his grip of her curls. 'Manners cost nothing.' He pulled her close into him. The rough leather of his apron grazed Kitty's bare arms, and she was even more overwhelmed by the odour of leather and sweat. Blackstock's free hand reached under the little flouncing skirt.

'Oh... ah... please, don't...'

'Be quiet!' His rough fingers probed her naked pussy.

Kitty fought a wave of pure panic. His callused hand felt rougher than the leather of the apron against her soft skin. As his finger probed deeper, she gave a little whimper.

'Well, well.' He chuckled deeply as tears trickled down her flaming cheeks. 'The little slut is dripping.'

'No!'

He shook his head. 'Don't contradict me, girl,' he growled, exploring further.

Appallingly, Kitty could not stop herself from pressing against his hand. It was as if her pelvis had taken on a life of its own. She gave a lost little cry.

'Oh, no you don't!' Blackstock withdrew his hand with a chuckle. 'Not yet, slut. There's a little matter of a belting first, remember? The boys will want to watch that. You'll have to wait until they've done their work. You don't mind waiting half an hour now, do you, pet?'

There was nothing Kitty could say, so she said nothing. There was nothing she could do, but stand in a quiet corner of the stables and try her futile best to look inconspicuous. Every time Blackstock passed, he would grin at her and wink lasciviously. Kitty would have given anything for a pair of drawers or a skirt of decent length. The head groom walked by, giving her another wink, and she relaxed for a moment. Then the sound of footsteps made her tense again.

'Blimey, Davy-boy, look what we got here!' A wiry sandy-haired boy broke into a great gap-toothed grin. 'Hello, Kitty, my darling. Been a while since you were sent to us. Been a bad girl again, have you?'

'Get off, Dick.' Kitty tried to push his hand away as the laughing boy felt beneath her skirt. His companion, a handsome lad whom Kitty did not recognise, just stood staring at her as if rooted to the spot.

'Finish your work first, Dick. There will be time a-plenty for that, once you've given Caesar his rub-down. Davy, you still have that tack to put away.' Blackstock chased the boys away. Then he licked his lips and winked at Kitty once again.

The maid got some respite after that, for some twenty minutes. Even so, it was an anxious and comfortless wait. From where she stood, she could see the leathering saddle. It was placed over a horizontal beam at just above the height of Kitty's waist. It had been there on each of her previous visits. The maid did not know whether it was kept there specifically for disciplinary purposes, or if it was a riding saddle that happened to be kept in a convenient place. It was even possible that Lady Alicia had sent instructions earlier, and Mr Blackstock's questioning of her business in the stables was simply his cruel joke.

Even worse than that were the straps. To her left there was a partition of rough planks, and this was festooned with all sorts of leather stirrup-straps, martingales and reins. Beyond this wooden wall there were three small stalls. These were unoccupied and Kitty did not want to think about their purpose. Nor did she want to think about the straps, which gleamed like well-oiled snakes of dark brown leather. Some of them were recognisably reins or other elements of harness, but Kitty did not know which ones were for use with horses and which had other purposes. She did know that the sight of so much supple leather, all of which could be employed to belt a girl's tender bottom, made her feel quite dizzy. Tearing her gaze away, she found herself looking at the saddle once again.

If the wait in the stables seemed to go on for ever, paradoxically, it also appeared to Kitty to be over all too soon.

'All right boys.' Mr Blackstock arrived, flanked by the grinning stable-lads. He advanced, drying his hands on a cloth, having evidently just washed them at the pump. 'One more little job before we finish for today.'

Kitty stepped back as the three men bore down on her, unable to suppress a little wail of terror. She bumped into the rough stone wall behind her and nearly lost her footing as she teetered on her high heels.

'Careful now, my dear.' Mr Blackstock caught her elbow and steadied her. 'Dick, get that buffalo-hide stirrup-leather. The inch and a quarter. Oh, and I want a running martingale and some bridle straps. Get me a couple of girth extenders, too.' The steadying hand pulled her towards the waiting saddle. 'Now, young lady. Would you care to step this way?'

Kitty stumbled, her legs seeming to be semi-paralysed, so the groom steered her over to the saddle and beam. 'Davy, go round and take her wrists. This filly is distinctly skittish and she just might try to bolt.'

A firm push in the small of the back propelled the maid towards the saddle. Kitty's wrists were caught by Davy on the far side of the beam, and she felt strong hands grip her waist and hoist her up. Mr Blackstock lifted her the few inches required and she sprawled belly-down over the saddle, held in place by the stable-boy's firm grip on her wrists. An even firmer grip grabbed her right ankle.

'We'll have these things off, I think. I have no mind to lose an eye!'

Kitty felt him remove her shoes, and then she gave a little wail of fear as she felt the bridle strap pass under her thighs, against the bare flesh just above her stocking-tops. This was pulled quite tight before another strap secured her ankles together. Kitty gave an alarmed squeak. Mr Blackstock had not strapped her down for her previous visits to the stables, and the procedure provoked a sense of mounting panic in her.

'Oh, please sir. This really is not nec - Ow!' There was a resounding smacking sound and Kitty felt pain lance through her left thigh.

'Keep quiet, or I'll put a bit on you,' Mr Blackstock growled. 'Dick, fetch me a curb chain and a lip-strap. Just in case.' Then he stepped into Kitty's field of view, holding a selection of straps. He put most of these down on a nearby work bench, but he retained two. One was a short double strap equipped with two buckles which he secured around her right wrist, threading one of the straps through a loop in the brow-band, a short length of leather with a loop sewn into either end. The groom then took another of the double straps from the bench and buckled it around her left wrist and the other end loop of the brow-band, creating a pair of leather handcuffs.

A hand on Kitty's bottom told her that Dick had returned, and she flinched as she waited for the inevitable pinch.

'Now, Dick, pass the ends of that martingale looped over the thigh strap to me, underneath the saddle,' Mr Blackstock instructed.

Below her, Kitty saw a hand holding both ends of a buckled strap emerge, and felt the pressure pulling her thighs forward. The belt was buckled over the strap joining her wrists, and then Mr Blackstock tightened it up.

Kitty yelped as she found her knees pulled forward and her wrists hauled down and back, forcing her to embrace the saddle. She was quite helpless now and she knew it. Her bare bottom was exposed to the world and she could only move her head. Worst of all, she was deprived of even the illusory feeling of security that having her feet on the ground might have conveyed.

'Pass me that stirrup-leather.'

Mr Blackstock doubled up the heavy-looking strap in one hand. With the other, he took a fistful of Kitty's blonde locks and hauled her head up until she met his eyes. He looked enormous, towering over her, the size of his great biceps and shoulder muscles emphasised by the bareness of his arms.

He tapped the strap against her cheek. It felt cold and hard, heavy and unyielding. Kitty felt suddenly faint.

'Now, girl, I mean to leather you good and proper. I shall give you a belting now which you'll not forget in a hurry. I shall give you something to take to show your mistress when I'm finished. I don't mind if you squawk, and you can wriggle all you like. It will make no difference to me!'

Kitty could only listen with bated breath to his heavy-booted tread as he strode across the flags that floored the stable-block. Her arms were hauled down by the strapping, to the point where she could not raise her head and see what was happening behind her. She gritted her teeth and closed her eyes tightly, her bottom-cheeks clenching in anticipation.

There was a low whistle, followed by a sharp crack. The strap caught her right in her most tender groove and a ferocious blaze of pain coursed through her rear. Though she had been given permission to cry out, Kitty was determined not to give her tormentors that satisfaction, and she clenched her teeth together to prevent an agonised yelp escaping.

'Good shot, Mr Blackstock!' Dick's coarse voice called out excitedly.

Leather strapping creaked in protest as Kitty writhed and wriggled. The fire across her bottom-cheeks subsided slowly, but Mr Blackstock seemed quite content to wait.

'Oh no, that was just to get my length, lad. Nothing but a practice stroke, that. Still, I reckon she might feel this.'

At last there came another low whistle, and another pistol-shot retort, followed instantaneously by a scalding eruption of pain. This stroke seared the tops of Kitty's thighs, and it was agonising. Kitty grimaced and shook her blonde locks violently. She almost ground her teeth together, but a hiss escaped her lips all the same.

'You see, Davy, some like to work the same area, but I like to spread them. Unless the count is low, and then I do my best to deliver them where they'll do the most good.'

'What is the count, Mr Blackstock?'

Despite the distraction of her throbbing backside, Kitty perceived that the stable-boy's voice sounded strained. So she tried to stop writhing and listen for the answer. Unfortunately, before replying, Mr Blackstock unleashed a third blistering stroke.

'Aaaooooohh...!' This time she could not stop the cry of pain escaping. If she had not been secured to the saddle, she surely would have jumped up like a jack-in-the-box. As it was, all she could do was writhe helplessly in her bonds. Kitty shook her head and kicked her legs back and forth, to the creaking sound of protesting leather, as if by doing so she could somehow disperse the pain.

'No count,' Mr Blackstock replied at last, to her horror. 'I shall give the wicked little chit just as many as I feel like. A dozen, maybe two - or even more. After all, there is no hurry. We'll give her a stiff dozen or so to start, and then see if she would prefer to play a different game.'

The thrashing continued quite relentlessly. The strap cracked across her bottom and thighs, time and time again. Kitty shrieked at the top of her lungs, quite helpless to prevent herself now, all resolve forgotten. She squirmed and wriggled, and fought the straps that held her so invitingly in position for the lash, all to no avail. The heavy stirrup-leather whistled through the still air of the stable-block, impacting mercilessly on Kitty's tender bottom, and she howled in pain.

Mr Blackstock was methodical and thorough, belting Kitty's hindquarters from the top of her bottom, right down to her stocking-tops. As he had promised, he was content to let her shriek her distress, and did not seem to mind how much she wriggled and writhed. Only when she got her heels up hard against her bottom, and kept them there, as if by doing so she could ward off blows on her thighs, did he intervene.

'All right, Dick, haul down on that ankle strap. Davy, your eyes look like they'll pop out of your head. It is a pretty arse, there is no denying. Go on, lad - if you like, step up and have a feel.'

Kitty whimpered as she felt the stable-boy's hand stroke her bottom.

'Nice, eh? I don't know how that arse stays so soft, considering how often the wicked chit needs whipping!' Mr Blackstock barked with laughter. Tears ran down Kitty's cheeks and she watched forlornly as they splashed on the flagstone below. She tried to ignore the pain that the boy's hand provoked as he pinched and probed.

'Bloody hell, Mr Blackstock. You could fry eggs on this bum; it's positively scorching!' There was a tone of wonder in Davy's voice. Kitty winced as his hands passed over the welts on her thighs. He stroked and patted her, before fingering the sheer material of her hose. 'I never seen stockings like these.'

'Course not - they're silk, you yokel.' Dick chuckled.

Kitty felt the boy tug at her suspender drops, as she watched another tear fall and splash on the flagstone below.

'What are these things, then?' There was a tone of rapt, almost awe-stricken, amazement in his voice. A young acolyte, initiated for the first time into a sacred mystery, could not have sounded more reverential.

'Suspenders.' Dick's voice from below was scornful. 'They're attached to the trollop's corset. Haven't you ever seen 'em before?'

'Take no notice of him, Davy,' Mr Blackstock said. 'I suppose you often got to fumble silk stockings and suspenders straps before you came up to the hall, eh Dick?'

'Well, I...'

'He never saw such things neither, till he came here, Davy. It's a new fashion, lad, instead of garters. That Mademoiselle Isobel in Hatherby makes 'em up. Anyway, let's get on with the job, shall we?'

Once more the sickening whistle echoed through the stable-block. Kitty howled with pain again.

'There's some beer in the jug - complements of Lady Alicia. Pour it out, Dick. There're three glasses there. Davy, you can unstrap the baggage's legs for her, now.'

Kitty slumped limply over the saddle, gasping brokenly and trying her best to stem the flow of tears coursing down her cheeks. Her bottom and thighs throbbed abominably. She had lost count of the belt-strokes she had received, but was sure it was close to two dozen in total. The agony was seeping away to a dull ache but every time her sore bottom was touched, even gently, waves of pain would lance through it again.

Mr Blackstock waited for his glass of beer, occasionally patting her proffered rear and provoking a new gasp from the maid. She felt the straps unbuckled from her legs and the loosening of the belt that kept her hands pulled back.

Mr Blackstock walked around the beam to her head. Kitty's attention was riveted to the stirrup-leather that still dangled from his hand. In the other he held his beer, and he placed this on the bench before turning back to the quietly sobbing girl. A callused hand lifted Kitty's chin until she found herself looking up into the big groom's eyes. His expression was one of amusement, but quite devoid of pity. Once again, the thick leather was tapped against her face.

'Now, sweetheart,' he said gruffly, 'have you had enough leathering? You could go another dozen easy, but I thought you might prefer to do something else.'

'Anything.' Kitty blinked up at him desperately. 'I - I'll do anything you like, sir. Please...'

The groom released her chin, allowing her to drop her chin again, and draped the stirrup-strap around her neck. Kitty shivered at the contact with the cool leather, closing her eyes and praying he would accept her offer.

'Funny,' the big man said thoughtfully, 'that's what they always seem to say!'

'All right, little missy, time to strip.'

Kitty eyed the three men nervously. She had had cold pump water splashed on her face and been given some to drink, and this indulgence had revived her somewhat. Even so, she swayed a little, her legs still unsteady, and was glad she was no longer in her heels. What did it matter if the stone flags were cold beneath her stockinged feet?

It was getting dark and the grooms had hung oil lamps on a beam above her, before settling on some bales of hay stacked in the corner. Here they watched, eyes bright with excitement as they drank their beer. It filled Kitty's heart with a sense of impotent indignation. It was so typical of her mistress: to send down cold beers to the men whom she had instructed to abuse her maid. It was like a message from the Marchioness, ensuring that Kitty remained aware of why, and on whose behalf, her ordeal had been ordained.

Anyway, she realised, dwelling on Lady Alicia's cruelty would not get her anywhere. She pulled off her uniform coyly. Kitty knew the men wanted a show, so she took care not to strip too quickly. She was all too aware of the leather strap, now doubled up again in Mr Blackstock's hand. She dropped the satin garment to a chorus of whoops and whistles and placed a hand uncertainly on her hip.

'The corset too, sir?' she asked hesitantly. She was wearing a heavily-boned back-laced corset of black satin. Kitty knew it would be a sore trial to unhook it on her own.

'Get over here,' the head groom grunted gruffly. Kitty swallowed hard and trotted over to him, horribly aware of three pairs of eyes devouring her curvaceous shape. Mr Blackstock took hold of the front of the corset and, with a brief grunt, unhooked the front. The corset fell away behind her. The suspender straps were still attached, so she felt her stockings tugged down behind by the weight of her stays. This was not her most pressing concern, however.

'All right, boys. You're going to see a proper B and B.'

'B and B?' Davy puzzled.

Mr Blackstock chuckled. 'Belting and buggering, lad.'

With a yelp, Kitty found herself propelled onto a nearby hay bale. She gasped as the prickly straw scratched her naked breasts and belly. She could feel the still-attached corset dragging along behind, her stockings now pulled down to just above her knees. Then she felt another tug and realised that the groom had knelt down on the corset. She hoped he would not damage it. If he did, there was no question about who Lady Alicia would blame. Kitty dared not even think about the state of her silk stockings.

'Hand me that saddle-soap, Dick.' There was the sound of rubbing and then she felt his finger on her anus.

'There's an art to ringing rose-holes, Davy.' Mr Blackstock spoke exactly, as if he was giving instructions on how to mount a skittish mare. Kitty gave a surprised gurgle as his finger gently circled her sphincter, massaging the tender tissue until the muscle relaxed.

'Ooh!' she moaned as the finger fondled the so-sensitive tissue.

'It's no good forcing it. You have to tease it gently till it's ready to let you in. *Uff!*'

She felt his big cock-head press against the ring of muscle. There was tightness and resistance for a moment and then she felt it slide in, surprisingly easily. Kitty remembered Mr Blackstock's cock as not particularly long, but thick as a girl's wrist. He must have lubricated her rose-hole well, she thought. That, or else Lady Alicia's training dildos must be having an effect on her at last. All the same, it was tight enough to make her gasp as she felt him ease in further. Worse, the force of the big man pressing down pushed her naked breasts and belly harder into the scratchy hay.

'You're reaming the little bitch proper, Mr Blackstock!' Dick called out excitedly.

And it was true. The groom's weight crushed Kitty's bare body into the hay as his fat cock inched into her, deeper and deeper. Lost now, moaning deliriously, Kitty could feel his belly rasping against the sore flesh of her bottom. Surely that was as far as it would go? she thought wildly. Then his hands closed on her hips and she gave a startled gasp as she felt him use his tremendous strength to pull himself even further in. She clutched the bale, burying her face in the coarse straw as Mr Blackstock buggered her magisterially.

'Oh, ah, oh, *oh!*' Kitty moaned and whimpered as her bottom-hole was mercilessly reamed. Her hands scrabbled desperately at the bale as she felt herself swept away into a sort of delirium. There seemed to be nothing in the world but the groom's great cock impaling her, nothing but the throbbing of her bottom and the piston-like motion of his thrusts.

'Oh, *yes... yes, sir....!*' she heard someone babble in the distance.

Finally the big groom grunted. There was a short series of even harder thrusts as he growled obscenities, and Kitty felt him shudder as he climaxed, and at last the reaming ceased. Kitty was engulfed by conflicting emotions. An odd sense of disappointment mingled with the desperation of her own unfilled need, and fought against an ebb tide of relief. Not that she was given long to think about it. Mr Blackstock withdrew without ceremony, leaving Kitty gasping on the bale.

'All right boys, you can play with her for while, but mind, she has to be sent back in time to serve them dinner in the hall!' the groom growled, picking up his glass of beer and wandering off towards the pump.

A strong hand took hold of a hank of Kitty's hair and hauled her up onto her knees. Blinking dazedly, she saw Dick sit on the bale in front of her. The boy was grinning and unbuttoning his breeches. Davy, who she realised must be kneeling behind her, relinquished his grip on her hair and reached around to take a double handful of her breasts.

'God, Dick, I ain't ever felt anything so fine as these.'

Kitty moaned as his rough hands clumsily squeezed her breasts.

'Aye, there are certain perks to this job, Davy-boy!' Dick patted the maid's hot cheek and she found herself looking into his laughing eyes.

'All right, easy, girl. You know how to suck this - I seen you do it.'

He slapped his engorged cock against her face, smearing the tears that had run down her cheeks, before sliding it down with obvious intent. Kitty opened her lips tentatively and let him push his ruby cock-head into her warm mouth. As she did so, she felt the boy behind her press his hardness against her throbbing bottom. Her own desire was getting truly desperate now, but she dare not ask for what she needed. She took more of Dick's stiff cock in her mouth and opened her legs invitingly, hoping against hope that the lout behind her would have the brains to take the hint.

CARROT AND STICK

It really was an outrage! To be treated like that, by such a horrid little tradesman. It really was too much! Amelia stroked her denuded mons as she fumed. Awful though the experience had been, she seemed unable to stop thinking about it. For all her shame and anger, her shaven sex fascinated her and she could not stop fondling herself. Amelia gently fingered her quim as she lay in the bath, experiencing a strange mixture of emotions from the sensation: part horror, part excitement, and part delight.

After her own shaving, Amelia had watched Clara receive the same treatment, and the image had burnt itself into Amelia's mind. Slowly, she licked her lips as she remembered the different elements of the scene: Clara's slender limbs; the black straps brutal against the white of her silk stockings; the bound girl's gurgling cries as Mr Catchpole worked with the shaving brush; the blonde fur being stripped away by the gleaming, relentless razor; the way the girl had whimpered at the touch of the cold steel. Amelia permitted herself a smile as she remembered her cousin's paroxysms while the barber's knowing hands had coaxed her into climax. The spectacle had almost made her own ordeal worthwhile.

The door opened suddenly and Amelia raised her hands quickly to her breasts.

'Don't think I don't know what you were up to, Amelia,' Jamie said, as he lounged in the entrance. 'You just can't keep those fingers from your sex, can you, you slut?'

Amelia held her tongue but, to her chagrin, felt her cheeks redden.

'Aha,' her tormentor said with a smile, 'it looks like I was right.'

Amelia silently cursed her traitorous face as he sauntered over to her.

'All right, you should be clean by now. Stand up.'

Amelia stared at him, and at the whippy-looking yellow cane he held. Jamie held his peace for a moment as Amelia struggled with herself.

Deciding there was little alternative, she got up sullenly, doing her best to cover her naked charms as the water drained off her into the slipper-bath.

'No, Amelia. I thought we had discussed this. Place your hands behind your head. I want to take a look at Mr Catchpole's handiwork.'

This was too much for her to endure. Rather than do as she was told, Amelia put her left hand, with which she had been attempting to cover her breasts, down with her right, which she was using to shield her quim.

'You really are a slow learner, Amelia,' Jamie said regretfully as he stepped behind her and unleashed a sudden stroke of the cane. The whippy stick cracked across Amelia's wet bottom. She gave a startled shriek of pain.

She tried to turn, to keep her naked rear away from him, but shuffling in the wet tub was slow, and his circling was quicker. Again the cane whistled through the air and thwacked across moist bottom-flesh. Amelia squealed again. When the third stroke caught her across her thighs, Amelia doubled up and howled. Then she raised her hands, though she still crouched wincing, knowing that she could not win this game.

'Ow! Ooh! That really stings, you - you - you...' As she blinked the tears of pain from her eyes, she met his gaze and the insult died on her lips as she watched him flex the cane.

'And so unnecessary, Amelia, my dear,' Jamie said calmly. 'Eventually you will learn it is best to obey right away. Now get your hands behind your head and stand up straight. Legs apart... Oh yes, that's much more appropriate. Would you mind terribly, Amelia, if I were to have a feel?'

Amelia moaned as he placed his hand over her wet mons and squeezed gently.

'Oh, yes, that's very nice. He did do a good job. Mrs Pritchard tells me you enjoyed it too, after all that fuss! Anyway, time to get dressed now. Lord Alex and Lady Alicia have asked me to present you to them after dinner tonight, and I have something particularly special for you to wear.'

'Not long now. Just wait till I see Uncle Alex. Just wait till he sees what Jamie has done to us. God, I hope we don't have to wait much longer. I'm dying for a pee.'

'Oh, Amelia, please don't make things any worse.' Clara blinked in appeal. 'Aunt and Uncle must have agreed to this...' She fell silent and leant against the dark oak-panelled wall with a chinking of chain.

Dressing for dinner had proved a grave disappointment to Amelia. Jamie had donned a smart dinner-jacket, complete with a white tie and white double-breasted waistcoat. However, for Amelia and Clara there was nothing but a fresh pair of stockings, clean knickers, and a new silk smock for each of them to wear.

'I thought you said there was something special,' Amelia had muttered as she put the hateful outfit on once more.

'Oh yes, of course.' Jamie smiled and produced from his jacket pockets a pair of sky-blue lacy garters and matching hair ribbons, and a similar set in pink. 'Here.' He handed the blue set to Clara. 'To match your lovely eyes.'

Amelia had fumed to see the silly girl's eyelashes flutter at the compliment. Then he had handed the pink set to her. 'To match your bottom when I spank it later, Amelia, and your blushing cheeks.'

Amelia had very nearly mutinied again, but he had strolled over to the cane cupboard and she hurriedly pulled the garters on. Betsy had then put the cousins' hair in girlish bunches with the ribbons, as Amelia watched Jamie out of the corner of her eye. The young man had emerged from the cupboard with a handful of dark-brown leather straps.

'What is taking them so long? We must have been here for over an hour.' Amelia shifted from foot to foot. The pressure in her bladder was starting to become acute. She was also increasingly uncomfortable. Jamie had strapped the girls' wrists behind their backs. Each wrist was secured to the opposite arm by a second strap, buckled just above the elbow, so that their arms were bound across the small of their back. This left their befrilled bottoms available and impossible to protect. Collars had followed, and chain leashes attached to these.

'Now, listen carefully, my pets.' Jamie had taken the leashes from Betsy and smiled at his captive's amiably. 'There are a lot of stairs and, without your hands available to save you if you fall, I want you to be very careful and try to trot along in step.'

Amelia had had just enough time to add this outrage to the catalogue she intended to bring to her aunt and uncle's attention before he had set off. After that, she had had to concentrate. There was no real reason why they should trip, though the heels on their white button-boots were certainly perilously high. However, the feeling of having no recourse to her arms, usually taken for granted, made her feel dreadfully insecure.

When they had finally got to the dining room Amelia had taken a deep breath, ready to present her long list of complaints. But to her utter fury, Jamie had produced a padlock and secured the leashes to an iron ring set into the wall by the dining room door. He had then kissed Clara on the forehead and told them to wait.

'I suppose they are having their dinner,' Clara mused, belatedly answering her cousin's last question.

Amelia glared at her. The position of her arms had tautened the thin silk over her breasts, and her pretty nipples were sticking out. The bunches made her look even sweeter and more vulnerable than usual. Amelia shook her head. 'And what about us,' she demanded, 'what about our dinner?'

'Oh Amelia,' Clara said softly, 'I - I don't think we are allowed to eat with... with... them.'

'Them? And who are they?' Amelia demanded furiously as the blonde girl quailed, her chain leash clinking as she cringed away. 'The adults? The quality?' Amelia spat the words, pulling herself to her full height and standing as erect and proudly as her bondage and shaming outfit would allow. 'I am an adult. I am nineteen and I am a baronet... I... I... I—'

'Of course you are Amelia, my sweet,' the Marchioness of Hatherby's husky, amused voice put in.

'Oh, Aunt Alicia.' Amelia was a little taken aback at Lady Alicia's abrupt appearance. Her ladyship was looking particularly resplendent in a mauve silk evening gown trimmed with cascades of white lace. Long mauve satin gloves complemented the dress, and her raven tresses were coiffed into an elegant arrangement. She smiled fondly at the tethered girls.

'And Clara, how lovely. My, how you have grown!'

'Jamie, he - he,' Amelia spluttered, 'he made us, he has dressed us like this, he - he chained us and left us here—'

Lady Alicia put a satin-covered finger to Amelia's lips. 'I know, and I know what a trial it must be to a girl of your spirit. Never mind. Look, he has given me the key.'

The woman winked and held up the padlock key, and Amelia felt her heart lift. Lady Alicia released the lock and took the ends of the leashes in her elegant gloved hand.

'Those men are having their cigars and port and—' she bestowed a radiant smile on the cousins '—no doubt discussing awful crudities.' She gave the leashes a firm tug and Amelia found herself stepping forward uncertainly. 'So you two little darlings had best come along with me.'

Amelia and Clara followed their aunt into the splendid drawing room.

'Aunt Alicia,' Amelia said as her aunt tugged them over to a comfortable chaise-longue.

'Yes, my dear?' Lady Alicia paused and half turned with a questioning expression.

'Do you think I - we - might have these awful straps and things removed? We've been trussed up like this for ages and it's ever so uncomfortable.'

To Amelia's distress, Alicia pursed her lips, as if considering this carefully. 'Not just yet, Amelia, I think.'

Amelia's heart sank as her aunt sat on the chaise, still holding their leashes, and indicated that the girls should get down on their knees. She tried another tack, for her need was becoming urgent.

'Please, Aunt, I - I really do need to be excused.'

'To be excused?' Alicia arched an eyebrow enquiringly.

'To go - I need to go.'

'But to go where?' Alicia idly picked a dressage-whip from the chaise with her free hand.

'To - to - to... I need to use the, the water-closet.'

'Oh!' Lady Alicia put the tip of the crop beneath Amelia's chin, lifted it and beamed. 'You need to go and do pee-pee! Silly girl, why on earth did you not say?'

'I...' Amelia blushed, abashed by her aunt's evident amusement.

'Did that beast Jamie not let you squat before had your bath?'

Now Amelia's cheeks turned crimson, and she knew Alicia was mocking her. Jamie had indeed offered her the use of a bucket in the nursery parlour before she had taken her bath. She had refused indignantly. Watching Clara tinkle into the bucket, frilly knickers around her ankles, as tears of pure embarrassment ran down the blonde girl's face, had not persuaded Amelia to change her mind. The nursery water-closet was kept locked now, and Jamie held the key, but she had told herself the chance was sure to come. If she absolutely had to, she had reasoned, she could even fill her bath a little more, once she got out of it. At least that would be in private. Unfortunately, Jamie's abrupt entrance had put paid to that particular scheme.

Amelia looked up at her aunt and pleaded with her eyes. The pressure in her bladder was getting worse all the time. For a long moment, she looked into her aunt's dark brown eyes and tried to fathom what the woman was thinking. At last, Lady Alicia leant forward and patted Amelia fondly on the cheek.

'You know, you really should have gone when you had the chance,' she said, and once again her beautiful face broke into a dazzling smile.

'I wonder what Hope Hall will be like?' Emma risked a shy smile at her companion as the carriage lumbered out of the reformatory gates.

Polly was seated opposite her. The interior of the coach was functional, even grim, with doors of black-painted iron, and the small windows were barred. However, the seats were of horse-hair and leather, and soft enough to mitigate the poor suspension over uneven ground. Emma was profoundly grateful for this, as the after-effects of her 'farewell' still lingered on the tender skin of her rear.

'At least we are quit of that place.' Polly gestured with her free hand in the direction from which the coach had come. 'You'll be all right, I expect.' The big girl gave Emma a wan smile.

'I'm sure you will be, too,' Emma said reassuringly.

The coach hit a rut and lurched violently, throwing both girls about on their seats. Only the handcuff, which manacled Emma's left hand to a bar set by the carriage door, prevented her from being thrown to the floor. She rubbed her wrist ruefully, for the violence of the motion had caused it to chafe against the iron bond. She looked at Polly, who had her own left wrist secured to the opposite door.

'I'm not so sure,' Polly said quietly. 'They obviously mean to make you a lady's-maid, eventually, but I think that the Marquis had special plans for me.'

'Oh.' Emma smiled encouragingly, although what she had overheard in the reformatory courtyard concerning her fellow passenger had puzzled her. 'Never mind, your job might be even better.' Polly showed no sign of cheering up, so Emma decided it might be best to change the subject. She looked around the prison carriage again.

'What were you in for?'

The big girl gave a resigned shrug. 'Oh, the usual. Gross moral turpitude. They caught me with a proscribed book. And you?'

Emma blushed, the shame of her conviction and the proceedings of the court still fresh. 'Immodesty and immorality,' she whispered and hung her head. 'I - they said I was pert to my mistress, when I would not... do something she asked... and, and then they said there were these stains on my sheets...' Emma blinked away a tear as she remembered the terrible injustice of it all. She looked up at the brown-eyed girl who was watching her sympathetically, and cheered up a little at the sight of a friendly face - a rather beautiful friendly face, at that.

'This is a surprise, anyway,' she said. 'When we arrived at the bridewell, we were just marched up from the train. I did not even know they had carriages like this.'

'They don't,' Polly said flatly. The coach passed under some trees and it became gloomier inside the padlocked carriage. 'I heard a wardress talking.' She looked at Emma. 'It seems this thing was sent by our new employers.' Both girls looked at the barred windows of the prison coach, and back at each other. 'Apparently, this splendid carriage is the property of Hope Hall.'

'I know it's hard, girls, but we all have to go through it.'

Amelia knelt next to Clara as their aunt, still holding their leashes in one hand and the long crop in the other, explained a little about their situation.

'Well, actually,' Lady Alicia continued, smiling smugly, 'it was different for me. But then, of course, I come from a different country.'

'Well, I don't see why—' Amelia muttered mutinously.

'Shhh, you must learn to speak when you are spoken to, if you wish to avoid... unpleasantness. There is a saying in Hatherby, which is "to bestow, first you must know". The Marquises of Hatherby and their families all have to taste the bitter dregs of servitude before they can be entrusted to wield the rod of true authority. In other words, if you wish power and privilege, you need to find out how it feels to be subjected to them.'

'So why isn't Jamie on a chain, then?' Amelia said sullenly.

Lady Alicia sighed, put down the crop and dropped the girls' leashes. She leant forward and lifted Amelia's face gently until the young woman was looking into her dark eyes. The older woman shook her head regretfully.

The slap was so sudden Amelia did not see it coming. Lady Alicia's left hand held her head, gently but firmly, as her right cracked across Amelia's cheek. 'Speak when you are spoken to,' she repeated slowly, eyes twinkling with merriment.

Rather than take up their leashes, she beckoned Clara to shuffle forward on her knees, and began unstrapping her bonds.

'Jamie,' she said, apparently electing to answer the question, despite having slapped Amelia for having the temerity to ask it, 'like Alex before him, attended public school.'

'Now,' she said to the unbound Clara, 'slip those silly frilly knickers off. I know they amuse young Jamie, but they give your pretty bottom a sight too much protection for the games we are going to play. Stand now, dear, and place your hands behind your neck. Look, Amelia, did you ever see such a pretty little sex? Mrs Pritchard tells me you enjoyed your shaving, by the way.'

Amelia blinked at Clara's shaven quim. As she was still on her knees, it was mere inches from her face. Her mouth felt dry. A potent mixture of fear and desire coursed through her veins.

'Very well. Clara, skip off and ring for the maid. Amelia, get up. I think we'll have your drawers off as well.'

Amelia watched glumly as her cousin tripped off towards the bell pull, the bottom of the girl's bare buttocks showing beneath the hem of the little smock as she moved. Her own panties were pulled down by Lady Alicia and she dutifully stepped out of them.

The leash-chain dangling from the collar felt particularly humiliating as she stood there, arms pinioned securely behind her, while Alicia's satin-clad hand fondly stroked her bottom. The chain descended, nestling snugly in the silk between her breasts, and then the cold metal brushed the naked flesh of her denuded quim. The sensation was quite unbearably tantalising and Amelia bit her lip as she tried to ignore the feeling, the pressure of her bladder, and her aunt's fingers exploring her bottom-flesh.

The maid arrived before Clara had returned to her aunt's side. A pretty blonde girl hurried in with a great deal of rustling of long, billowing silk skirts, carrying a large silver tray.

'Ah, very good, Kitty. Bring that over here.'

Despite herself, Amelia watched the maid's approach with some fascination. She was a very pretty girl with frizzy blonde locks which were barely restrained by a white lace maid's cap. The billowing skirts emphasised the girl's narrow waist, and her full breasts seemed about to burst out of the low-cut bodice. Apart from the fact that the girl's nipples could be seen peeking from the lace trim of the cups, the uniform might have been respectable, if old-fashioned. The element that made it seem peculiar was the sleek leather collar encircling the girl's slender throat, and matching wrist-cuffs. However, Amelia was most struck by what was on the tray.

To one side there was a plate with expensive-looking sweets; on the other, a stiff-looking paddle of black leather, and a rubber dog's toy shaped like a bone. The paddle was perforated with regular small holes, and something about it caused a prickle to run down the back of Amelia's neck.

'When training girls, I am a strong believer in the carrot and stick approach - or rather, in this case, bon-bons and paddle. Amelia, sit next to me and watch. I suspect you are not quite ready for this yet. Clara, get on your hands and knees.'

Alicia took the rubber toy from the tray. 'Now,' she said, 'I want you to retrieve this without getting from your knees or using your hands. Understand?'

Amelia watched as her cousin, blinking anxiously up at the woman on the chaise, gave a tentative nod. Clara licked her rosebud lips uncertainly.

'Now,' Lady Alicia instructed briskly, 'don't move a muscle until I say, "fetch".' The Marchioness threw the little rubber bone right across the drawing room. It bounced unevenly against the far wall before coming to rest under a chiffonier. Amelia followed its progress and then looked back at Clara kneeling on the floor. Clara was looking up at Lady Alicia nervously. There was silence for a moment as the four women in the room waited, each one of them, so it seemed, holding her breath.

'Fetch!' Lady Alicia said at last.

Clara looked up at her, at the bone, and back again, with pleading eyes and ever redder cheeks. For a moment Amelia thought her cousin was going to beg to be excused this duty, but it seemed that something in Lady Alicia's eyes dissuaded her for, with a small sigh, she turned and crawled across the carpet towards the toy.

Amelia watched her, rapt. Clara's bottom was quite exposed, her quim peeking back at the women grouped around the chaise. When she reached the chiffonier, Clara had to get her shoulders and head right down, arching her back and lifting her bare behind most prettily.

A moment later, the blonde girl emerged, the rubber toy between her teeth. Amelia could not suppress a smile as Clara crawled reluctantly back, eyes downcast and pure humiliation written across every inch of her lovely face.

'Here, girl!' Lady Alicia put out her hand and took the bone from Clara's mouth. 'Hold this for me, Amelia.' The woman held the saliva-slick thing up in front of her face. Amelia opened her mouth and took it reluctantly.

'Kitty!'

The maid who had been standing silently, bent at the waist, creaking slightly, and proffered the tray.

'What is it to be?' Lady Alicia moved her gloved hand from over the sweets to the paddle, and back again. 'Carrot or stick?' Her hand went back and forth hesitantly a few more times, fingers flexing. 'Paddle or bon-bon?'

She sighed theatrically and picked up the paddle. 'Recalcitrance and hesitation. When I say "fetch", you must go like an unleashed setter or I shall imagine that you do not wish to please me. Turn around, raise your bottom. That's it.'

Crack! Crack! Crack!

The little black paddle whipped down three times in quick succession and Clara shrieked with pain. She wiggled her bottom as if it were on fire, gasping and grimacing comically. Lady Alicia placed the paddle back on the tray and took the rubber bone from Amelia's lips.

'Stop that silly noise now, Clara.'

Amelia stared at her cousin's buttocks. The paddle had raised what looked like dozens of little blisters on Clara's bottom-cheeks. Clara was shaking her head furiously, still gasping from the pain.

Lady Alicia threw the bone again. This time it bounced around the casement window, coming to rest by the crimson velvet drapes.

Amelia looked at it, then at the still-wincing Clara, at the quietly smiling Marchioness, and at the impassive maid. The clock ticked on the mantelpiece and Lady Alicia's gown rustled a little as she shifted on her seat.

'Fetch!'

This time Clara fairly scurried across the room, grabbing the toy and turning quickly before crawling quickly back.

'Here, girl!' Lady Alicia Feversham took the toy once more and placed it in Amelia's mouth as Kitty bent and proffered the tray again.

Amelia held her breath and kept her eyes on Clara as her aunt's fingers hovered. The blonde girl was flushed from her exertions now, and panting a little, and there were some tears visible on her pretty face. Her eyes followed the movements of Lady Alicia's hand attentively.

'Carrot or stick? Carrot or stick? I have to admit that that was a lot better. But you could do better still.' The mauve fingers picked up the paddle again. 'Turn around and lift your bottom.'

Clara gave a despairing sob, but did as she was bid.

35

Crack! Crack! Crack! Crack! Crack!

Amelia watched, astonished, as the wicked device punished Clara's cheeks again. Her cousin howled in agony as the paddle cracked across her bottom and her thighs. Five hard blows punished Clara's hindquarters. Amelia, sitting helplessly bound, watched open-mouthed and felt her blood freeze. How Clara kept in position, she could not imagine. The blonde squealed like a stuck pig and wriggled her behind furiously, but somehow she managed not to bolt. Amelia saw her cousin's knuckles whiten as she pawed desperately at the carpet. Her slender shoulders quivered violently as she convulsively curled and uncurled her toes.

Lady Alicia placed the paddle back on the silver platter, took a bon-bon and calmly placed it in her mouth. She allowed Clara several minutes to recover. Amelia watched her cousin's bottom and thighs bloom with a fresh crop of the little blister-like swellings. Most of her hindquarters were a furious scarlet, now.

By the time Lady Alicia had finished her bon-bon, Clara had stopped howling, though she was still sobbing. Amelia stared at her cousin's bottom, wondering if it felt as sore as it looked, and how long she might hope to avoid finding out the answer for herself.

'Come here, Clara!' Lady Alicia ordered crisply. Clara turned quickly and raised her tear-splashed face apprehensively. Lady Alicia produced a lace-trimmed handkerchief.

'Now, cousin, you must stop this silly blubbing.' Tenderly, she wiped the tears from Clara's face. 'What is the matter, did I make your little bottom a bit warm?'

'I, ah, it... it's agony!' Clara gasped.

'Oh dear,' Lady Alicia said mildly. She stroked Clara's cheek. 'Well then—' the steel in her rich voice was unmistakable '—you had better try a little harder to please me, had you not?'

'Y-yes... Aunt Alicia,' Clara sniffled, her eyes wide with terror.

'Good girl!' Lady Alicia bestowed a dazzling smile and took the rubber bone from Amelia's lips. 'Now, dear, would you care to try the game again?'

'I think we must be there.' Emma pressed her face against the iron bars of the coach's window. The coach had stopped and the driver was talking to a man who had opened heavy iron gates. Both men seemed to be laughing but she could not hear what they said.

The coach lurched forward and through the gates and the girls could hear the wheels scrunch on a gravel drive. Emma tensed in anticipation of their imminent arrival at the hall, but she had not reckoned on the size of the grounds. The coach trundled on as both girls tried to peer out, but it was dark and there was little to see.

Finally, as the coach neared the hall, Emma made out its shape in the moonlight. A looming fortress-like tower was her first sight of the hall as the carriage approached its ancient west wing. Before it reached this ominous-looking keep, however, the coach turned sharply to the left. They found themselves jolted as the wheels rattled over cobbles, and then it lurched to a stop.

They were not furnished with lights, but there was sufficient illumination from without for the girls to exchange an apprehensive glance. Polly's face and dark soulful eyes looked even lovelier in the moonlight. As the key rattled in the padlock of the door on Emma's side, she reached across and gave her companion's hand a farewell squeeze.

'Good journey, girls?' The sandy-haired youth who had manacled them into the carriage looked in, grinning. He climbed in and unlocked the handcuff securing Emma. 'Step outside, if you please.'

Emma did as she was told. A stern-faced, black-clad woman awaited her, next to a big balding man.

'Yours, I think, Mrs Pritchard. I can't see this little chit winning the Silver Cup!'

'Emma Swift?'

'Yes, ma'am.' Emma gave an awkward curtsey.

'You'll need to be swift here, girl, if you wish to save your tender skin.'

There was a creaking from the carriage as the boy and Polly descended. The man and woman looked from Emma to the tall girl.

'And this must be your filly, Mr Blackstock. Come along with me, Emma.' The woman turned on her heel and hurried off.

Emma half-turned to follow her, then looked back at her new friend.

'Polly Thomas, sir.' The big girl gave a curtsey in her turn.

As Emma turned to scurry after the receding back of Mrs Pritchard, she heard the groom growl, 'Not any more, you're not.'

'That's it. Good girl.' Lady Alicia beamed at Clara who was flat on her belly and fervently licking the woman's stockinged toes. 'The little darling really tries to please, don't you think, Amelia? She just needs some rigorous training to stop that silly thinking about orders. Soon, I am quite sure, the little love will learn to just obey!'

Amelia could neither see nor guess what Clara could do to be more submissive or obedient. For the last few throws of the rubber toy, she had waited for the order to fetch, poised like a retriever, as Lady Alicia stroked her golden hair. Then she had shot across the room and grabbed it in her mouth, hurtling back on hands and knees as fast as ever she could. Trembling, Clara had awaited the judgement. Twice she had been given a sweet and time to eat it as tears of relief and gratitude welled in her eyes. Once more she had been judged deficient and received another five hard cracks across the bottom with the paddle. Amelia had never heard her cousin, or anyone else, howl quite so heartbreakingly before.

Amelia's need to urinate had not grown any less pressing as she sat watching her aunt train Clara. Part of her was delighted by the sight. Part of her was truly frightened for, at any moment, she knew she might replace Clara as the object of Aunt Alicia's spite. Mostly though, she did not really care what was happening to Clara, but just wanted the performance to end so she might get the chance to go and seek relief.

'Very well, Clara, put my shoes back on. I think it must be time for us to join the gentlemen. Kitty, you may go up to my chamber now and prepare yourself. I doubt if I will be very long.'

Amelia was aghast as her aunt picked up her leash. She looked down at her still-naked and shaven quim, and back up at Lady Alicia.

'Please, Aunt, you can't. I mean—' The cold look in Aunt Alicia's eye stopped her mouth, but she continued pleading with her eyes.

The woman patted her on the cheek consolingly. 'Amelia, don't make such a fuss. You don't have anything down there that these gentlemen have not seen! Now, come along girls. No, Clara, no need to get up.'

It was an odd little party that made its way down the corridor; the elegantly turned-out Lady Alicia, rustling in her mauve silk gown and lingerie, Clara crawling in her little smock and stockings, scarlet bottom glowing like a beacon, and Amelia, similarly attired, arms still in bondage, trotting along stiff-legged on Lady Alicia's leash.

'All right, girl, get those clothes off and get into the bath.'

The scullery was stone-flagged and gloomy, but at least it was not cold. A tin bath had been placed and filled in the middle of the floor. Emma looked up at Mrs Pritchard uncertainly, and started to unbutton her grey reformatory dress.

'Get undressed.'

The stable smelled of leather, hay and horse-sweat. Polly looked up furtively at Mr Blackstock and the two grinning stable-boys. She could not stop the blush, but there seemed to be nothing else for it. Dropping her gaze, she began to unbutton the coarse uniform.

'Ah, splendid! The ladies at last. Amelia, my dear, and Clara too. May I say you both look radiant.'

Amelia stared at the floor as Lord Alex greeted them, and tried not to pout too obviously. She was having difficulty standing still now, the insistent pressure of her bladder becoming more and more uncomfortable by the minute. However, this was not so distracting as to materially lessen her sense of shame. She could feel the hem of her smock against her belly, just too high to cover her freshly shaven quim. Furtively, she leant forward, in a futile attempt to lower the material enough. There were three men in the smoking room: as well as Jamie and Lord Alex, who she had expected, there was a well-built man in a dog-collar, who had been chatting when the girls' entrance brought the gentlemen's conversation to a sudden halt.

Lady Alicia bent and placed the handle of Clara's leash in her mouth. 'Clara and I have been playing fetch. I'm afraid I had to smack her bottom a little bit. Scamper over there now, mischief, and show Master Jamie your behind.'

Clara did as she was told. Amelia glanced up long enough to see that the three men's eyes were locked onto her cousin's still-red rear. Then Lady Alicia clapped her hands together.

'But, for heaven's sake, where are my manners? I forgot that you have not been formally introduced. Miss Clara Tattershall and the Honourable Amelia Colinbrooke, may I introduce our rector, the Reverend Richard Dawes. I expect you might have heard of him, for he is rather famous.'

Heard of him? Amelia was thunderstruck - of course she had! How could any girl not know the name of the author of *Dawes's Domestic Discipline*, a copy of which sat on the shelves of every house of quality in the country? Who did not know the name of the man who had written a dozen best-selling works on every aspect of corporal chastisement, with especial regard to the punishment of girls? The man whose disciplinary skills had been called upon by the highest in the land, and whose cane had been applied, so it was rumoured, across the bottoms even of royal princesses.

Amelia was no coward, yet even so she might well have preferred not to meet the man at all. To meet him so, half-naked and helplessly bound, was enough to make the bravest young lady quail. There was nothing for it, though. She took a deep breath and looked up, determined not to reveal the extent of her trepidation.

He was quite a handsome man. At least, his visage was less diabolic than she had imagined. He was clean-shaven, with rather short brown hair, greying at the temples. His face was ordinary - except for his eyes. They were grey, a cold slate grey, and there was something about the intensity of his gaze that caused Amelia, just for a moment, to forget to breathe. It was as if the man looked straight into her soul, searched and judged and found her wanting.

He kept his eyes on her for a long moment, and Amelia found herself mesmerised, unable to look away whilst he kept her locked in his gaze. Then he looked down at her lower belly.

'Charming,' he said at last and took another pull at his cigar. Then he looked down at Clara, who was wincing as Jamie stroked her martyred bottom.

'Well, Jamie, it looks like you are teaching them a thing or two.'

'Oh, it's early days,' the young man said. 'And Clara is a good girl, really. Would you not agree, Aunt Alicia?'

Lady Alicia murmured her heartfelt assent to this as Jamie gestured with the stub of his cigar towards Amelia. 'Of course,' he said languidly, 'that little minx is a different prospect altogether.'

'Oh, yes,' the Reverend Dawes said quietly, 'yes, indeed. That I can see. For one thing, the way she is fidgeting, one might conclude that she had ants in her pants.' He paused. 'That is, had she any pants within which to contain such minuscule arthropods!'

Amelia's cheeks burnt as the company roared with laughter. Just as this was fading, there was a tap at the door and Mrs Pritchard entered.

'The secure carriage has arrived, milord. You asked to be informed.'

'Quite right, thank you, Pritchard - and the filly?'

'Is in the stables now, sir.' She turned to Lady Alicia. 'The new maid has been put to work in the kitchen.'

Lord Alex stood and bowed to the Reverend Dawes. 'Going to beat you this year, Richard! Please excuse me, I need to go and check my secret weapon.' He stood and hurried out.

'Would you think me very rude if I were to leave you with Jamie and the girls now, Richard?' Lady Alicia asked. 'I also have some pressing staff matters to attend to.'

The Reverend Dawes expressed his perfect satisfaction at being left with Jamie and his charges and Lady Alicia withdrew, to the accompaniment of a great deal of rustling.

'This is the way it's going to be, see.'

Polly was completely naked now. Her long hair had been pulled into a ponytail by Mr Blackstock's surprisingly deft fingers, and a rope halter put around her neck. He had led her into a little stall. Open at the front, this consisted of a stone back wall and two partitions of planking, about two yards in length, and four feet apart. The floor of this was strewn with straw which tickled her bare feet as he led her into it and secured the rope on a large iron ring.

'You are to be trained to run with a cart. You are to be Lord Alex's pony. It won't be forever, but it will be pretty tough. Lord Alex is determined to win the cup this year, and that is going to mean a lot of very hard training.'

He used her hair to pull her down until she was kneeling in the straw. Then he left her for a moment, returning with a length of thick-looking leather strapping. 'Now, there's something you must understand. His Lordship believes you get the best out of a girl if you treat her strictly, like a pony. I don't know if there's anything in this method. The Reverend Dawes don't hold with it and he's won two years on the trot, to coin a phrase.' The big man grinned at his own joke and slapped the strap against his massive thigh. 'But, anyway, it's what his lordship wants, and so it's what his lordship gets, understand?'

'Y-yes sir, I think... Ooh!'

The strap cracked across her upper arm.

'Wrong! Ponies don't talk, you silly mare. You may nod or shake your head in response to a direct question. Otherwise, from now on, a single word from those pretty lips will earn you a leathering.' He slapped the strap against his leg again and grinned. 'Ponies don't try to cover up their titties, neither.'

Hurriedly Polly dropped her arms, although this made her breasts feel horribly vulnerable to the terrifying groom.

'Good girl,' he growled and motioned her to turn around. Polly faced the stone back wall and felt his rough hands explore her body. 'Well, there is a little muscle here.' He slipped his hand between her legs and squeezed her thigh firmly, appraising the flesh in a brusque professional manner.

'Will she do, Ben?' Polly froze as she recognised the languid tones of Lord Alex.

'Perhaps, your lordship, but there's a lot of work to do. These long legs will eat up the ground, but she'll have to put on a lot of muscle if she is to have a chance of staying on the second ascent of Holly Hill.' He gave the back of Polly's right thigh a stinging slap, by way of illustration. She bit her lip and made herself stay in position.

'Get her up for me. We can trot her properly in the morning, but I want to have a look.'

The groom took her by the ponytail and guided her to her feet and out of the stall into the open area of the stable-block. Lord Alex held a lantern up, his bewhiskered face illuminated by it, his sharp eyes gleaming in the lamplight. Polly was not sure if she was more frightened of the lord, or the groom holding her halter and his wicked strip of leather.

'Yes, yes,' Lord Alex spoke a little hoarsely. 'Damn me, Ben, I think the filly might just do it. Now, I want her fed well. We need to put some meat on those thighs.' He stepped forward, holding the lamp up, and Polly suppressed a whimper as he reached between her legs as the groom had done a moment earlier, but this time from the front.

'Steady, girl. Easy, now, easy,' Mr Blackstock whispered in her ear. His hand stole around her back and rested on her hip, gently preventing her from stepping back as Lord Alex felt her thighs. 'Have you decided what to call her yet, your lordship?'

'Mm, yes. She's such a pretty filly, I rather thought I would name her "Blossom".'

His strong hand started to move up her thigh. Despite herself, she gave a gasp and flinched, but Mr Blackstock's strong arm held her steady. His hand stroked up and down reassuringly, without relinquishing its hold.

40

'Easy now, there's a good girl,' he murmured as Lord Feversham's finger probed and she whimpered nervously. Then, on finding a well-lubricated welcome, it slid inside her sex.

The low insistent voice was almost hypnotic in the soft glow of the lamplight. 'Easy, Blossom, easy girl. Easy now, Blossom, my beauty.' The naked girl leant back in the groom's grip and a lost cry escaped her lips in response to the touch.

The Reverend Dawes placed his hand on Amelia's stocking-sheathed knee and sighed. 'You mean to say, she refused the bucket? Really, girl! That is shocking!'

What was shocking, Amelia thought furiously, was that she had to stand in front of this man, nearly naked, as he idly caressed her thigh with one hand and toyed with her leash with the other. The Reverend had finished his cigar but was still sitting comfortably as she trembled, partly from fear and partly from a sense of outraged decency, before him.

'Clara here pulled a face or two, but she squatted obediently enough in the end,' Jamie said. The girl in question knelt with her head on her master's knee as he stroked her hair. 'Amelia is, I regret to say, refractory, disobedient and very, very stubborn. It will be a long hard road with her, I fear.'

'No doubt strewn with thorns, eh, girl?'

Amelia winced as he pinched the bare flesh of her right inner thigh, just above the top of her stocking.

'You know, I am setting up a little disciplinary course for wayward girls later on in the year, at the Rectory.'

Amelia found herself pinioned by those cold grey eyes again. Fear suffused her and she seemed to be experiencing difficulty in breathing once again. The hand moved up her thigh, fondling the bare flesh appreciatively.

'Yes, you mentioned it. Just six trainees at a time, is that right?'

'That is correct. More, and I might not be able to give each candidate sufficient personal attention.'

The eyes bored into hers. Amelia felt herself sway. For some reason her knees did not want to support her.

'Might do her good,' Jamie said thoughtfully.

'Might do her a lot of good.' Reverend Dawes gave Amelia a smile and squeezed her thigh. She could not quite suppress a low whimper of trepidation.

'Unfortunately—' the Reverend Dawes drew the word out, '—it would be impossible.'

Amelia breathed again. Her sigh of relief was audible and he cocked a questioning eyebrow.

'I only mentioned the idea to a few friends and I already have a full course and a waiting list.' His hand reached Amelia's shaven quim. It was impossible to step back as he held the leash taut. To her surprise, his fingers were gentle, fondling rather than probing. 'That damned book, you see.' The Reverend laughed, self-deprecatingly. 'I get so many requests to demonstrate my methods, I would spend the entire year travelling the country if I acceded to them all. That was the idea of the course, you see. At least for six months I shall get to stay in Hatherby.' He laughed but his eyes did not, remaining fixed on Amelia's.

'So your course is to be six months?'

'That's right. Six months...' his fingers left her quim and stroked up until they rested on her lower belly, just above her nearly bursting bladder, and as he spoke he pressed gently but firmly, one prod with every separate syllable '...of most rig-o-rous' the pressure was almost too much to withstand 'disc-i-plin-ary train-ing.'

THINGS THAT GO BUMP IN THE NIGHT

Lady Alicia enjoyed her chambermaid's ordeal from a comfortable chair. Fifteen minutes earlier, she had opened and closed the bedroom door and then stolen back silently on stockinged feet, at pains not to let an unguarded movement set her leather corset creaking and alert Kitty to the presence of her mistress. The Marchioness of Hatherby observed her maid's growing distress with bright eyes, idly fingering her fine black dressage whip.

Kitty whimpered. The heat was growing, the warm glow evidently becoming uncomfortably hot, the guttering candle sending pulses of heat towards the maid's twitching bottom.

'No... please...'

Lady Alicia smiled. Kitty was forbidden to speak. The girl began to desperately wriggle within the limited scope her bonds allowed, though fidgeting was strictly prohibited.

'Please... it's burning... mercy... somebody...'

The observer could see there was, as yet, no danger. The heat was real but Kitty's imagination no doubt amplified it tenfold. The chains clinked as she strained and wriggled ever more frantically. Lady Alicia luxuriated in the spectacle. She would never tire, she thought, of tormenting this maid.

Sheer black stockings set off kitty's long legs, her plump and creamy thighs surging from the tight stocking-tops in a way that seemed to Lady Alicia positively poetic. Though her waist was cinched to nineteen inches by the corset, her breasts and bottom were firm, round and full.

'Ooh... aah... Mistress, where are you? Mercy. Please, somebody, help me!'

With a convulsive jerk, Kitty yelped in pain and one of the nipple clamps popped off.

Lady Alicia smiled a smile of purest malice and stood up, crop in hand.

'Mercy, mercy, please, put it out! Put it *out!* Somebody help me, please...'

Lady Alicia stood close by, watching intently as her maid babbled and begged increasingly incoherently. Finally, as Kitty started shrieking, but before the skin nearest the flame began to redden, she raised the crop and slashed it down. With consummate skill, she hit the candlewick with the tip of the crop, extinguishing the flame with a single stroke.

'Stand still.' Her voice echoed around the chamber. 'And for God's sake stop that awful mewling noise!'

The straw was a little ticklish but otherwise surprisingly comfortable. The naked girl lay under a horse-blanket, for the late spring night was still a little chilly. She was still tethered by the rope halter around her neck although, as her hands were free, it would have been a simple matter to untie herself. Not that she could have run, for she had been hobbled with iron cuffs connected by three large links of chain. Anyway, the girl, no longer quite sure if she was Polly or Blossom, had no real desire to run away.

It was frightening, certainly, and confusing, this strange new world where, it seemed, she was supposed to try to behave as if she were a pony. Almost like a pony, anyway. She smiled to herself in the dark, doubting if Lord Alex did what he had done to her to his four-legged mounts. The memory of his insistent finger, and of the groom's powerful hands and irresistible grip, caused the strangest sensations to course through her body anew. She reached down, her thighs clamped upon her hand, and a low moan troubled the night air.

It took Kitty a few moments to realise what was happening, longer to recover some composure, but awareness of her mistress's presence quickly had effect and she stood, panting and gasping, flooded with relief that was sadly short-lived.

'What a disgusting spectacle! Squawking and mewling like a scalded cat.' Lady Alicia grasped the end of the candle in her leather-gloved hand and pulled it out unceremoniously, letting it drop into the bowl.

Kitty was quivering all over, unable to see but aware of both her mistress's displeasure and her own exposed condition. She tried not to think of what Lady Alicia might be about to do with her crop. The blindfold was yanked off and there was a blaze of light. Suddenly Lady Alicia stood before her, resplendent in a long black leather corset, long gloves and thigh boots, stiletto-heeled and brilliantly polished. The Marchioness flexed her awful switch, her lovely face contorted with fury.

'Speaking without permission! Fidgeting!' She struck the loose chain and dangling nipple clamp with the tip of her crop. 'Look at this! I've rarely seen such a disgraceful exhibition. Have you anything to say, you pitiful creature?'

'I'm sorry, mistress... I was fr-frightened,' Kitty sobbed.

'I shall have to take you to the Tower again, if this recalcitrance continues.'

'Oh please, mistress, I promise I'll be more obedient.'

'Hm. Well, we'll see. You will have to be whipped, so mind you take it well - but first I have need of that tongue of yours.'

Lady Alicia snapped off Kitty's restraints. Movement sent vicious jolts of pain through the girl's stiff arms and legs, but she was allowed no leisure to massage them. Her hair was grabbed and she was hauled over to the centre of the room where Lady Alicia forced the maid to her knees, standing with legs wide, exposing her sex. With the end of the crop, she raised Kitty's chin, until her eyes bored into Kitty's own pleading orbs. 'You know what to do, don't you?'

'Yes, mistress.'

'What?'

'I... I have to lick your... your pussy, mistress.' For all her time at Hope Hall, Kitty blushed at this.

'Do you want to?'

Kitty swallowed hard. 'Yes, mistress,' she whispered, cheeks aflame.

'Then ask me nicely!'

'P-please... may I lick your pussy, mistress?'

'What a little slut you are Kitty, begging to lick me. You ought to hear yourself, you whore. I ought to make you lick my arse - it's no more than you deserve - but I find myself in need of some relief.'

Snapping her fingers, she pointed down and Kitty leant forward and kissed between her mistress's legs, softly, fervently. She inserted her tongue, cat-like, between the labial lips and lapped upward to the place that always made her mistress frenzied.

'Christ! That's it, go on, you little slut.' Lady Alicia bucked wildly, uttering bloodcurdling threats and blaspheming. Kitty's face was smeared with juices as she sought to keep her tongue in contact with the flesh around the clit. Lady Alicia was pumping her pelvis so violently now, smacking herself into Kitty's face, that the maid could only stick her tongue out blindly, hoping to hit the right spot.

'Oh, yes! You little whore, where's that tongue of yours? Get it in!'

She grasped Kitty's hair in both hands, letting the crop dangle from her wrist. Lady Alicia shrieked and bucked as if possessed by demons, grinding Kitty's face into her crotch until the girl could neither see nor breathe, then let out a final scream and her whole body shuddered as Kitty wormed her tongue deep at the finish.

A low moan was followed by a filthy oath. Lady Alicia took a moment to recover from her climax, retaining but relaxing her grip on Kitty's tresses. Kitty kept her mouth glued to Lady Alicia's nether lips well after the orgasm had subsided, knowing better than to move away unbidden. Finally, Lady Alicia shook herself.

'Well, you little slut, are you going to kneel there licking my slit all night? Get up. We've a whipping to attend to.'

The rhythmic bumping from next door appeared to be reaching a crescendo. There was a high clear cry like that of some exotic bird, then a girl's voice, shouting, 'Oh yes, yes, sir. Oh yes! Oh yes! Oh yes, master!'

Amelia put her hands over her ears but it was no good; she could still hear it. All she could do was lay and fume as she perspired between the pungent sheets of latex. Infuriating as the sounds of Clara and Jamie's coupling were, at least they afforded some measure of distraction from her own rapidly increasing discomfort. The rubber sheets felt strange and clammy against the bare skin of her breasts and back and legs.

Once again she shifted, provoking odd sounding, rubbery creaks from the sheets. The tacky-feeling latex rasped her erect nipples almost painfully as she moved. There was no doubt about it, it was getting hotter and hotter in her little latex prison.

A last scream of pleasure came from the room next door. Amelia scowled and tried not to think about the clammy feeling of rubber on her skin. It felt strange, yet smelt even stranger. A perverse cocktail of latex and sweat assailed Amelia's nostrils until her head was spinning. She tried in vain to recoil from the viscid embrace of the rubber sheets, and her latex cocoon was getting stickier by the minute. It felt as if she were being enveloped; sucked into the obscene maw of some great clammy nightmare creature.

Lying still was the best plan, controlling her breathing and trying not to perspire. Amelia tried to ignore the grunts and gasps that came from her cousin's room, but she had to think of something, apart from how sticky she felt, and most of all, about the smoking room. She would just refuse to think about it ever again!

'So pleased to make your acquaintance, madam.' Reverend Dawes had bowed low in a mocking politeness - after her humiliation. 'I do hope we shall meet again very soon.'

Lying in her sticky little bed, the memory of his devouring eyes impaled her. How she hated that man! Then she groaned, and pressed her hands harder against her sex. It was as if her hand had taken on a will of its own. She did not want to do what her fingers seemed compelled to do, for she knew it was risky.

Amelia moaned as the tips of her fingers found their target. Her body writhed in response to her own touch, and her squirming was making the rubber slick with perspiration. The clamminess of the sheets eased by degrees into a much more slippery embrace, as her perspiration provided ever more copious lubrication. The image of the Reverend Dawes's fingers fondling her sex vied in her mind's eye with the vision of his transfixing gaze. Oh, how she hated him! Amelia bucked and moaned as her fingers worked harder and faster. The man was a devil, a brute! She devoutly wished for nothing more to do with him.

Amelia gave a strangulated groan as her legs thrashed back and forth in their enfolding envelope. The point of no return was suddenly upon her. Amelia bit her lip as her climax started.

'You filthy swine!' she cried, the hateful figure of the Revered Dawes, a cane gripped in his hand, somehow the only thing she could think of as the first shock-waves of her climax started to engulf her. Her cries became completely incoherent as she thrashed wildly in the sheet's moist latex embrace.

Emma could not sleep, though she was very tired. It was well that she was not claustrophobic, for her bed was in a sort of cupboard in the corridor off the kitchen. Just long enough to lie flat in, with a couple of feet of height and slightly more width, it was much like being locked into a chest. She comforted herself that there were air-holes in the wooden door which let fingers of yellow gaslight into her little prison. At least she was comfortable. The sheets and cotton nightdress felt luxurious after the coarse reformatory bedding, and the mattress, though thin, was a real improvement on bare bridewell boards. It was neither discomfort nor confinement that was keeping her awake.

The truth was that she missed the company, if not the conditions, of the reformatory. Night in her dormitory had been full of sounds: the moans of girls whose bottoms had been welted that day, trying to find a comfortable position; the clank of manacles, for each girl was tethered nightly to her bed by an anklet and stout iron chain; the low murmur of friends risking a furtive gossip, and the gasps of those daring girls who would not, or could not, obey the strict reformatory rules regarding self-abuse. Above all, there had been the breathing of her fellow inmates and the sense that her ordeal was being shared.

Here, Emma felt alone. Mrs Pritchard seemed as cold as she was imperious. Cook, who had set her to work at once, was a big jolly woman who wielded a wooden spoon with vigour. Emma slipped her hand over her bottom, feeling to see if the tenderness had abated yet. The skin still felt a little sore. Cook had a strong arm and her wooden spoon had been very big and extremely hard. The first time she had ordered Emma to hoist her skirts, it had just been a few sharp cracks. The second time, it had been a few more, and the new girl had had to hop about for several minutes, clutching her hot cheeks, before returning to scouring pans.

The third time Cook took the spoon to her had been terrible. Emma had missed a minuscule mark on one of Cook's copper pans and the big woman was furious. Grabbing the hapless kitchen-maid by her earlobe she had hauled her around the big table and sat down on her chair, forcing Emma over her knee in the same well-practised movement. Emma's skirt had been lifted and her new cotton drawers pulled brusquely apart, almost before she knew what was happening.

The wooden spoon came down and down again in quick succession. Emma had squealed and squirmed in the large woman's grip, all to no avail. Once she got her hand back protectively, but her knuckles had been instantly rapped.

The paddling continued until Emma shrieked herself hoarse. Her bottom was sore, and she had kicked and bucked increasingly desperately. All in vain. Cook's arm had been relentless, and her imprisoning grip tremendously strong.

Finally, sobbing and gasping for breath whilst desperately clutching her hot buttocks, Emma had been thrust off that capacious lap.

'Get on with your work,' Cook had ordered curtly. Blinking tears from her eyes, Emma watched the woman place the big spoon back on its hook. Then she had hurried back to her pile of washing-up.

Another day of that tomorrow, she thought and sighed, wondering what else the day would bring. What had happened to poor Polly? Emma thought, a little sadly. When would she see her friend again?

There was another muffled bump. Lucy strained her ears, lying so still as she listened that she even ceased to breathe for a few seconds. Whatever the sound had been, it was not followed by those so familiar footsteps. She sighed. Innumerable mysterious noises haunted the long nights at Hope Hall, and they might have been designed to drive a girl to distraction.

Not that there was much she could do but lie still and listen. Lucy was in no state to get to sleep. She writhed slowly in bed, in her plain little attic room, trying not to moan aloud, trying to assuage the maddening tingling between her legs. Not for the first time, she cursed the cruelty of the master who had ordered her wrists cuffed and secured to a stout leather collar and her ankles secured, well apart, to the foot of the bed. The collar was chained to the head of her iron bedstead and there was no way to move more than an inch or two in any one direction. The only pressure she could get against her clitoris was from the insubstantial weight of the blanket. This was rough enough to prickle her bare skin, but not heavy enough to use to attain relief.

Lucy whimpered. She wore a short cotton nightdress, but this had gradually ridden up as she writhed in the little bed. It was diabolical. If she stayed quite still her shift would not ride up, and she would not have to endure the prickling of the rough horse-blanket against her swollen, shaven mons. However, she found this quite impossible to achieve, and every time she was put into this situation the same thing happened. Her own involuntary movements caused the garment to work its way up until the hem was ruched around her waist. The tickle of the rough blanket against her tenderest tissues would then drive her further into a state of frenzied desperation.

There was another noise and she froze again. Yes, surely that was a footfall on the stair? A heavy tread. It must be him, coming to take pity on her, surely?

It had been late when Lucy had been summoned to serve brandy in Lord Alex's private study. Lady Alicia was elsewhere; no doubt finding new ways to vex her little blonde maid in her boudoir. Usually, Lucy would consider this to be a favourable situation. If she was alone with Lord Alex, even if she had to endure a whipping, there was more chance that he would screw her afterward and thus she would attain some measure of relief before being pinioned for the night. A good chance but, unfortunately, no guarantee.

That night, he had read for a long while, sipping brandy and smoking a cigar as she stood to one side, silently awaiting her master's pleasure. The Marquis had been perusing the very latest work, delivered by the author himself, the Reverend Dawes. This volume was a collection of improving anecdotes, entitled *Bridled Lust - The Suppression of Vice in Nubility, From Chastity Belts to Chastisement*. From time to time, Lord Alex had jocularly read out passages that took his fancy, or informed the maid of what he considered an especially interesting fact.

'I say, listen to this, Lucy my pet! "When Dr Fergus MacCuip was appointed governor of the penal colony on the island of Latigazo, he was shocked to find the female prisoners greatly addicted to self abuse."'

He had paused and turned to look directly at Lucy, who had dropped her gaze demurely. 'Rather like you, eh, you little monkey?' Lord Alex laughed and Lucy had been unable to stop the blush spreading across her cheeks.

'"He was at a loss as how to control this vice, as he found that whipping the culprits only seemed to make them more determined to masturbate." Ha, we know all about that particular phenomenon, do we not, Miss Nimble Fingers? Perhaps he should have had them trussed like you at night, eh, girl? That would have stopped the vixens' tricks, I'll warrant!'

Lord Alex had taken another sip of brandy before returning to his passage. '"Until one day he treated a cook who had inadvertently rubbed her eye after preparing a dish with the island's famed diablo peppers, a fearsome local variety of the *habenero*, widely respected for its blistering ferocity. Even though the girl had washed her hands before touching her eye, it had swollen painfully. This gave Dr MacCuip his great idea. That night, he required that the girls in his charge chop up peppers. Then they were sent to bed. A few minutes later, the howls of agony from the first culprit rent the tropical night. Then the next girl sang out, and the next. Dr MacCuip sat and listened with satisfaction to the symphony of shrieks as he laid his plans for making chilli sauce production a mainstay of the penal colony's economy."'

Again Lord Alex had paused and taken a pull at his cigar. '"The product was a great success. It was called Firefinger Sauce, and to this day features a dusky maid with watering eyes on the label!"'

There could be only one eventual result of Lord Alex reading such material. Eventually he had closed the book with a snap so decided that it had caused Lucy to start. There had been a long pause, long enough for her to wonder, with mounting panic, what he planned to do with her.

'It's late, so I think I will just give you a spanking, sweetheart. Pull up those skirts and get over my knee.'

Lucy found the short skirts of the 'tutu' which she sometimes had to wear most shamefully revealing, yet the full skirts and petticoats of her full uniform had drawbacks of their own. Pulling up the voluminous material far enough to expose her bottom was not easy. Failure to do so adequately was certain to earn extra slaps. Somehow she had bent, billowing skirts and all, over her master's lap, but the tutting told her that she had not succeeded in baring her bottom to his satisfaction.

Crack!

His hard hand stung her right thigh.

'Ooh!'

'Be silent, girl. I told you to lift your skirts.' There was a deal of rustling silk as he struggled with the copious material. 'These long skirts are a bother. As are all these petticoats. Still, your bottom does look peachy like that, against the folds of white cotton. You really must stop clenching it, though. You know that by now.'

There had been a warning growl in his voice and Lucy had somehow managed to relax her bottom-cheeks. Then she had been spanked. Lord Alex was a big man, extremely strong for all his indolent airs, and his hand was very, very hard. Lucy had tried to stay silent, as she was supposed to when her master spanked her, but all too soon found that the cries of pain were being forced through her tightly gritted teeth. Again and again his hand had come down, cracking across her bottom-cheeks, and then the backs of her thighs, where these were bare above the tops of her silk stockings.

Lord Alex had gruffly ordered her to be quiet, but her bottom stung like fury and little yips and gasps of pain spilled out with every smack as the pain built up and up and up... Perhaps he had been feeling merciful - more likely the reading had aroused him to the point where his own need had become urgent. Whatever the reason, for once, a short spanking was all Lord Alex had required her to endure.

'All right, get on your knees. Frig me, girl, quickly now.'

As fast as she could manage, the skirts slowing her down considerably, Lucy had sunk to her knees at his left side. A little hesitantly, but deftly nonetheless, she unbuttoned her master's breeches and took out his long thing. The sight of it, as always, made her feel a little dizzy. He had not ordered her to suck it on this occasion, so she had not. Instead, the maid leant forward and pumped a dainty fist up and down as she delicately teased his balls with her free hand.

'Oh, God, yes, that's it. You're getting better at this, you cheeky little bitch,' he had murmured between grunts of pleasure. 'Practice makes perfect, eh? You saucy baggage!'

Lucy's heart had skipped a beat at his words. She had been whipped enough times in the past for not getting this job right. Still she hardly dared hope it, but it seemed she might give satisfaction this time. She licked her lips anxiously and concentrated on the task in hand with renewed attention.

'Oh, God, yes!'

It had begun twitching in her hand and she could have sworn that the blue veins marbling the shaft were throbbing. Lucy had felt a surge of panic flood her. He had not given her any instructions for this stage. If he spurted and made a mess she might well earn a whipping, yet it was not her place to decide whether to catch his spending in her mouth, her hands or, as Lord Alex sometimes preferred, over her breasts. What was she supposed to do with it this time?

'All right, girl, take it in your mouth.'

Her question answered, Lucy had placed the glans between her lips in the very nick of time, for she felt the hot spurt hit the back of her throat a split second later.

Once she would have choked - but no longer. Lucy had been trained to swallow. Dutifully she accepted the fluid, keeping her head bowed and trying to ignore the burning of her bottom and the throbbing in her loins.

He had not taken her and she had known, only too well, what that was going to mean.

The footsteps were coming closer. Lucy took a breath and then froze again, trying not to set off any creaking of the bedstead. Surely it was he, coming to have mercy?

Lord Alex had picked up his book again as Mrs Pritchard had taken her to be manacled in bed. It was not impossible that his reading might have got her master aroused again. The image of Lord Alex on top of her, crushing her, his cock impaling her and taking her to blessed release, flooded the girl's fevered mind. She tried her best to ignore it. If he did not come, the picture would drive her completely to distraction.

Lucy gave a low, frustrated moan.

The footsteps had stopped but, to Lucy's horror, they had not stopped outside her door. From the sound of it those keys were rattling in the lock of Kitty's door, which was situated next to her own. No! She could not bear it! Listening to the little slut cry with pleasure as Lord Alex took her would be unendurable, though it was a torture she had had to endure more than once before.

There was a muffled sound like a hand impacting on soft flesh. Kitty's clear voice cried out with pain. There was a deep laugh. It was Lord Alex, all right.

Tears formed in Lucy's eyes; tears of jealousy and humiliation, but most of all, of sheer frustration. The itching was terrible now. Her pussy was due for shaving in the morning and stubble dusted the swollen tissues. The tiny hairs caught in the rough fibres of the blanket, exacerbating the chafing sensation until it sent her half-insane. If only there were more weight, she might have pressed her clit against the fabric and... But it was no good. The blanket was too insubstantial, and the incessant rubbing only tantalised her even further.

Something made her pause. It was the sound of the key in her door! Lucy groaned, barely daring to believe what she was hearing. The door swung open and Lord Alex stood in silhouette against the well-lit corridor.

'Well, Lucy. Not disturbing you, I hope.'

'Oh... Ah... No, no, sir,' she managed.

She felt the bed move as he sat on it and drew the blanket up slowly. Lucy had to bite her bottom lip to stop herself from crying out with desperation.

'Just thought I would check. Tsk, tsk, it's ridden up again. I hope the blanket was not vexing on your skin, my dear.'

Relief flooded her as the blanket was lifted and cool air fanned across her shaven sex.

'What's this? It looks damp. Heavens, girl, you're all wet. I think I had better explore further.'

'Oh God, please... sir!'

'Getting a little whiskery again, aren't we? It's shaving day tomorrow, is it not?'

'Oh, ah, yes, sir...!' Lucy managed, trying not to think about the barber, due in the morning to put the maids through their twice-weekly ordeal by shaving brush and razor. A strong forefinger probed and slid inside her lubricated sex, and Lucy was powerless to prevent her lower abdomen bucking up to meet his hand. The chains restraining her clinked and the leather collar and cuffs creaked as her body fought against her bonds. Lord Alex laughed at the mewling, bucking creature that his maid had become, but Lucy was too far gone to care about anything, except one...

'Oh, fuck me, please, sir. Oh, God, fuck me, master.' She babbled and begged between incoherent howls of desperation.

Lord Alex did not grant her wish but he let her clit rub against the heel of his hand as his finger thrust deep inside her pussy. His other hand pushed her little nightdress up even further and squeezed her breasts. Lucy fought the wrist-cuffs and the ankle restraints with ever-growing frenzy as her master's hands took her to the point of orgasm, and then beyond.

Pleasure exploded through her body. The chains of Lucy's restraints and her iron bedstead rattled violently as she convulsed within the confines of her bondage, and shrieks of ecstasy filled the little room. She had been so desperate for so long that the climax came like an explosion of white light, wiping away awareness of anything but itself.

For a few seconds, at least. Soon enough, she came gasping back to awareness, of her state of helpless and naked bondage, and most of all to the smiling presence of Lord Alex, sitting on the bed and watching her.

'There, now,' he said in satisfied tones as she began to get her breath back, 'that's better, isn't it?' He pulled the nightdress down, covering her nakedness, for which Lucy was profoundly grateful. Even in the afterglow of her orgasm, the way she was restrained made her feel terribly vulnerable to his whims.

Lord Alex pulled the blanket up, bent to plant a fond kiss on Lucy's forehead, and then checked the chain that fixed her collar and wrist-cuffs to the iron bedstead.

'Dear me, this is a bit loose. I do hope Mrs Pritchard is not getting slack.' He produced a small key and unlocked the padlock that secured it, shortening the chain by a couple of links so that Lucy could move even less than before. He stroked her cheek before bending to kiss her gently on the lips. Then he rose and went to the door, turning to blow her a kiss before he locked it for the night.

'Good night, my dear. Sleep tight, as they say!'

SADDLE SORE

Cautiously, Kitty placed the tray on the little rosewood table and darted an anxious glance towards her mistress.

'You may pour,' Lady Alicia instructed, continuing to look out of the casement window. Trying to control the trembling of her hand, Kitty poured the Earl Grey, anxious in case she should spill a drop. When it was safely done, she stood awaiting further orders, sneaking a furtive peek at her mistress as she stood bathed in sunlight.

Lady Alicia presented a truly magnificent spectacle, her black hair pulled into a bun which emphasised her sultry Spanish beauty. Her breasts were full and her hips generous, her waist laced tight into a long black corset. Apart from fine drawers of black silk and matching stockings, her only garment was a black lace negligee which she had allowed to fall open, letting the sun's rays caress her bare breasts and thighs.

Finally she turned to the maid. 'Well, girl, how did you enjoy your trip to the stables yesterday?'

Kitty felt the blush suffuse her cheeks. She hesitated, hardly knowing how to answer.

Her mistress regarded her gravely for a moment. 'So answer me, little one - did Mr Blackstock belt you well?'

Kitty's bottom lip began to tremble. 'Yes, ma'am,' she whispered huskily, staring at the floor.

'Let's see. Turn around and drop your drawers!'

This instruction was easy to follow. The skirt of Kitty's uniform was so short it rode up as she bent, and she had only to pull her knickers down to leave her bottom exposed.

Lady Alicia grunted her satisfaction. 'Yes, he did, didn't he?'

Kitty quivered at the memory as her mistress leisurely perused the evidence of her thrashing.

'All right, you can pull them up. Let that be a lesson to you not to spill my tea!' The maid adjusted her dress with huge relief. By the time she stood upright again, her mistress had returned to her vigil at the window. 'Tell me Kitty, when Mr Blackstock was belting you, were any of the stable-boys present?'

Kitty blushed a deeper shade of scarlet and the knot in her stomach tightened. If she had dared, she would have refused to answer, but Lady Alicia's enquiries were not to be ignored. 'Y-yes, ma'am,' she whispered, hanging her head in shame as she remembered the boys' comments... their hands... their things...

'I see. And what were they doing during - and after - your punishment?'

Kitty sniffed disconsolately but she knew she had to answer; Lady Alicia had an uncanny talent for finding out the truth. 'They - they touched me... and they - they played with themselves. They made me kiss their... their—'

'Played with themselves, you say?' Lady Alicia interrupted. 'What do you mean? Surely you aren't accusing them of self-abuse?'

Kitty glanced up to find her mistress's gaze upon her. Her tone was shocked but her eyes were sparkling and there was a hint of a smile on her lips. 'Come here!'

Kitty approached her mistress with trepidation, but Lady Alicia merely motioned her to look down into the courtyard. Below, outside the stables, a boy of about nineteen was forking manure into a barrow. As the day was hot and the work hard, he had stripped to the waist. Though slender, his body was wiry and gave the impression of strength. His dark hair had been cropped, giving him something of the air of a convict. His body was nearly hairless, his pale skin glistening with sweat as he laboured in the warm sun.

He put down the fork and bent to lift the barrow, the seat of his cord breeches tightening as he did so. Unaware of the women's gaze, he lifted the barrow and wheeled it out of sight.

Lady Alicia turned to Kitty and her eyes were bright. 'What about him, the new lad - did he abuse himself?'

Kitty noticed that her mistress had slipped a hand inside her silken drawers. She looked down, remembering the boy laughing and slapping his cock against her tear-streaked face. After the buggering from Mr Blackstock, Kitty had been left desperate with desire. The stupid boy had failed to understand, or had refused, the invitation she offered with her open legs. Instead she had to suck him, which gave her no chance of relief. Kitty had to stop herself from smiling; revenge was going to taste sweet.

'Yes, ma'am,' she said, trying to sound reluctant. 'He - he frigged himself while I was getting whipped.'

Davy followed the blonde maid up the stairs, his eyes fixed on her behind. Below her knickers, above the tops of her stockings, he could see the traces of Mr Blackstock's belt inscribed in shades of mauve. The sight, together with the memory of Kitty bucking under the belt, her bottom bouncing from the impact of the strap, combined to make his manhood swell inside his tight breeches.

Davy had never been inside the house before and wondered at the size of it as Kitty led him down a long corridor, her perilously high heels click-clacking on the tiles and echoing around the hallway. He had no idea why he had been summoned. A wild hope that yesterday's delights might be repeated competed with a strange sense of unease. Finally the maid stopped, and turned to look at him haughtily. As she knocked, Davy thought he caught the hint of a smile. The little trollop wasn't so full of herself yesterday, he thought, but his amusement was short-lived. A husky female voice bid them enter.

Davy was astonished. He had had little experience of women. What he had seen of Kitty with her drawers down for the belt had been something of a revelation to him. Certainly, he had never seen anything like Lady Alicia. She stood resplendent in the sunshine by the window, hands on hips. Her proud breasts were upthrust by the corset, veiled only partly with a film of black lace through which her jutting nipples glowed like rubies against pale cream skin. Davy blushed to see so much of so grand a lady, then blushed deeper as the riot of silk and lace and perfume in the room made him all the more aware of his own coarseness; his stench of sweat, horses and manure, his rough stained breeches and the patched smock he had thrown on when Kitty had come to fetch him.

Lady Alicia regarded the red-faced stable-boy with distaste. 'You - what is your name, boy?'

'Davy Falconer, if you please, your ladyship.'

'You will address me as "ma'am", do you understand, boy?'

'Yes, ma'am.'

'How long have you been at Hope Hall, Falconer?'

'I started last week, ma'am, if you please, ma'am.' Davy found himself unable to wrench his gaze from her nipples. Visions of chewing them made his mouth go dry and his cheeks flame brighter.

'Well, Falconer, I have to tell you that reports have come to me of appalling behaviour on your part. I wish to find out if these reports are true.'

Davy felt a sudden dread. What had he done? He tried to think. He thought of Kitty's smile but, no, it couldn't be. The other stable-lad had done the same, had egged him on; he had thought it must be normal at Hope Hall - permitted, encouraged even...

'I have been told that whilst this maidservant was being chastised yesterday, you had the gall to masturbate. Tell me now, boy, and tell me the truth. Did you or did you not abuse yourself yesterday?'

Davy reeled in shock. Lady Alicia was terrible in her anger. For all her flouncing silk and lace there was steel in her voice. He did not know what to say. He had frigged himself while the chit was being whipped, though surely she had been too distracted to see? Did making her suck him count? he wondered. At any event, there had been others present, as guilty as he and yet witnesses, for all that...

'Yes, ma'am, but I weren't the only—'

'Silence, boy!' she roared. 'I have no wish to hear excuses from masturbating brats. At Hope Hall self-abuse is punished, and that means you are going to be thrashed.'

Davy was thunderstruck. The thought occurred to tell her ladyship to go hang, to go and get himself another job. Somehow, though, the words would not come. Maybe he was mesmerised by Lady Alicia's splendour; perhaps the hope of more delights like watching Kitty's whipping was too intoxicating to forgo. Anyway, as Davy told himself, he was a tough lad who could take a beating from any woman. His only real fear was that he would be ordered to drop his breeches. In front of Lady Alicia and a sniggering Kitty, that would be too humiliating to endure.

To his relief, Lady Alicia indicated a whipping-triangle ready set up in the corner of the room, and coldly ordered him to remove his smock. A birch or cat on the back, he thought, suppressing a smirk. I'll show these women how Davy Falconer takes that! He allowed Kitty to buckle the restraints around his wrists. He grinned insolently at her, but she seemed disturbingly self-satisfied. He suffered himself to be secured, standing with arms above his head against the triangle. Nor did he struggle when the maid fastened his ankles close together. Only when Lady Alicia came close, close enough for him to smell her intoxicating perfume, so close that her jutting nipples grazed his naked back, did his self-assurance start to waver. She reached around and took his nipples between sharp nails, and for the first time Davy shivered.

'You stink, boy, do you know that?' Lady Alicia whispered huskily into his ear. Her overwhelming presence assailed his senses. Her lacy negligee brushed against his bare back, tickling terribly. He could feel her nipples, as hard as unripe strawberries, boring into him. Musk-rose perfume made his head reel as her nails bit hard into his nipples and her teeth nipped at his ear. Davy groaned.

'Answer me, boy. Do you realise that you stink?'

'Ow! Yes, ma'am.' He gasped as she twisted his nipples viciously between her crimson talons.

'Sweat, stale spunk and horse-shit, you dirty masturbating boy - you stink of shit!'

Davy was trembling now, panic growing, but then she released his nipples and reached down around his waist to unbuckle his belt.

'No!'

'What's the matter, boy? Don't you want Kitty to see?' Lady Alicia undid his breeches and pulled them down to his knees. 'I thought she already had. Kitty, look, what a pretty bottom!'

Davy's face burnt. He was shamefully exposed.

'What's this, boy? Don't tell me you have the gall to entertain impure thoughts even here, in my very bed-chamber?' Lady Alicia took the stable-lad's erect cock between her nails, digging in until he moaned with pain. 'Kitty, fetch me a cane!' She put her lips to his ear again, gouging his rigid member with her nails as she whispered, 'I'm going to thrash you now, boy. I'm going to cane you till you cry. I'm going to beat you until you beg for mercy.'

Davy took a deep breath when she released him to take the rod, swearing to himself that she would never hear him beg. He was no coward, nor was he unacquainted with the rod. Yet as she slashed the long cane through the air with an ominous *whoosh*, his whole body tensed. His cock and balls had felt so vulnerable to her talons, he wondered if there was any limit to what this terrifying creature might decide to do.

Finally the cane fell, slicing across his bottom with a sickening *thwack*. A hiss of pure pain escaped from between Davy's gritted teeth. As the waves of pain slowly subsided he tensed himself for the next stroke. But Lady Alicia was in no hurry, content to let the agony from the first cut slowly fade.

'Stop sniggering Kitty, unless you want the same! Go and fetch the harness, then get that uniform off.' He heard the cane *whoosh* through the air again, the sound making his stomach clench so hard it hurt, but no impact followed. Only after several preparatory swishes, each one ratcheting his nerves to screaming pitch, did she finally lash into him again.

Afterward, Davy could not have said how long the thrashing lasted, nor how many strokes his bottom and thighs received. Lady Alicia beat him leisurely, with long pauses between each stroke, but she was pitiless and her arm was strong. She whipped his bottom and the backs of his thighs, working down until the cane cracked across his legs a little above the knees. Then she worked up again, taking no pains to avoid striking the crimson marks of previous strokes.

When she reached the tops of his buttocks, Davy waited in apprehension as his tormentor took a break to refresh herself with tea and cake. Then the strokes started again, over cheeks already beaten to redness. Soon after she resumed the torment, Davy heard himself beg. Begging quickly turned to pleading for mercy, and pleading to howling helplessly as the cane came down again and again.

Lady Alicia released him herself, cooing insincere condolences to the sobbing boy. Davy slumped to his knees and found his face pulled into the black silk of his mistress's drawers. The sweet sensations of warm silk and perfume vied with the dreadful throbbing in his hindquarters, creating a state of mind close to delirium. Lady Alicia stroked his neck firmly, pulling his face into her crotch.

'There now, boy, your whipping's over. You can stop crying now.' She caressed him as the pain slowly subsided. Davy felt foolish yet wildly excited. Trembling with anticipation, he nuzzled her warm flesh through the warm silk which blotted out his vision.

'We have another treat before you go, my lad.'

Something in her tone made him suddenly fearful. She grabbed an ear and pulled his face out of her crotch, forcing his head round. Kitty was behind him. The maid had taken off her uniform and wore only a long black satin corset and stockings. The gorgeous sight of her full breasts and creamy thighs caused Davy's stiff cock to twitch.

Then he saw it and his blood ran cold.

Kitty had buckled a harness of leather straps around her midriff. She was smiling down at him, fondling an obscene black strap-on cock.

Icy fingers of pure terror gripped Davy's heart. Lady Alicia's talons closed vice-tight in his hair as Kitty moved towards him.

'Oh... please no...' The rubber cock slapped hard against his face as the women's laughter pealed around the bed-chamber.

'I do not permit self-abuse, my boy, for I feel it is such a waste!' Lady Alicia yanked his head back until he had to look into her pitiless eyes. She bent and he felt her finger run down the furrow between his bottom-cheeks, then probe. Davy's sphincter clamped convulsively around the penetrating digit. He heard her throaty chuckle once again.

'Hm, he's very tight. I think we had better send to the stables for some saddle-soap.' Davy whimpered despairingly as his mistress smiled down at him. 'Don't worry, boy, I'll see to it that the other grooms know what we intend to use it for.'

'I say, aren't the meadows looking splendid!' Jamie slashed his whip through the air, neatly decapitating a buttercup. Amelia's bottom tensed in automatic response to the hiss of the crop, and she sensed Clara flinch beside her.

There was certainly truth in his observation. The meadows on the far side of the ornamental lake were ablaze with wild flowers. Golden buttercups vied for attention with crimson poppies, while mauve vetchlings and the creamy froth of meadowsweet provided a palette of subtler colours. Not that Amelia was in any mood to appreciate the scene.

For one thing, the soft sward was difficult to walk across in the precariously high heels of her button-boots. For another, the little smock and frilly knickers, so humiliating in the nursery, were even more mortifying out here in the open air. Anyone might see her here: gardeners, estate workers, and stable-boys.

Amelia's cheeks burned anew as she remembered the cat-calls that had followed the cousins as they tottered across the cobbles of the courtyard. The knowledge that she would have to return, probably passing the stable-block again, squatted like a stone in her stomach.

Then there was the fact that the mission they were on was far from cheering. Betsy bustled along behind Jamie and the cousins, laden down with trugs and secateurs. One glance at the maid's burden reminded Amelia of the task they were intent on.

Jamie had announced the expedition after luncheon. 'We need to put up some birches for you girls. It's not the best time, as they are in leaf, but that cannot be helped. It looks like a lovely afternoon. What do you say, girls - shall we go up to the groves and cut some switches?'

'Yes, sir,' Clara had said softly, after a moment's hesitation. Amelia had nearly slapped the silly little bitch.

'Amelia, you don't seem keen. Have you another plan, perhaps? Were you hoping to pay a visit to the Reverend Dawes, for instance?'

The very mention of the name had made her face go red. The jovial suggestion filled Amelia with utter dismay.

'No... please,' she had said quickly, terrified now that he would send her, on some pretext or other, to the rector.

'So you would rather come with Clara and me to cut birches?'

'Oh, very well, I suppose.'

'Amelia!' Jamie's expression had decided her to re-phrase.

'Yes... please... sir,' she had said, forcing the words out one by one.

'Jolly good.' Jamie had given her bottom a friendly squeeze. 'I'm sure we will have a lovely afternoon.'

The little party strolled on in the warm afternoon sun, through the meadow, and then to the park beyond. Herds of graceful fallow deer moved off as they approached, disappearing into the dappled shade of the oaks that fringed the pasture.

'I say, look,' Jamie pointed with his switch, 'there's Lord Alex, exercising his new filly!'

Amelia stared, astonished. A well-maintained drive cut through the deer park, some way from their party. Along this a tall girl was running, pulling a little sulky in which Amelia could just make out the well-built frame of Lord Alex, enthusiastically waving a whip.

'But—' Amelia blurted, '—she's completely naked!'

Jamie put his head back and laughed heartily. 'What would you have a pony wear, you silly girl? Anyway, she's hardly naked; she's in harness.'

Lord Alex must have spotted them, for he raised his carriage-whip in greeting before returning to his work. Jamie returned the salute with his own whip.

'Great heavens,' Jamie murmured as they stood and watched. 'Well, he did say he had found himself a thoroughbred filly.'

The naked girl ran a hundred yards or so, her long legs seemingly eating up the pathway, despite the fact that she was hauling Lord Alex's weight. Then she was pulled up and made to turn before being galloped back in the other direction. This time, they could hear Lord Alex urging her on.

'Gee up, go on! That's it, faster! Faster!' His voice could be heard clearly across the park, despite the distance. Amelia could also hear his whip crack as he used it to urge his mount to greater efforts. It seemed to be mostly for show; cracking to either side of the straining girl in warning.

Not all the lashes were so benign, however. There was a crack that could only have been the sound of leather upon flesh, and the girl gave a cry of pain which her bit could not completely muffle. The stroke made her stumble and sway between the shafts and, for a moment, it looked as if the sulky might go over.

'Tsk, tsk - now she'll get it,' murmured Jamie. 'She will have to learn to take those encouraging kisses in her stride, if I know Lord Alex.'

The driver pulled his mount up. Amelia could not hear the words, only the sharp tone of Lord Alex's voice, but she understood the language of the whip well enough. Three stinging strokes were laid across the pony-girl's naked back and Amelia flinched in sympathy. Lord Alex gave his mount no respite, but turned her, and once again the tall girl cantered off along the drive.

'Well, girls,' Jamie said as he followed the sulky's progress, 'pleasant as this is to watch, we do have work to do.'

The young man led the girls on through a gate which gave onto a pretty woodland ride. Almost at once, the pathway began to climb steeply through the woods. The trees lining the woodland ride on
either side were mostly oak, though hornbeam soon became more common.

'It is a remarkable estate still, is it not?' Jamie said, waving at the woods. 'All this is still within the walls. Of course, it used to be truly vast in the old days.'

Amelia concentrated on keeping her balance. The path was a rough farm track. The sun-baked clay that had given some solid footing for her heels was rapidly becoming sandy. Glancing round, she noticed that silver-barked birch trees had begun to make an appearance, lining the pathway. Amelia had always loved the delicate grace of the birch, but today their beauty gave her no pleasure. Instead they seemed ominous and tainted.

'One wonders how long these groves have been maintained,' Jamie mused as they followed the path upward. He led them from the main path. It was brighter here, for the birch foliage was light, the trees were small, and the afternoon sun was shining. The woods were full of birdsong, but for all this the place seemed terrible to Amelia. Just as in the Whippery, the very brightness of the groves only increased their sense of menace.

The birches here seemed to be shrubs rather than trees, for the most part consisting of regular-sized evenly spaced bushes. Jamie instructed the cousins and the maid to take a trug and pair of secateurs each. Then he led Amelia to one thicket of birch.

'These are coppiced so we can reach the shoots,' he explained. 'Not usually a long-lived tree, the birch, but these beauties are ancient. The coppicing lengthens their lives.' He pulled a long limb free and indicated for Amelia to snip it off. 'It makes you wonder, doesn't it—' his face was rapt '—how many birch rods has this old stool provided for Hope Hall?'

Amelia cut the next bough that he indicated and placed it in the trug.

'It must be hundreds, anyway,' Jamie continued. As he imparted this cheering information, he patted Amelia on her behind. 'Think about all those well-flogged bottoms while you are cutting.'

'Easy girl, easy. That's it, good girl, Blossom. Looks like you've had a good run. Time to rub you down, now.' The stable-boy led her back into the same stall in which she had passed a restive night. There he began unbuckling the harness of brown leather straps, which was all she wore.

'Whoa, whoa, easy, girl.'

Blossom swayed, her legs like jelly, as the last part of the harness came off. He steadied her with a hand on her elbow.

'The master worked you hard this afternoon, eh?' He gave her a smile as he perused her naked body, gently touching one of the welts which Lord Alex's driving-whip had left across her back. Guiding her down onto her knees, he unbuckled the bridle and eased out the bit. She gave a little sob of relief.

'Just rest easy there, Blossom, girl.'

Dick hung the harness with a lot of similar tack and went out of sight, leaving her kneeling naked in the straw. It occurred to her that, for the first time since she had arrived at the stables yesterday evening, she was neither chained nor bound. She could see the invitingly open double doors of the stable-block a tantalisingly few feet away, and the mad thought entered her mind, just for a moment, that she could make a run for it.

The idea was absurd. Where would she run to, naked and friendless? How far could she run, in any case? Lord Alex had had her harnessed to his sulky and made her race around the estate all morning, flogging her enthusiastically every time she had flagged. Blossom had been made to run until she could barely stand, let alone flee.

There was something else that kept her trembling, naked in her stall, more potent than exhaustion and more powerful than fear. Blossom had not liked her name being changed, yet she had accepted it. It was galling to be treated like an animal, yet it was strangely seductive.

Lord Alex had proved that he could be a brutal master as he had flogged her to ever greater efforts, yet he had taught her that he was her master. Something strange had stolen into her soul out in the park. Blossom knew now that she belonged to Lord

Alex. It was not the place of property to run away.

So the open door and the freedom from restraint held no appeal; it made her feel unsafe and uncomfortable. The urge to escape was deeply unappealing, yet it tugged away at her. She turned her face the other way. The stall was open with three sides formed of rough-hewn planks. It was too small, she realised, to hold any but human ponies. This fact increased the feeling of enclosure, and she turned right around until her back was to the open side, until her heart stopped hammering.

'Good girl.' Dick had returned with a gleaming steel bucket full of water. 'No, not like that.' He caught her hands and pulled them back, then gathered up her long mane of brown hair.

Blossom understood. She bent and put her face into the water, drinking directly from the bucket. The water was indescribably delicious, the coldest, sweetest, most soothing drink she had ever had in her life. All too soon, the hand in her hair pulled her head back and out of the bucket.

'Whoa! That's enough, girl. That's enough - time for your rub-down, now!'

If the water had been bliss, what followed was more like torture. Dick produced a rubber curry-comb, a brush that looked like a hedgehog made of stiff rubber spines. He proceeded to scour every inch of Blossom's body with it.

'Easy, now - stop wriggling, you bad girl. Hold still or it will be the worse for you.'

'Oh, ouch, please, ooh!'

'No talking!'

The currying turned into a wrestling match as the rubber spikes abraded the soft flesh of Blossom's breasts.

'Looks like you have a handful there, boy!' A deep male voice boomed around the stable.

'Aye, Mr Blackstock. She's a big girl and she's wriggling like a salmon, but the master said I was to curry her proper!'

'Here, lad, I'll hold her while you scrub.'

'Ooh... ow... mercy.'

'Stop talking or I will put the bit on you, girl!'

Blossom fought against Mr Blackstock's iron grip as the curry-comb began to scour the tender flesh of her inner thighs. Dick scrubbed, Blossom wriggled and kicked, and Mr Blackstock held her down with consummate ease. Eventually she somehow recovered control over herself again, and ceased struggling and crying, gritting her teeth as the rubber comb bit into her calves.

Blossom's whole body was an angry scarlet now, the colour of a well-smacked bottom, and her skin felt as if it had been rubbed raw. When Mr Blackstock finally released her, she collapsed, sobbing brokenly into the straw. She wiped the tears from her face and tried to get her breath back. The two men were standing over her naked body, watching her in silence, and awareness of them grew as the pain of the currying faded to a not unpleasant glow.

'Damned pretty filly, if you like them big and leggy.' There was a thickness in Dick's voice and, though she kept her eyes downcast, she could see his hand stroking his groin.

'Not a bad-looking piece, I'll give you that. We'll have to have some entertainment later, when you've cleaned her up.'

'Are we allowed?'

Mr Blackstock gave a harsh barking laugh that made Blossom flinch. 'By God, yes, boy, as long as we don't interfere with the training. After all, this job has to have some perks. Don't worry, that business with Davy was just her ladyship's little joke. If she fancies giving you a dose, she'll think up another reason. You see, lad, when her ladyship takes a fancy to your arse... Let's just say she generally gets a little of what she fancies!'

Blossom peeked up. Dick's usually florid face had gone pale. Mr Blackstock laughed again.

'I wouldn't worry about it too much. It looks to me like she's more interested in young Davy.'

'That's it, Clara, good long limbs - they'll make a birch that will fetch you properly, my sweet.'

Amelia tried to ignore Jamie's relaxed and amused voice, and concentrate on her doleful task. It was not easy.

'Betsy, what on earth is this? Great heavens, girl, you should know how to cut a Hope Hall rod by now! This little twig is only good for one thing. Do you know what that is?'

'A - a bosom birch, sir.'

'That's right. A little bitty titty-teaser. Now, I will have no waste. Strip those leaves off and get those titties out, and we shall demonstrate to the girls why it is advisable to cut their switches good and long.'

Amelia glanced down at her trug in alarm, trying to gauge if any of her leafy boughs might be adjudged too small, and trying to quell the sensation of near-panic that gripped her vitals. She decided against the branch that she was going to cut and reached out to take another, more substantial one.

'I say, Jamie, well met. What a glorious day!'

The voice of the newcomer made her hand freeze for a second, and Amelia was not able to stop her outstretched arm from trembling slightly.

'Glorious indeed, Reverend. Ah, you have trugs with you, I see. I suspect that you are on the same mission as we.'

Amelia swallowed bitter bile as the two men chuckled behind her.

'It really is remarkable. However many dozen birches I put up each winter, I always seem to get through them and need to come and cut more by the end of spring.' He sighed theatrically. 'The wickedness of the world, Jamie, makes constant demands on my store of rods.'

Amelia laid the cut branch in the trug, which was on the ground, conscious that in bending she must display her bottom to the watching men. However, she need not have worried.

'I must own that your nursery-maid is possessed of an extraordinarily well-developed pair of breasts,' the Reverend said crisply. 'However, one wonders if she has some reason, other than sheer exhibitionism, for displaying them so wantonly?'

'Indeed so, Reverend. She has been cutting light, for which there can be but one remedy. Amelia, Clara, leave your tasks and come over here.'

Amelia turned at last to find what she had half-expected and much dreaded. The Reverend Dawes's glittering gaze immediately locked onto her eyes. It was only for a moment, but for that moment she was sure that her heart had altogether stopped. It was only with a real effort of will that she could obey Jamie's instruction and walk towards that terrible gimlet gaze.

Fortunately for Amelia's progress, the prospect of Betsy's bared breasts drew the Reverend's attention away. The nursery-maid was blushing crimson. The top of her apron had been let down, the buttons of her uniform undone and the top two clasps of her corset unfastened. Her breasts had done the rest, pushing forward and out of the constraint of her clothes. Betsy kept her head bowed as she proffered the bundle of birch twigs, freshly stripped of their leaves, in a visibly trembling hand.

'Old Banks, the woodsman, has kept these coppiced for forty years to safeguard the Hall's supply of rods. I'll not have his work wasted by cowardly trollops who seek to save their skins by cutting twigs before they are grown to size!' Jamie declared.

'Quite right. Faith, Rose, watch and learn and note well the size of limbs required, unless you wish to receive the same.'

The Reverend's presence had so compelled Amelia's attention that she had scarcely been aware that he had not arrived alone. Now she ventured a glance at his companions. A lovely girl with long blonde hair and a demure expression stood next to a robust-looking young woman with a shock of red curls. Both wore smart black maids' uniforms. Neither girl replied, but both kept their eyes downcast, and Amelia saw the redhead swallow glumly.

'All right, Betsy.' Jamie took the proffered twigs at last. 'Cup them with your hands and lift them up for me. Thank you.'

The nursery-maid paled. She cupped her breasts and pushed up from below. The woodland seemed to have gone very quiet, as if even the birds in the trees had stopped to watch. Amelia stared at the white expanse of flesh. Betsy's breasts were flawless, the snowy rounds only interrupted by the deep rose of her nipples. Whether her breasts were shivering, or the quivering of her supporting hands transferred the motion, they trembled in the dappled sunlight as Jamie raised the rod.

Swithk!

The birch twigs whispered through the fresh air and bounced across the proffered breasts. Betsy's face contorted with pain. She jammed her eyes closed and shook her upper body vigorously, bending almost double as she did so.

'Back into position, Betsy. There's a good girl.'

'Ooh, ah, s-s-sorry, sir.'

By the time the nursery-maid managed to regain the ordained position, a tracery of fine red lines had bloomed on the milky flesh of her breasts. The rosy nipples seemed to have grown, too, pushing out more prominently than before.

Swithk!

A high-pitched gasp of pain escaped from Betsy's lips.

'I think that fetched her,' the Reverend Dawes said conversationally. He casually took out his cigar case and opened it. Betsy was bent double again, her antics providing evidence for the truth of his observation. She shook like a wet dog and gave a series of little grunts of pain. It was a full minute before she could stand and proffer her breasts again. Her nipples were jutting out like pink thimbles now, and the crimson tracery was so vivid that her breasts looked as though they were constrained in a film of crimson lace. The welts were fine, the skin remained unbroken, but the nursery-maid's birched bosom looked sore. Amelia's own breasts tingled in sympathy as she stared. She watched a tear trickle down Betsy's cheek.

Swithk!

'Ooh!' Betsy doubled up once more.

Jamie peered disdainfully at the bundle of twigs, half of which were now broken. 'Good Lord, you must have titties like iron, Betsy.' He threw the makeshift birch rod down, shaking his head. The young man shrugged in the direction of the Reverend Dawes. 'Breasts like old boot-leather. I doubt she felt a thing.'

The object of this observation clutched her breasts, hopping from foot to foot and shaking her head from side to side as she hissed with pain.

'Adjust your dress now. Make yourself respectable,' Jamie ordered dryly. 'Come along, you wanton girl, we do not have all day.'

It was not difficult to understand the reason for the delay. First Betsy had to regain control of her body. The tears were coursing freely down her face and the tracery of tiny welts bloomed angrily on her breasts. These she was kneading, as if she could somehow massage away the pain. When, at length, Betsy regained control, she had to stuff her breasts back into the tight grip of her corset, not something easily or painlessly accomplished. The maid winced and grimaced as she struggled with her stays, until Jamie gave a sigh and helped her force the garment closed.

'Aiee...!'

'For heaven's sake, be quiet, girl. And button yourself up.'

Betsy obeyed, but she did so slowly and with considerable wincing, and for the remainder of the afternoon, Amelia noticed, the least movement of the nursery-maid's arms would cause her face to crease with pain again.

ALL WORK AND NO PLAY...

Kitty hurried through the hall, a fistful of silk in either hand, as she hoisted up her billowing skirts to keep the hem of her uniform from sweeping the floor. The black silk of the gown, together with the six starched petticoats which flounced out her skirts so widely that she might have almost have had crinoline beneath, produced a veritable symphony of rustling as she bustled along.

Mrs Pritchard had gone to town after luncheon and thus it was her duty, as senior upstairs servant in the housekeeper's absence, to greet the visitor whose carriage she had seen approaching from the blue drawing room. The honour of this office was new to the maid, and it made her heart swell with pride, but it also made her somewhat apprehensive. She wished, once again, that the bodice of her uniform was not so perilously low-cut. As she looked down, she could see her breasts jiggle in front of her, pushed up by her corset and barely contained by the wisp of lace above the garment's supporting quarter-cups.

Even more, she wished that Mrs Pritchard had not insisted she wear the leather collar and cuffs again. The visible tokens of her servitude seemed so inappropriate for one in such a position of responsibility.

These feelings only increased tenfold as Kitty turned into the grand entrance hall and saw the figure standing there. His look was frankly villainous. Not a big man, five foot eight at most and wiry in build, he was unshaven and as tanned as a gypsy fruit-picker. He wore a stained white suit with frayed collar and cuffs and had not even bothered to respectfully remove his battered Panama hat. Kitty rustled right up to him, only to confront green eyes that twinkled at her villainously.

'The tradesman's entrance is at the back, through the courtyard,' Kitty said primly, trying to draw herself to her full height without simultaneously thrusting out her breasts. She silently cursed the collar that was bound to undermine her effort to assert authority.

The man just looked at her for a moment. Casually, he put his hands in his trouser pockets. This action pushed his jacket open a little, just enough for Kitty to glimpse the little whip thrust casually into his waistband.

'Is it, sweetheart, is it?' he said at last, smiling and flashing a gold tooth that made him look even more like a pirate. He turned and looked around the impressive entrance hall, showing no sign of being prepared to leave.

Kitty prevaricated for a moment, in a real quandary. Why today? she wondered fretfully. Mrs Pritchard would have known how to deal with this grubby beggar. If she did not get rid of him, she would certainly be in trouble. There was no option but to try again.

'I'm afraid I must ask you to leave,' she said, aware that her voice was sounding distinctly shrill as it echoed around the marble entrance hall.

The man cocked his head enquiringly and studied her, perfectly unperturbed. 'Oh, must you now, my sweet?' he mocked.

Kitty felt the blood rise to her cheeks as his gaze dropped from her face to her breasts.

'Haven't seen you here before.' He kept staring at Kitty's breasts, and licked his lips hungrily. 'I'm bloody sure I would have remembered a nice ripe pair like that.'

He stepped forward and Kitty tried to step back, but the voluminous skirts slowed her, and his hand moved fast. Kitty gave a startled shriek as he grabbed her left nipple through the flimsy lace of its constraint. He pinched it between thumb and forefinger.

'Ow! Ouch! Let go, you're... Ow!'

Still smiling, the man gave her nipple a vicious twist and pulled down, forcing her to sink to her knees. Kitty found her face next to the whip. It was made of yellow-brown braided leather, worn in places and, from the looks of it, much used. The man retained his painful grip on her nipple but casually withdrew the whip with his free hand. Kitty found her chin lifted by a loop of the thing, the braided texture coarse against the tender skin of her throat. He tilted her head back until she was looking up into his laughing eyes.

'Now then, you saucy little trollop,' he said in quietly menacing tones, 'why don't we inform that bitch Alicia and her old bugger of a husband that they have a visitor, eh?'

'Hold it straight, now, Betsy. No, higher than that and for heaven's sake keep your hand still. You know you'll just get extras if you flinch, you silly girl!'

Perspiring as much from fear as from the warmth of the day, Betsy tried to keep her palm steady. She stood in the centre of the nursery parlour in nothing but her corset and the new black silk stockings. She was trembling as she waited for her master to bring down the tawse again. Betsy closed her eyes and silently prayed.

There was a decided clink and an anxious sob from the side. Betsy opened her eyes to find her master's amused gaze upon her. He gave her a wink.

'Don't go away,' Jamie said.

Betsy hated the belt on the hands; worse, in fact, than almost anything else. She gave a sigh of relief, grateful for the respite, however brief.

The cousins also wore nothing but their usual uniform of white silk smocks and stockings. Both had their hands pinioned behind their backs, in the now-familiar fashion. Both had been silently straining to achieve the task that Jamie had previously ordained.

When, a little earlier, that young man had sentenced Betsy to the belt, he had also announced that the cousins would not be allowed to watch the disciplining of the nursery-maid. In order to prevent peeking, he had made use of a simple but effective expedient. Producing two golden guineas, Jamie had held one against the wall, level with Amelia's eyes. The girl had then been made to stand on tiptoe, with feet wide apart, and hold the coin against the wall by pressing it with her nose, something she could only achieve by straining visibly. Clara had then been made to follow suit.

'Good girls, that's it. Drop the coins and I'll stripe those pretty bottoms!' Jamie had growled, giving Amelia's bare behind a friendly pat. He had then instructed Betsy to place silver platters on the floor between the cousins' straining legs. The sight of the two girls, bare bottoms twitching in anticipation, calf and thigh muscles taut and trembling with the effort, was something Betsy only wished she had the leisure to enjoy. Whether Clara's shapely slenderness or Amelia's more generous curves and long legs were the more appealing, she would have been hard put to choose. However, Betsy's own travails were too pressing for her to gain any real enjoyment from the cousins' plight. At least, so she had thought, before she heard that sharp metallic clink.

Furtively, she looked at the platter between Clara's legs. There was nothing there, and the blonde girl was still obviously straining. However, from Amelia's silver tray came an accusatory gleam of gold.

'Pick it up,' Jamie said firmly.

'I... but—' Amelia turned, looked at Jamie, then at the tray and the coin upon it, and briefly up at the tawse swinging in his hand. Betsy watched her lick her full lips. Now Amelia had turned, the shapely contours of her breasts could clearly be discerned through the thin silk of the smock. Betsy swallowed, wishing she had a pair of nipple clamps with which to worry the teats which pushed so impudently against the fabric. That, and an hour or three to play with the haughty Miss Amelia on her own. Well, she thought wryly, even a humble nursery-maid could dream!

The object of her reverie swallowed nervously and got down - a little awkwardly, for she could not use her arms for balance - to her knees. Master Jamie moved around behind her, and Amelia signalled that she was only too well aware of this by letting out a little whimper of fear.

Betsy knew, from bitter past experience, that it is no easy task to pick a coin up with one's teeth when one's hands are tightly pinioned, wrist to opposing elbow, behind one's back. That Amelia found the task difficult was obvious. Her bottom, the nursery-maid had to admit, was a real beauty. The sweet cheeks were twitching, the muscles clenching convulsively in anticipation of the tawse. To get her head down, Amelia had to stick her bottom out in counterbalance, but it was clear that she hardly dare attempt the final thrust.

There was a horrid dry whuffling sound as the leather tails disturbed the still air, followed by a vicious-sounding snap, as two leather tawse tails cracked across the inviting bottom. Amelia emitted a pained squeak, and Betsy watched the girl's pinioned fingers flex helplessly in their bonds.

'Come along, Amelia. I said pick it up.'

'Oh, ooh, ooh, ow, ow...'

'Good God,' Jamie said, 'at this rate, we'll be here all day.' He grabbed a handful of auburn ringlets and hauled the gasping girl roughly back to her feet. Then he thrust her up against the wall.

'Feet apart, now - wider, wider. All right, stand still.' He stood back and raised the tawse and, for a moment, the whole of Hatherby seemed to hold its breath.

Crack! Crack! Crack!

Three times in quick succession the heavy tawse impacted on Amelia's bottom.

Crack! Crack!

Twice it snapped ferociously across the backs of her thighs. The leather tails hissed through the air, Amelia squealed, and Betsy felt her own bottom flinch involuntarily in sympathy.

After the fifth stroke, Jamie allowed the girl a minute to jump about and squeal. Prevented by her bonds from rubbing the wide stripes that dissected her bottom, her hands fluttered futilely. Amelia hopped from foot to foot as if engaged in some demented dance, furiously tossing about her shock of auburn ringlets.

A few minutes later, Jamie knelt, smiling, and retrieved the coin.

'Ow! Yow! Hoo, ha, that - ooh, oh that... st-st-stings!' It was several more minutes before the girl could be compelled to cease jiggling and jumping from foot to foot. Amelia gasped and gulped, as the welts ripened to a fiery red. Betsy winced in sympathy as she watched her, all too aware that the tawse that had caused such agitation would be snapping away at her own palm very soon.

Too soon, for the nursery-maid, Amelia recovered her composure. Sniffling, the girl resumed her position, pressing the coin to the wall once more with her nose. Amelia's welted bottom and thighs quivered visibly beneath the hem of her gown, as she stretched upward and her muscles strained at their task again.

Jamie turned back to the nursery-maid, tawse swinging slowly in his hand. 'Well now, Betsy. I do apologise for that interruption. Your hand seems to have dropped a little - keep it up, now, and quite still.'

Betsy supported her right wrist in her left hand, holding her palm up and both arms out straight in front of her. To do this she had to press her upper arms in against her breasts. Her arms squeezed her breasts together, forcing them up in a way that made her terribly self-conscious. Not for the first time, she wished her breasts were not so large.

The tawse was even harder to ignore, however. Betsy licked her lips and watched the thick tails swing. Jamie raised it once again, and she held her breath and closed her eyes tight, praying for deliverance as she awaited the inevitable impact.

There was a timid knock at the door. Betsy did not dare to breathe. A pained whimper came from the direction of Amelia, a strained grunt from Clara, and then a resigned sigh from Jamie. Cautiously, Betsy opened one eye. She watched Jamie lower the tawse and turn towards the door. Betsy breathed again.

'Come in!'

A pretty face in a maid's cap peeked anxiously around the parlour door. Betsy recognised the new kitchen-maid, Emma, blinking nervously into the room. The girl looked at Amelia and Clara; her eyes widened with surprise and then she looked away. She stared at Betsy with wide eyes. Blushing, she dropped her gaze to the floor.

'Well girl, what is it?' Jamie demanded.

'Please, sir.' Emma's voice was soft and hesitant; her fingers kneaded at her apron. 'I... I've been sent.'

Only another hundred yards or so to go, Lucy told herself as she fought to stop her heel turning over again. She managed to right herself just in time, but only avoided a worse disaster by the silk of her stockings for, as she fought to regain her balance, the tray swayed, causing glasses and decanter to lurch perilously. Chains tinkled, glass skeetered on silver and clinked together, and leather dug painfully into tender flesh, as the maid fought to stay upright and safeguard the contents of the tray.

There was a gnarled wisteria trunk entwined around this corner of the hall. The flowers were long gone but a pair of blue-tits flew busily about the leaves. Lucy watched them for a few seconds; they seemed so free and merry as they danced through the air, playing tag under the warm afternoon sun. If only she dare take a moment to recover. No - Lucy knew her mission to fetch refreshments had already taken too long. If she knew her master and mistress, they would be getting impatient, and know them she did, only too well. There was nothing for it. She had to struggle on.

The trouble was that these high stiletto heels were not designed for gravel pathways. At least that was one of her troubles. Unfortunately she had others, too. Lucy had been stripped down to her long black corset and stockings for her master's amusement after luncheon. But the removal of her uniform had only been the start.

'You have been getting slack and sloppy, girl,' Lady Alicia had told her pleasantly. 'Alex suggested taking you to the west wing—' Lucy had stiffened at the mention of that terrible old tower '—but I have persuaded him to exercise restraint.'

This had turned out to be one of her ladyship's little jokes for, though restraints had been employed, it was the maid rather than master who was destined to be exercised in them. First a leather belly-belt, equipped with several D-rings, had been pulled tight around the narrowest part of her already tightly laced waist. Light chains were affixed to her wrists and ankle-straps, all four meeting and running through a central ring on the front of the belt. It was a diabolical device. The chains were long enough to allow a certain freedom for her feet or her hands, but not both together. Too large a step would tug her hands down, too much movement of her arms restricted her feet. She could totter on her heels, holding the tray at waist-level, only if she restricted herself to taking tiny steps. It was uncomfortable, but feasible, to walk like this so long as she did not stumble, but keeping her balance took tremendous concentration; concentration which was rendered nigh-impossible by the saddle-strap.

It was a thick rounded thong of rawhide. Fixed to her belt at the front, the leather was passed between her legs and pulled tight, before being secured to the back of her waist-strap. Standing with the thing bisecting her tender tissues was a sort of purgatory. Hobbling, as it rasped against her throbbing clitoris, was sheer hell. It is true that there had been a moment, as she shuffled off to fetch the wine, that had been briefly close to heaven. However, Lucy knew that another such eruption now would undoubtedly make her drop her burden, and the last thing she needed now was another such release.

If only the saddle-thong had not been fixed so ferociously tight. If only there were a few inches more slack in her restraining chains. If only the heels were not so narrow and high. Lucy winced as she hobbled around the final corner, trying to blink away tears of pain. She could see her master and mistress in the distance, and could imagine the impatience on their faces. Gritting her teeth, she hobbled forward grimly. Little steps, little steps, she repeated to herself silently, like a mantra, only steady, little, tiny steps.

Chink, chink, chink, went the chains. Creak, creak, answered her corset, as she tried to bend at the waist in order to allow herself more slack. The sun was warm on her nearly naked breasts. Wasps were buzzing ominously about her, and the saddle-strap was cutting her in two. Little steps, little steps, only tiny little steps.

A little further, a glance risked at her master, and Lucy saw displeasure in his face as he flexed his crop. That glance was very nearly her undoing, for she teetered on her heels precariously. Desperately, praying silently, she struggled once again to keep her balance. The glasses chinked against the bottle as the contents of the tray went sliding again. Lucy thought her heart had stopped for a moment as she scrabbled against gravity and unyielding steel chain.

Fortune smiled, for once, and somehow she held both balance and burden. With a relieved sigh, Lucy tottered off again.

She was perhaps twenty feet away, perspiring under the Fevershams' impatient gaze, when she heard the call of greeting. Lucy looked up, as did her mistress and master. Approaching the bench from the other direction came Kitty, resplendent in full uniform, and a man wearing a dingy white suit and battered Panama.

Grateful for the distraction, Lucy put her head down and focused on attaining the last few yards. She forced herself to ignore the chafing saddle-strap and concentrate on making even, tiny steps.

'What have you done to that poor girl, you wicked pair of blackguards?' the man called out jovially.

'I - I'm sorry ma'am, master. This man - he—'

'Do you know this baggage wanted me to use the tradesman's entrance, Alicia? Where do you get your staff?'

Lucy tried not to let the conversation distract her as she clinked and creaked the last few feet.

'From the reformatory, generally, which you know as well as I. Oh God, why are servants always such awful snobs?' Lady Alicia cried joyfully. 'So, Jack, you have finally returned!'

She had made it. The saddle-strap still dug in bitterly but at least Lucy no longer had to walk. She stood as Lord and Lady Feversham exchanged joyous hugs and affectionate insults with the newcomer. Once she had recovered her breath she glanced at Kitty, who had turned very pale.

'I'm so sorry about the maid, Jack,' Lady Alicia purred. 'I shall thrash her for her impertinence. Unless you would rather—'

'Oh, yes,' Jack enthused, laughing and giving the blonde maid a hungry leer. 'I would definitely rather pay off that particular account myself!'

'Of course. I shall send her to you at a convenient moment.' Lady Alicia said merrily, clapping her hands together in delight. 'Well, Jack, this calls for a toast in celebration. Lucy, what are you doing, standing there like a ninny? Hurry off and fetch another glass for our guest!'

The kitchen-maid stepped uncertainly into the nursery parlour. She was small and delicately pretty with dark brown hair pinned back under her cap. The girl's daintiness made Betsy feel huge and positively ungainly by comparison.

'Yes, girl?' Jamie demanded.

'Cook sent me to find his lordship, sir, and ask for—' the girl blinked anxiously '—for a taste of the cane, sir.'

'Well then, why are you here?'

The girl hung her head and stared, somewhat dolefully, at the floor. 'It took ages to find his lordship, sir. You see, sir—' she peeked up at Jamie, her voice little more than a timid whisper '—I got lost...'

'For God's sake, girl, I did not ask for your life story!' Jamie snapped impatiently. 'Get to the point.'

The kitchen-maid quailed a little at this outburst. 'Well, sir, when I found his lordship he was, he was—' a blush touched the girl's pale cheeks '—he was busy.' She swallowed hard as if remembering something awful. 'He said that I should come here and ask you to... to...'

Betsy understood what had happened. It was something of a ritual for new girls, and she remembered her own introduction to the vastness and complexity of the hall only too well. Stumbling, lost from corridor to unknown stairwell, finally reaching her goal only to be sent off somewhere else in search of punishment, she had been in tears long before the first stroke had been struck. All the same, looking at this pretty little morsel, she was surprised that Lord Alex had sent her on. The master must have been occupied with something interesting, Betsy mused, to have passed up such a dainty little treat.

'Very well, girl, I am busy too - but I expect I can find the time to thrash you. Betsy, you won't mind if your belting waits a little longer?

Betsy blinked back at him. 'N-no, sir.'

'Good. Then everyone is happy?'

There was a groan from Amelia and a slightly panicked gasp from Clara, which suggested that the blonde girl's coin might be starting to slip. Betsy peeked at the little kitchen-maid, who had gone very pale, and then back to her master, who threw the tawse down onto the chaise longue, where it landed with a sickening thump.

'I asked if everyone was happy?' Jamie demanded more forcefully.

There was a ragged chorus of unconvincing, 'Yes, sir.'

The young man smiled. 'Jolly good,' he said with a satisfied air. 'Betsy, get that bloody sack off her, will you? You, girl, what is your name?'

'Emma, sir,' the girl said softly. 'Emma Swift.'

Betsy hurried to help the girl take off her functional grey kitchen-maid's uniform. Beneath, her underclothing was all white, except for soft black woollen stockings. Her undergarments were plain but clean, and obviously new. She wore a thin cotton camisole beneath her corset, which acted as a halter for her breasts. The corset made a trim waist even trimmer. The girl blushed furiously, but did not protest as she was

67

undressed. She kept glancing fearfully towards Amelia.

'I see you find Miss Amelia's condition interesting, eh, girl?' Jamie had apparently noticed her fascination.

'Ah, sorry, sir, I didn't mean—'

'Not at all. Come over, if you are interested.'

Emma peeked up at Betsy, as if looking for help. The nursery-maid was neither willing nor able to supply it, and did not meet her gaze.

'Come on.' The note of command in Jamie's voice was more obvious now, and Emma walked across to his side.

'It looks a bit hot, does it not?'

Betsy could see most of the bottom in question as Emma stood to one side of Amelia, and Jamie at the other. The stripes that the tawse had left were still glowing. Jamie put his hand on Amelia's left buttock and squeezed, drawing a gasp of pain from her.

'It feels warm, too. I tell you what, Emma, why don't you kneel down? Steady, Amelia. Drop the coin again and I'll skin you! Right, Emma, shuffle a bit closer; now you can see what you were so fascinated by. Get a good look, girl.'

His hand closed on the back of the maid's neck, forcing her face inches from Amelia's quivering bottom; he lifted the hem of Amelia's smock with his other hand.

'Feel for yourself how hot it is. Put your face against it. Cheek to cheek, so to speak. Come on, you nosy little chit, do as I say!'

The maid did as she was told with palpable reluctance. Another pained whimper escaped Amelia as Emma laid her cheek against the surface of the girl's well-tawsed bottom. Jamie made her stay there for a minute, pressing her face against the hot bottom-flesh, obviously enjoying the tableau.

In truth, it was a pretty sight - at least Betsy found it so. Amelia stood, her whole body quivering as she strained to hold the coin against the wall, arms bound behind her. The girl's shapely legs were set off by her sheer white stockings and her curvaceous figure was barely veiled by the thin little smock. Emma knelt, the picture of imperilled innocence, in her white corset and drawers. Her flawless little cheek was just touched by a blush, almost as if the fiery glow of Amelia's bottom might be contagious. Even so, the girl's face seemed pale against the rosy surface of Amelia's bottom. Betsy could have stood and watched the scene all day. Longer, so long as it postponed her own appointment with the tawse.

Jamie appeared to find the picture pleasant, too, for he stood and contemplated the scene for several long minutes before taking a deep breath. 'Now, Betsy, if you can persuade young Emma to stop nuzzling other girls' arses, I would like you to bend her over, palms down on the nursing chair. I suspect you know the drill.' Jamie broke the spell as he opened the big cupboard to peruse his extensive collection of canes.

Betsy, naturally, knew the drill very well. There was a line in the pattern of the carpet some two feet from the low seat of the armless nursing chair. Taking Emma's bare arm firmly, she guided the girl over. The kitchen-maid's skin was warm and silky under her hand and she could feel the girl tremble slightly as she steadied her.

'Toes behind that line, please.'

The girl glanced sideways at Betsy's breasts. Betsy pinched Emma's arm crossly in response.

'Ow!'

'Come along, place your hands on the seat,' she insisted gruffly.

Emma's corset groaned a little in complaint as she bent, but it was neither so long nor so tightly laced as Betsy's, and she got down without difficulty. The nursing chair was low, and Emma's cotton-clad bottom now the highest part of her. Betsy reached out to pull the girl's drawers apart.

'That's enough, Betsy. I'll do that.'

Trying not to show her disappointment, for she had no wish to be accused of petulance, Betsy held her tongue and stepped away.

Jamie had selected his favourite, a flexible four-foot length of kooboo, and he cut this, once, twice and three times through the air as he approached the lovely bending girl. The sound that the cane made as he swiped it made Betsy's own bare buttocks clench reflexively in response, and she gave a silent prayer of thanks that it was Emma's and not her bottom that was proffered, ready for the kiss of the rod.

Jamie handed the cane to Betsy, who held the awful thing gingerly, as if it were red-hot. Emma gave a frightened little gasp as the young man pulled her drawers open at the back, and exposed a surprisingly plump bottom for so slight a girl. He tutted, failing to get the folds of cotton to fall back to his satisfaction.

'Emma, my dear, you won't mind if we drop these altogether?'

'Er, no, sir - I mean, um, yes, sir - that is, I mean...' Whatever the maid, in fact, did or did not mean mattered little, for his fingers had reached round to untie the drawstrings even as she tried to give an answer.

'Good, good,' Jamie said, apparently taking her confused mumbling for assent. In a trice, the cotton drawers fluttered down the girl's legs to fall in a drift around her ankles, and her hindquarters were completely exposed.

Emma was too petite for Betsy's idea of the proper female form; still, the buxom maid had to admit, the girl had a pretty bottom and shapely legs. The kitchen-maid's buttocks were impudently chubby, almost pure white rounds. Her pale thighs were well fleshed for their size, and her skin looked deliciously creamy, above the black lambswool of her stockings.

Jamie whistled his appreciation. 'Small but not so skinny!' he said admiringly. 'What a pretty little behind you have, Emma. I shall really enjoy administering this flogging.'

He laid the yellow cane across the plump buttocks, producing a reflexive twitch from her muscles, and an anxious gasp from the bending girl.

'Lovely, quite lovely,' the young man said, watching the nether cheeks flinch in anticipation. 'That bottom is as plump and sweet as a ripe peach.'

He stepped back and held the stick out, prodding the sex that peeked back between Emma's legs. She squeaked, but held her position dutifully. Reformatory girls, thought Betsy with a knowing smile - they always came at least partly trained.

'What do you say to a round dozen then, Miss Mischief?' Jamie called out as he took up his position.

'Um, I, er, please...'

'Just say "yes please, sir," you silly little bitch.'

'Yes please... sir.' The kitchen-maid's voice was now no more than a hoarse, thoroughly frightened-sounding whisper.

Betsy looked from the apprehensively twitching bottom to the face of her master, and saw the rapt smile of one entranced as he raised the cane.

Whoosh... thwuck!

The familiar yellow blur shimmered through the air, and the chubby little bottom-cheeks wobbled visibly from the impact. Emma hissed and her knees dipped, ever so slightly, before she got back into the prescribed position. Jamie waited, and thus the nursery waited. The only sound a pained panting from Emma.

The tramline welt bloomed as Betsy watched. It was almost horizontal, dissecting the girl's bottom-cleft just above the middle of her cheeks. The nursery-maid tried to swallow but found, for some reason, that she did not have enough saliva.

Jamie raised his rod again.

Whoosh... thwuck!

'Ooh, hoo, hoo, hoo...'

Emma's knees dipped deeply and she wiggled her bottom vigorously. This time, getting back into position was clearly a real trial. Jamie waited as the girl regained control of her tongue, and forced her now violently trembling legs to straighten.

Whoosh... thwuck!

The yellow blur came sooner this time, taking Betsy by surprise. It seemed to have caught the kitchen-maid out, too.

Emma howled. She dipped her knees and back, then straightened up again, several times in quick succession. The howling subsided into a gasping and the humping motion into stamping of her dainty feet as the third weal bloomed across her upper thighs.

'Come along, girl,' Jamie said impatiently. 'Resume the position; I haven't got all day.'

Still gasping with pain, the kitchen-maid forced herself to straighten her legs and stick her bottom out towards the man wielding the rod. This time there was no mistaking her reluctance. She pressed her hindquarters out hesitantly.

As Jamie raised his cane, the girl's whole body froze. Furtively, Betsy quickly brushed the fold of flesh sheathing her clitoris, as the yellow flicker rippled the air and the girl's buttocks bounced to the sickening sound of impact once again.

'*Aiee...!*'

Betsy blinked as she watched the girl react to the stroke. Again, there was the strange bucking dance but this time, as well as stamping, Emma put her left leg back up and across her right thigh, as if somehow she could shield her hindquarters from the blistering onslaught of the cane this way.

Jamie did not even have to tell her. As the girl regained control from the waves of pain that had carried her away, she forced her body back into the ordained position. Her welted bottom twitched violently in accompaniment to a slew of gasps and sniffles.

Betsy hardly knew how she got through the caning; every time the implement whooshed through the air she gave herself a furtive touch, pulling her hand away before Jamie could turn and catch her. How Emma endured the beating without recourse to restraint was an even greater source of wonder. That the small girl felt the thrashing was evident from her shrieks. After each stroke she seemed to find it ever harder to present her trembling thighs and flinching bottom for the next.

Yet, somehow, the kitchen-maid managed to stand relatively still for the full twelve. At the end, this was only achieved with the help of dire threats of further strokes should she fail to get back into position, but she did indeed get into that position.

The twelfth stroke was the worst. Even as she heard the slightly higher-pitched sound as the cane cut through the air, Betsy knew that this one was going to be tight. The *thwack* of hard rod on firm flesh rapped through the nursery only a little more emphatically, but there was no mistaking the ferocity of the final cut.

The sound that first emerged from the girl's lips was not a scream. It was an almost soundless gasp, as if the pain were so intense that she could not get the air out of her lungs. Nor did she move; she seemed to have been turned to stone for a full second. After this brief interlude, it was as if a coiled spring had been released. Emma first jumped high into the air before falling to the floor, her legs convulsively thrashing.

The little maid gurgled and shrieked and gasped, clutching and furiously kneading her bottom as she writhed on the floor, so violently that her corsets creaked in protest.

Betsy glanced at Jamie, who was watching with a satisfied smile. He allowed the kitchen-maid to wriggle on the floor for several long minutes, apparently content to watch her squirming in distress, until her cries had subsided to a low sobbing.

'Ooh, it h-h-hurts, s-s-so m-m-much...'

'All right, girl. No need for all this fuss. Get up now and kneel on the chair; let us see that bottom!'

Sniffling and panting heavily, wincing as she moved, the kitchen-maid slowly got onto her knees on the chair. Her hands moved away from her bottom-cheeks with reluctance. She gripped the back of the chair so hard her knuckles whitened. Her pretty head sagged and her slender back was racked every few seconds by a new rictus of convulsive sobs.

Betsy stared at the sight the girl presented. Twelve scarlet stripes now barred Emma's bottom and thighs. Just twice the tramlines crossed where the strokes had made an agonising intersection, but overall the welts were remarkably parallel. The painter of the pattern stood and admired his handiwork with a satisfied expression. His left hand worked busily in his trouser pocket as he waved the cane with his right, as if conducting some silent melody.

'There now,' he declared at last. 'A well-grilled bit of rump, if I ever saw one. I should think Cook will be well satisfied with those when you show her!'

This comment only provoked a fresh torrent of sobbing from the kitchen-maid. Jamie bent and planted a tender kiss on the nape of her slender neck.

'There, there, never mind, sweetheart. I tell you what.' He pointed at his bedroom door with the cane. 'Cut along to that room and wait for me. I have a job or two to do.' He looked at Betsy with a smile that froze the buxom maid's blood. 'But when I've finished, I'll come and give you something to make it better!'

The kitchen-maid turned and looked at Jamie with wide eyes and a solemn expression. Her gaze followed the pointing cane to the door it indicated, then back at the cane again. She swallowed hard, and then stood and bent to retrieve her drawers.

'No,' Jamie said quietly, and waved the tip of the stick admonishingly. 'No, I don't think they will be needed, my dear.'

The girl took a deep breath, a last appalled look at the still-straining cousins, and trotted off to Jamie's bedroom, wincing with every step.

'Right.' Jamie retrieved the tawse from the chaise longue, put down the cane and beamed at Betsy. 'Where the devil were we?' He winked as Betsy's stomach turned a somersault. 'Oh, yes. Now then, Betsy, back to business. Stick that hand out. Steady.'

The dreamy glow that had enveloped Betsy as she watched Emma being thrashed turned back to terror in an instant. Her hand trembled violently as she held it up, and even gripping the wrist with her free hand could not persuade her perspiring palm to stop quivering completely.

There was something about Jamie's demeanour - that and the ruthless way he had caned the kitchen-maid - that told Betsy with a sickening certainty that he was in a mood to fairly skin her. Oh, how she hated it on her hands. As her sense of panic mounted, she wondered if there was any way to persuade him to belt her bottom instead.

He took up his position. The thick leather strap swung idly in his hand. Her fingertips quivered expectantly.

'Keep it steady, now, Betsy. I want to give your hand a really good crack this time,' Jamie said conversationally.

Betsy closed her eyes tight and held her breath. The seconds that ticked away seemed to slow to minutes as she waited. It was so hard not to snatch her hand away. The struggle to keep her upturned palm in place was so difficult she was amazed that her knees did not give way beneath her. Another second crawled by... another... another... each cranking up the tension evermore unbearably.

There was a distinct metallic clink, followed by an awful pause.

'Clara! You naughty girl!'

Betsy opened her eyes and peeked cautiously. Jamie was shaking his head resignedly and looking at the blonde girl. The nursery-maid glanced down to see Clara's guinea gleaming on the platter between her feet.

Jamie sighed. Turning back to Betsy, he shrugged and winked at her. Then he rubbed his right shoulder as if it were getting stiff.

'Good God,' he said. 'Did you ever hear that expression, Betsy,' the young man asked ruefully as he turned back towards Clara, 'no rest for the wicked?'

THE REVEREND DAWES'S DRAWERS

'Ah, Monsieur Jamie, how good to see you. These must be the young ladies we spoke of on the telephone, no? Miss Clara and Miss Emily, no? How pretty.'

'Mademoiselle Isobel.' Jamie gave a short bow and gestured towards Clara. 'This is Miss Clara and—' he indicated her companion and corrected the mistake '—Miss Amelia.'

Amelia had heard of Mademoiselle Isobel, the celebrated couturier and corsetier. Her emporium was the largest and most fashionable establishment in the three counties, and was the sort of boutique more likely to be found in a major city than in a little town like Hatherby. So grand and modern was the emporium that it was even furnished with a telephone and the new electric light!

In the flesh, Mademoiselle Isobel proved to be a pretty, dark-haired little woman in her thirties. Amelia, unable to suppress the competitive streak in her character, was forced to admit that the lady displayed her trim figure to perfection in an elegant gown of dark green silk. The chic propriety of the woman's attire made Amelia's present situation all the more unendurable. Her state of mind was not helped by the way Mademoiselle Isobel perused the cousins, who had been leashed, bound and humiliatingly exposed once again. The woman's green eyes twinkled with amusement as she studied the blushing girls.

'Yes, you were right to bring the little dears to me, Jamie. No doubt you need to keep them on a tight rein, but do you think that, for the fitting, they might be unleashed?'

To Amelia's joy, Jamie assented easily. The various straps and collars that bound the two girls were unbuckled and unlocked by Betsy, and she was soon able to move her unbound arms with relief. There were customers and shop-girls all around, and she moved to lift her hands to shield her breasts, all too aware that the flimsy silk of her smock was failing, as usual, to veil her nipples properly.

'Keep them at your sides, Amelia,' Jamie said sharply.

Somehow managing to suppress the urge to glare mutinously at him, Amelia sullenly bit her lip but did as she was told.

'You mean to keep them in these pretty little frocks for much longer, Jamie?'

Fervently, Amelia closed her eyes and prayed. Surely Mademoiselle Isobel would point out the impropriety of their costumes? Perhaps she was about to suggest more suitable attire for girls of their age and status to their tormentor? After all, even the common shop-girls scurrying about the boutique were elegantly and modestly dressed!

'Oh, yes.' Jamie's voice was a self-satisfied drawl that curdled Amelia's blood. 'These frocks will do them for the rest of the summer, certainly. After that, we shall have to see.'

Until the end of the summer? But that was months away! Amelia had to bite her tongue to prevent a bitter protest. One day, someone would pay for this ordeal, she promised herself, as she struggled against competing tides of fury and despair.

'Yes, yes.' Isobel clapped her hands delightedly. 'Most suitable for such pretty little girls. But you were right to be concerned about the corseting. They must be laced up tight. It will enhance their charms and help to curb their youthful appetites for mischief. I suggest we run them up some short waist-cinchers which will leave their titties and their pretty bottoms entirely free for disciplinary and training purposes. Now, if you would care to follow me?'

Amelia hoped fervently that they would be led to private fitting-rooms, but the Frenchwoman took them to one side of the shop where some seats had been set out. This was clearly the lingerie section of the emporium, for there were racks of frilled and ruched underthings all around, and there were several mannequins, all with impossibly narrow waists, on which were displayed various styles of corsetry.

The chairs were arranged around a little wooden platform, and behind the seats were several full-length mirrors. Amelia caught sight of herself, a pretty, auburn-haired young lady in an absurd and indecently abbreviated dress, and saw her own cheeks start to redden. Quickly she looked away.

'Now, take off your little smockies, *mes petites choux*.'

Amelia looked at Clara. The blonde girl blinked helplessly at her, eyes wide with panic, a blush suffusing her cheeks. Both cousins looked around. Mademoiselle Isobel's emporium was large, and they had the corsetry section to themselves.

However, there were half a dozen other customers, both gentlemen and ladies, in the other sections of the store. It was evident that these gentlefolk had only to look over in their direction and...

'Ah, the pretty little things are shy, I see.' Isobel clapped her hands in what looked to Amelia ominously like delight. 'Charming, and quite natural, of course. But such foolishness cannot be countenanced here, my dears. Come, quickly now, or shall I have to call my staff to disrobe you. The fuss will no doubt attract the attention of everyone but... Ah, good. Good girls, that is more sensible.'

Amelia pulled the smock over her head reluctantly. Not for a minute did she doubt the little woman's word, nor the sick certainty that any struggle would ensure the undivided attention of all the customers and staff at present in the shop. Clara had already taken her smock off and was handing it to an elegantly dressed shop-girl. This young lady folded the slip of silk and waited for Amelia to hand over her own garment with, it seemed to the semi-naked girl, the suggestion of an insolent smile.

The worst thing about her situation was that Amelia was aware of exactly what sort of spectacle she presented. Clara, admittedly more slender than her, and with golden rather than auburn ringlets and curls, stood trembling, covering her bare breasts with not a thing to hide her shame but a pair of frilly white knickers and similarly hued silk stockings, gartered just above the knee. Turning away in distress, Amelia saw her own more bounteous naked figure reflected in the mirror.

If her own blush seemed less pronounced than her cousin's, this could only have been because the contrast between her flaming cheeks and her auburn locks was less marked than that of her cousin's. Clara's pale coloration and golden curls made her blush stand out like a beacon. All the same, Amelia truly believed, Clara could not have felt any more mortified than she.

Still, as she was about to discover, there was worse to come.

'Now, Clara, stand upon this for me.' The corsetier indicated the little platform. It was no more than two steps high, just enough to put Clara's waist just below the level of Mademoiselle Isobel's head. Yet, it was enough, Amelia realised glumly, to draw the attention of other shoppers.

'Place your hands behind your head, *ma cherie*.'

Clara had always shown herself to be far more submissive than her cousin, and her pride was certainly less pronounced. Yet, Amelia knew, her nursery companion suffered dreadfully from shyness. She supposed that that was why, for once, it was the usually timid and biddable Clara who balked.

'Please, must I? I - oh, Jamie. I mean, sir... Ow!'

Jamie stepped forward and delivered a hard slap to the bare flesh of her upper thigh. 'Do as you are told, you wicked girl,' he hissed furiously. 'Don't you dare to show me up in public! Now, obey

Mademoiselle or I promise to make you a very, very sorry little miss indeed.'

Hesitantly, Clara exposed her lovely apple-sized breasts. Amelia could see the girl's bottom lip trembling, and was not surprised when tears began to course down her cousin's flaming cheeks. For all that, Clara's flesh was pale; the pure white of the luxuriantly frilled knickers and her stockings revealed the pale peach tones of her flawless flesh beautifully. The sight was so poignant, Clara's sweet, vulnerable beauty so heartbreakingly delicious, that, just for a second, Amelia forgot her own travails.

Oh, cousin, she thought to herself, dry-mouthed. My sweet, trembling little dove. What I would not give to be in Jamie's place and have you on my leash. How I would make you cry if you were mine! How I should whip that pretty little bottom! How frequently and pitilessly I would flog you, until you wept for mercy!

Unfortunately, Amelia's reverie was short-lived. Jamie remained in striking distance of Clara's thighs just long enough to ensure that Mademoiselle's instructions were obeyed. Then he strode over to Amelia and stood behind her, so close that she could feel the heat of his breath on the back of her neck.

Amelia found it hard to concentrate on the tableau before her, however entrancing she found the sight of Clara standing sobbing on the box. A hand stole around her waist and pulled her back a half step. Another hand gripped her frill-wrapped bottom firmly, and the first one moved up until it clasped her left breast. Only by a real effort of will did Amelia suppress the urge to push his impertinent fingers away.

'I do hope you will be better behaved than your cousin when your turn comes for fitting, Amelia,' Jamie murmured in her ear. 'Because, of course, I shan't be so lenient with you as I was with her.'

Amelia tried hard to ignore his fondling as she watched the corsetier use her tape measure on Clara. The semi-naked girl stood, hands behind her head, trembling visibly as the little woman deftly measured waist, bust and hips, Calling out figures to her elegant assistant.

'Twenty-two, Monique. Lovely slender waist. Should lace down to sixteen, in time, Jamie. Eighteen inches would be more than generous.'

Amelia knew something of tight lacing. The cousins' finishing school could not have been accused of being lax in that regard. On hearing this, she suppressed a sigh. It was not difficult to guess that hard trials lay ahead.

'Bust thirty-three, Monique. B cup.'

'Not like these ripe handfuls, eh, Amelia?' Jamie had brought his other hand up and around to take her right breast, and he squeezed hard then lifted the naked globes in his palms, as if weighing them. 'Must be at least a D!' he chuckled in her ear.

Then Amelia, who thought she had seen the worst that lay before her that day, was disabused. Mademoiselle Isobel placed her tape measure around her neck and put her hands on Clara's hips. The girl gave a shocked little squeak as she realised what was happening, then the woman pulled her frilly knickers right down to her knees.

'I say, good show!' a male voice called out, and there was an outbreak of sporadic clapping. Aghast, Amelia realised that most of the other customers had drifted across the shop to the lingerie area, no doubt to enjoy the display. Clara, seemingly not daring to defy Jamie and Mademoiselle by covering her nakedness, yet too mortified to hold her position, had buried her face in her hands and was sobbing quietly. Something told Amelia that, when her own turn came, Jamie would be unlikely to allow her even that escape.

Mademoiselle Isobel had already demonstrated how deftly and efficiently she could work. Yet it seemed to Amelia that she dawdled deliberately, prolonging Clara's agony unnecessarily, and making sure that her customers had a treat. Amelia could not deny that as a display it was delightful, but the stomach-churning knowledge that she was bound to be the next performer turned the sight from a pleasurable vista to one that struck fear into her heart.

Both cousins had been shaven that very morning, and Clara's neat pussy-lips looked mouth-watering under the shop's electric lights. Her slender thighs trembled violently now, pressed firmly together. Mademoiselle had to do something which Amelia did not follow, but which made Clara start and give a little cry of pain, before the blonde girl could be persuaded to stand with her feet apart.

'By God, what a delightful little quim. Jamie, does that belong to you?' an amused lady's voice put in, to general murmurs of agreement.

'Not exactly, Mrs Treadwell, but I am charged with looking after it at present. This one, too.' Jamie dropped his left hand to pat the front of Amelia's frilly knickers, to general laughter.

Amelia did not want to watch, knowing that her fate was sure to follow Clara's, yet she could not stop herself. Monique handed Mademoiselle Isobel a thin leather belt, which she proceeded to tighten around Clara's waist until the girl grunted with discomfort. What was she doing? Amelia wondered. What had this to do with corset fitting? Unfortunately for her peace of mind, the answer came all too soon.

'Stop blubbering and hold this, Clara,' the elegant woman said sharply, and reluctantly Clara lowered her hands and did as she was told. She held the end of the tape against the buckle of the belt, which Mademoiselle had ensured was at the centre of her belly. The woman took the tape between the whimpering girl's legs and up again to place it at the back of the belt.

'I always equip my corsets with anchor points back and front, to which a saddle-strap may be attached, should one be required. I shall also furnish these with attachments for a back-board. Deportment sometimes needs to be enforced by physical means with young girls like these.' Mademoiselle Isobel spoke brightly to Jamie and winked.

As the young man was still close behind her, fondling her breasts, it almost seemed to Amelia as if the wink had been directed at her.

'Now, hold it very firm, *ma petite!*' the woman instructed and tugged the tape until it disappeared, to a ripple of merriment amongst the customers and a little squeak from Clara, between the shaven lips of the blonde girl's labia.

Eventually the measurement was taken, a process which to Amelia's reckoning took several minutes, involving a distressing and gratuitous amount of fiddling and tugging at the tape, as Clara gasped and moaned. When the tape measure was finally retrieved and carried off by the elegant Monique, the naked girl was finally allowed to step down from the box. As she stepped unsteadily down to a raucous cheer from the assembled customers, Amelia looked into Clara's eyes, but could not have said if Clara was aware of her. There was something strange in the naked girl's expression; distant, as if she had somehow gone past shame and entered into some strange dreamy state, which had caused her eyes to become glazed.

Amelia had no more leisure to think about her cousin for, at that moment, she was propelled towards the little stage herself. Reasoning that the only way to get through this ordeal was to get it over with, Amelia stepped up onto the box and put her hands behind her head. Yes, it was humiliating. Yes, it was shameful and indecent to be so exposed, breasts bobbing naked for the *hoi polloi* to gawk at. Yet she was the Honourable Amelia Colinbrooke and, if she were to be forced into this dreadful display, she could at least exhibit dignity in her manner. Most of all, she was determined her tormentors should not see her cry.

'Waist twenty-five inches. Not so svelte as Clara, eh, ma petite choux? I am sure she will go down to nineteen inches without undue difficulty, anyway, Monsieur Jamie. Your nursery-maid, she is a big strong girl, yes? She looks like she could lace, yes? *Pouf*, with such muscle to hand, this minx should lace down to eighteen.'

Twenty-one inches had been Amelia's record at school, and the prospect of being cinched down to eighteen was so awful that she swayed on the platform for a moment, her knees going weak. She was given no time to dwell upon the dismal prospect, however.

'Bust thirty-six inches, cup double-D.'

There was a chorus of ill-mannered whooping from the customers, and several coarse comments about grapefruit from both male and female voices. Amelia had been trying to ignore the audience, keeping her eyes firmly closed, as if by not seeing them she could make them disappear. The remarks about her breasts provoked a strange reaction. A sort of furious curiosity seized her. She knew that she should just try to ignore the brutes, but something compelled her to take a look at her tormentors.

Unfortunately, the moment she chose was not a good one. Amelia did not recognise the three men and two women, all elegantly dressed, who were watching her with expressions of mingled admiration and amusement. There were also three shop-girls in sight, one of whom was bashfully modelling a corset.

The scene filled Amelia with impotent fury. Those elegant ladies with their superior expressions, who did they think they were?

At that moment, two things happened simultaneously. Amelia felt Mademoiselle's hands on the waist band of her panties, and at the same time watched with horror as the Reverend Dawes entered the shop. Time seemed to slow to a crawl as she watched him turn towards the lingerie department, and his eyes locked on to hers.

'No!'

Her resolution to endure the fitting fled, and she tried to bend to retrieve the frilly knickers as the corsetier pulled them swiftly down. To the amusement of the onlookers, Amelia bent, scrabbling for her panties, then suddenly straightened up again with a yelp. Mademoiselle Isobel must have had some sort of pin or needle secreted in her hand, because Amelia felt exactly as if she had been stung by a wasp. The sudden pain in her left buttock banished awareness of all else for a few seconds, even her sense of shame. A second sting, in her right buttock, caused another squeal, and Amelia found herself standing up, clutching her bare behind protectively, and blinking away the tears she had determined not to shed.

'Ah, you silly girls, you think Mademoiselle Isobel has never done a fitting with a reluctant young lady? La! Now, *ma petite*, be nice and hold the tape for me, and do not make me use my little encourager again!' The woman's voice was high and gay, but Amelia did not doubt that she would instantly employ the needle to gall her again if her client did not co-operate. Grunting as the little belt was tightened around her waist, Amelia did her best not to sob and to ignore the voices below her.

'I say, Jamie! Good day, sir. A corset fitting, is it? Very good. That's the impertinent child, Amelia, is it not?'

'That's right, Reverend! And we will fit her with rubber bloomers, next.'

The laughter of the male voices was joined by Mademoiselle Isobel's high peal. Chewing wormwood would not have been more bitter to Amelia.

'Reverend Dawes, your drawers are ready,' the corsetier said as Amelia took the tape in trembling fingers and held it to the buckle of the belt. 'Monique, run and model a pair for the Reverend.'

'Me, madame? But—'

'No buts, Monique. Yvette and Eloise are busy. Run along, girl. Quick as you can.'

Amelia heard the woman sigh as she felt the tape tugged tight.

'I spoil my girls, *messieurs*, and you see the result? I expect you wish to test the garment properly, Reverend. It might help to dissuade Monique from giving herself such airs!'

Amelia could not prevent a gurgling sound as the tape was worried deep into the cleft between her legs. The rubbing tape was provoking the very strangest feelings as she helplessly clutched the end of the thing. As with Clara, the process seemed to take forever. Amelia's awareness of her shameful nudity seemed even more mortifying, somehow, now that she felt the baleful gaze of the Reverend Dawes on her naked body. Felt, rather than saw, for she could not bring herself to look at him. She could not and did not look down at the source of the maddening sensations but, having just watched Clara go through the same ordeal, Amelia was appallingly certain that all other eyes were fixed on the smooth flesh of her now ripely swollen mons.

She bit back a sob of relief as she felt the tape measure tugged out from between her labia. As Mademoiselle Isobel unbuckled the belt, Amelia ventured a glance at Clara, who had been allowed to pull her knickers up before leaving the platform, and then given back her smock. The blonde girl now stood staring into space with that faraway expression on her face. Much as she hated her nursery costume, it was a lot better than nothing. Amelia's fingers fairly itched in anticipation of being given permission to retrieve her own panties and smock.

'All right now, *cherie*, pull off your knickers for me altogether, *vite!*'

Amelia was too aware of Mademoiselle's needle to refuse. So she bent, pulled down and stepped out of the frilly knickers, trying not to show her distress too much to the audience. As she had not been ordered differently, she let her left hand move over her shaven quim and her right across her breasts, hoping against hope that Jamie would not order her to uncover herself. To her relief, for once, she was not disappointed.

'You wished to see some rubber pantaloons now, Monsieur Jamie? Shall we repair to the rainwear section?'

The little party walked over to another part of the shop. For no good reason, that Amelia could see, the Reverend Dawes came with them, swapping jocularities with Jamie. Amelia hurried through the shop, which was thankfully less busy now than it had been earlier, desperately trying to hide her nakedness and fervently wishing she had another pair of arms.

The rainwear section of the shop smelt powerfully of rubber. The pungent odour of latex seemed to be haunting Amelia, and the scent was so strong here it made her feel a little giddy.

There were several racks of mackintoshes and some shelves stocked with galoshes in this part of the store, but there was also a plethora of other garments that, to Amelia at least, seemed to have little to do with protection from the elements. The naked girl was given a few moments to wonder at her surroundings, as the two men and Mademoiselle Isobel began discussing the various sorts of rubber pantaloons which the Mademoiselle took out from a massive set of drawers.

Some of the rubber garments hanging from the racks looked just like dresses, other items like uniforms for nurses or maids. There was latex underwear garnished with copious rubber frills, rubber gloves and stockings, and great enveloping capes. Amelia glanced over at her cousin to see what she made of this bizarre array, but Clara was still staring into space distractedly.

'Now, rubber knickers must be very tight.' Isobel's voice was brisk but there was no mistaking the note of amusement in it. 'We have various designs, you see. These are the new style, legless panties. Or we have the bloomer type with the directoire leg, which I would recommend as more secure. Try these on, *ma petite*. They should fit you, I think!'

Why the Frenchwoman should think anything of the sort was a mystery to Amelia. It was clear to her from the beginning that the rubber bloomers were far too small.

'Oh, no, Mademoiselle, I really can't - these are too tight.' The note of panic in Amelia's voice was due to Mademoiselle Isobel's position behind her bare bottom and Amelia's suspicion that the needle was itching in her hand.

'Of course they are not too tight, silly,' Isobel said in an amused voice. 'It is just that you need talcum powder.' She clapped her hands. 'Yvette, leave that now. Bring me the talcum powder and a brush.'

The powder was duly brought and with it a make-up brush. It was so soft that its touch proved all but unendurable. Mademoiselle Isobel had to ask Jamie to hold Amelia down as she applied the talcum powder over her legs and thighs.

'Ooh, no, I can't stand it. No, please, not there - it tickles so, *aiee...*!'

'Ah, but you will need it in those ticklish places later, or the rubber will stick and then where will you be, *cherie?*'

'Oh, oh, please, no more. Mercy...!'

'Be still, Amelia, and stop fidgeting, or I shall have to punish you most severely when we get home.'

'A wilful child! I see you have your work cut out with this one, Jamie. The doleful results of sparing the rod can be seen in such comportment amongst so many modern misses, I am afraid to say,' the Reverend Dawes put in sympathetically.

Eventually the powder was applied to Mademoiselle's satisfaction and, with a great deal of effort and some help from Jamie, the rubber bloomers were eventually pulled up. To say that they fitted like a second skin would be the height of understatement, unless that be epidermis stretched taut over swollen flesh. The bloomers gripped Amelia tight about the legs, and clasped her mons even more firmly. She closed her eyes and tried to think of something other than the chafing of the rubber as it stretched over her clitoris. This was not easy, for she was made to parade up and down.

'Yes, these are just the thing for bedwear, Mademoiselle. I think the legless ones will be better with the smock. Do those come with frills?'

'*Oui, Monsieur*. Note the elastics above the knee and at the waist are just a little tighter than the rest. That sometimes chafes, so should be used with petroleum jelly. These yellow ones are semi-transparent, as you see, but both also come in black, white, pale blue and pink, though all of those colours are more opaque.'

Let me take them off. For pity's sake, let me take them off. Amelia pleaded with her eyes but she did not dare to speak. She was getting more desperate with every stiff, peculiarly squeaking step. If I cannot take the damned things off, she thought, at least let me stand still!

'Pick your legs up, Amelia.' Jamie's voice was sharp. 'I did not tell you to shuffle. Pick those legs up now.'

Amelia was trapped in a nightmare. Forced to march, naked, up and down, she was unable to ignore the presence of the Reverend Dawes, who seemed almost to devour her with his awful eyes. Yet every step brought her closer to disaster. Every step stretched the rubber sheath over her clitoris, just a little tighter. Every step brought disaster inexorably closer. It was as if she were being forced to march right over a cliff.

'Ooh. Ahhh. Aiee!' The inevitable happened at last, forcing a strange strangled shriek from between Amelia's lips. Just for a second her ordeal, her tormentors, the whole world vanished, wiped out by an incandescent flash of ecstasy.

Amelia came to herself all too soon. It was too appalling. She found herself on her knees in a fashionable shop, wearing nothing but a pair of clammy rubber knickers. Jamie, the Reverend Dawes and Mademoiselle Isobel were all looking down at her with amused distaste.

'Good Lord, Amelia, what an extraordinary performance!' said Jamie, but it was the Reverend Dawes whose verdict she waited for, head bowed.

'The girl is evidently an incorrigible wanton, Jamie. I am about to test a new design of flogging drawers, that Mademoiselle Isobel has been good enough to run up to a design of my own. Perhaps we should see how these rubber items stand up to similar wear and tear!'

Amelia stood waiting glumly next to Clara, both girls standing to attention, hands held neatly, as ordered, at their sides. Her smock had finally been restored to her, but her loins were still gripped in the clammy rubber embrace. The legs of the bloomers descended below the hem of the silk smock, and Amelia was only too aware of the bizarre sight she must have made.

The party had traipsed back to the lingerie section of the shop, where Mademoiselle Isobel took coffee with the gentlemen. Monique seemed to have been gone an age, and Amelia wondered what could have taken her so long. The shop-girl's reluctance to model the Reverend's order had been obvious, and Amelia wondered if the girl might have stolen out of the emporium and run away.

Such speculation was curtailed by the arrival of the young lady in question. Monique still wore her dark brown hair in an elegant coif but, instead of a fashionable full-length dress, she now wore only a lace-trimmed sleeveless white cotton shift, the hem of which just covered her knees. The girl's anxiety was palpable, her reluctance to approach the company plain. Yet there was something odd about her gait apart from this; a stiffness that reminded Amelia of the difficulty in walking that the rubber bloomers had caused her.

'Ah, there you are, Monique. Yvette! Trot along and fetch a number three cane for the Reverend - oh, yes, and a bucket of water and a sponge. Run along, *tout de suite!* Now, Monique, but you are not modelling chemises today, *ma petite*. Come along now! Off with it. I am sure that the Reverend is eager to see what we have done with his design.'

If the girl had seemed unwilling to approach, she pulled the shift off, over her head, with even more obvious reluctance. Her expression was solemn, even dignified, and only the barest hint of a blush showed around her cheekbones, but Amelia saw her fingers tremble as she folded the garment to place it neatly on the wooden platform.

Despite herself, Amelia stared in astonishment. Monique wore a white coutil corset laced tight about a neat waist and equipped with lace-trimmed cups to support her full breasts. However, it was the shop assistant's lower body that compelled Amelia's attention. She could not have conceived of anything tighter than the latex monstrosities that gripped her own loins yet, if anything, these cotton drawers appeared to grip the girl in an even fiercer constraint.

'Ah, yes. I thought I had better order some flogging drawers for the attendees on my course. For the sake of propriety, you know. After all, it is not always desirable for single gentlemen to beat nubile young females on the bare!' The Reverend chuckled to himself, although Amelia could not see what was so amusing, nor what relationship her own treatment had to the propriety of which he claimed to be concerned. Still, she reasoned that she was in enough difficulty already, so she kept her observations to herself.

'You see, they are fashioned in two pieces, a front half and a rear, with leather strips serving to reinforce the seams at either side.'

Amelia could see. The drawers had legs about half the length of the girl's thigh, leaving just an inch or two of bare flesh between the end of the drawers and the tops of Monique's black silk stockings. From the bottom of the leg to the waistband, thick leather strips ran, equipped with metal eyelets, much like one might find on the lacing of a corset. Laces connected the front and back panels on both of Monique's flanks, and it was clear that these had been used to adjust the drawers until they were astonishingly tight.

'Face front, girl!' the Reverend ordered gruffly, taking the four-foot length of yellow cane from Yvette, who had arrived hurriedly back.

The force of the lacing had pulled the thin cotton of the front panel so tightly over Monique's quim that a fold of the material had disappeared between her legs, and the girl's dark pubic curls could plainly be seen, flattened by the thin fabric.

Amelia blinked twice at the sight, not surprised to note that Monique's pretty brown eyes were watering and her bottom lip was quivering as she stood stiffly to attention. The Reverend leant forward and prodded the girl's quim gently with the tip of his rod, provoking a terrified little squeak.

'You see, Jamie, with these, the girl's state of mind may be monitored, yet as no nakedness is entailed, even the most prurient-minded could scarcely claim any impropriety.' He continued prodding for a few moments and Monique moaned again.

'Hold your tongue, girl,' Mademoiselle Isobel said sharply. 'I expect the Reverend will give you something to groan about, presently!'

'All right, turn and bend over. Place your hands on the platform there,' the Reverend Dawes ordered in a slightly strangled tone. Monique obeyed, and Amelia caught her breath at the sight the girl displayed. She had a full bottom, and she might have as well have been naked for the extent to which the flogging drawers disguised the charm of her behind. She bent, corset creaking in protest, shapely legs straight, and as she bent the drawers appeared to tighten even more, though that seemed scarcely possible.

'What is that, cotton?' Jamie put in, his voice slightly hoarse as well.

'The finest cambric. Usually we use it for the ladies' pocket handkerchiefs,' Mademoiselle Isobel said.

'That's why we need the leather strips,' the Reverend Dawes explained enthusiastically. 'The front and back panels are so fine, and the stress on them so great, I expect that quite a few will rip through wear and tear and...'

He unleashed a yellow blur and the white-sheathed bottom quivered with the impact. The thwacking sound as the cane bit home made Amelia's own belly tense in sympathy. Monique's legs bowed slightly for a second and then straightened up again, but an 'Ooh!' bore witness to the ferocity of the stroke.

'The idea is,' the Reverend continued conversationally, as he lined up his next lash, 'that the lacing strips can be re-used. When the panels split or rip, they can be replaced. A tedious job, perhaps...'

He struck again. Amelia saw no more than a yellow flicker, the cane cut through the air so fast, but she heard the thing crack across Monique's bottom and saw the buttocks quiver with the impact. This time, the shop-girl could not stop a squeal and she stamped three times with her high-heeled shoes before managing to straighten up into the prescribed position once again.

'But not a skilled one. Mademoiselle can provide the panels, fashioned to the contours of the miscreants, and girls who split their drawers may be employed in sewing in new rears. Or fronts, should they split in that department!'

He struck again. This time the cane whipped across the girl's thighs and a strange whinnying sound was forced out of her mouth. Monique stamped her feet and wiggled her bottom desperately, and she had to be spoken to sharply by Mademoiselle before she would straighten her legs and assume the proper position again.

'A most ingenious arrangement,' Jamie murmured with admiration. 'Still, this pair has not split yet.'

The Reverend turned and smiled, flexing the cane between his powerful hands. 'Quite right,' he said. 'They seem to be standing up well, so far. Silk would be stronger, but I was hoping to keep to cotton, both for reasons of economy and because I do not want my girls giving themselves airs.'

At this, he looked straight at Amelia and she hurriedly dropped her eyes. The effect of this was that her gaze fell on her jutting breasts and the nipples that were sticking out, visible against the thin silk, as they seemed to do distressingly frequently. You can keep your silk, she thought mutinously. But she hardly breathed until the Reverend's attention moved back to the trembling Monique.

'However,' the Reverend Dawes said with a dramatic flourish, 'there is another test yet. You, girl, give me that sponge.'

The material constraining Monique's bottom and thighs was so thin, and so taut, that Amelia could already clearly see the welts that the Reverend's cane had raised on the girl's hindquarters; lines of pink glowing through the snow-white stuff. Monique gasped as the man applied the soaking sponge, thoroughly wetting the whole target area. Then she started whimpering strangely.

'Is it shrinking?' Jamie asked in awe.

'A little bit. I don't think these can get much tighter, really,' Mademoiselle chuckled.

What was not in question was that wetting the cotton made it more transparent. The welts showed through lividly now, and Amelia licked her lips. The now wet gusset revealed every detail of Monique's quim.

The Reverend stepped back and placed the cane across the moist material sheathing the fullest part of Monique's bottom. The shop-girl gave a little wail of fear and Amelia watched the plump cheeks clench in anticipation.

'Relax them, girl. I'll have no clenching - relax them.'

Somehow Monique managed to comply and, without more ado, the Reverend lashed the proffered bottom once again. There was a subtly different sound as the cane impacted on bottom-cheeks constrained in wet cotton, and another shriek from Monique's lips. This time she stood and clutched her bottom, deaf to Mademoiselle Isobel's shocked admonishments. The girl shook her pretty head, and hopped from foot to foot for a full minute before turning a tearful and shamefaced look towards the man wielding the cane.

'Feel that one, miss?'

'Ooh, oh, yes, sir. It was terribly tight, your reverence, sir. Ooh. Ouch.'

'Tighter than the others?'

'Y-yes sir, quite a bit... ah... stingier on the wet.'

'Excellent. Well, bend down again, girl.'

'Ah, again?' Blinking away tears, Monique looked first at the Reverend and then at Mademoiselle, before turning back with obvious reluctance to the platform and taking up her position once more. The Reverend Dawes strode over to her and patted the damp seat of her drawers, causing the girl to wince and suck her breath in. The large man chuckled as he squeezed her bottom flesh appraisingly.

'No splits. Excellent; these will do very well.'

Monique's bottom was moving in response to his probing; as his fingers moved down the cheeks to pass between her legs, she let out a groan. Amelia wondered crossly what this fingering could have to do with the Reverend's professed concern for the proprieties. Corporal correction was one thing, but it seemed to Amelia that this fondling was improperly intimate, and that Monique's moaning and writhing displayed an indecent response to such liberties. Of course, she reasoned as the girl's cries became more desperate, Monique was nothing but a shop-girl and little better could be expected from common sluts of that sort. Still, it was appalling that Amelia had to stand and watch the low-bred brute caress his trollop to what was obviously a climax, and she vowed to revenge herself on Monique, should the opportunity ever come her way.

At least she did not have to watch for very long. The girl soon started grunting and gasping in a most undignified manner and finally fell, squealing to her knees. She was given but the briefest of interludes to recover, then packed off to extricate herself from the whipping drawers and dress. Amelia sighed with relief as she watched the girl scurry away.

'A most satisfactory experiment,' the Reverend said genially as he toyed with the cane. 'I should like a dozen pairs initially, Mademoiselle, and two dozen extra back panels. Now, it only remains to enquire how the rubber version functions.'

Those predatory grey eyes locked onto Amelia's and suddenly her heart was hammering again.

'My dear.' The Reverend Dawes inclined his head politely and indicated the platform with his cane. 'Perhaps you would care to step this way?'

A ROD IN PICKLE

The joyous pealing of the distant church bells could be clearly heard from the nursery as the cousins were dressed in their Sunday best. Yet the sound failed to cheer Amelia. For one thing, the corsets had arrived from Mademoiselle Isobel's on the previous day, and Betsy was lacing her into the stays with a relish matched only by the nursery-maid's considerable strength.

'Oof... ah... Please, Betsy, it's like a vice already... Ooh.' Amelia hung onto the bedstead for dear life, as the maid hauled at the laces with all her might.

Clara, already laced into her own white satin waspie, stood watching, looking startled and breathing carefully, to one side. All she wore was the corset and the usual silk stockings, this time supported by the new suspender drops with which the stays had come equipped. Thus, the white lace trim of the corset, the suspender straps and the silk stocking-tops provided the most delightful frame for the blonde girl's shaven quim.

Unfortunately, Amelia had no leisure to enjoy this prospect. Betsy placed a plump knee in the small of her back, to get even more purchase, and both girls grunted as the laces were forced tighter, and then tighter still.

When, a little later, they joined the rest of the Hope Hall household in the courtyard, Amelia felt no happier about the day. The collected maids all gloried in their full uniforms for once, hoisting long skirts out of the mire under Mrs Pritchard's disdainful gaze. They did not even have to undergo the humiliation of wearing collars. In contrast, once again Amelia and Clara had been given the absurd smocks to wear. Clara had then been issued with the usual frilly knickers but Amelia had had to endure even worse.

'Now then Amelia, don't make a fuss, girl,' Jamie had said, smiling contently.

So it had been rubber bloomers again. The latex legs showed below the hem of the smock and they squeaked insistently as she walked, provoking all sorts of witty comments from Lady Alicia. And they rubbed, and rubbed, and rubbed. The worse thing of all was that Amelia knew only too well to whom she was squeaking towards across the park. There was no forgetting whose cold grey eyes would be waiting at the church.

All of which would have been sufficient to explain her distracted expression during the hymns, and the way she stared stonily at the back of Mrs Justice Ormorund in the pew in front of her during the sermon. But there was worse.

The Reverend Dawes had chosen a favourite line from Proverbs as his inspiration for the sermon.

'There is a rod in pickle for the arrogant, and stripes prepared for the backs of fools,' he snarled, with barely disguised relish. It was not an especially cheerful text and, glancing furtively around the church, Amelia noticed that a few female cheeks had paled, and she observed several slender hands tremble on their hymnals as the rector of Hatherby expounded on his theme. 'A whip for the horse, a bridle for the ass and a rod for the fool's back!' the rector exhorted from the pulpit, cracking his hand against the oaken structure as he did so, producing retorts that echoed around the church and provoked visible flinching among certain of the more comely members of the congregation.

The Reverend Dawes's lip curled as he elaborated on the words 'whip for the horse', and his grey eyes stared so hard at someone seated to the rear that Amelia, along with most of the rest of the congregation, turned to look at the trembling girl in a modest maid's uniform sitting at the back of the church. She recognised the red-haired Rose from their encounter in the birch groves. Rose kept her eyes downcast, but Amelia could tell from the girl's blush that she was perfectly well aware of the Reverend's attention.

A plump blonde farm girl received similar treatment when the good rector turned to the value of bridles when dealing with asses. Then, to her horror, Amelia found herself frozen to her pew by the man's basilisk stare, as he expounded on the value of rods when it came to the backs of fools, with all too evident enthusiasm.

'Arrogance, disobedience, wilfulness, all are forms of foolishness, and all may be mitigated by the application of the firm corrective rod!' he boomed as Amelia hung her head, horribly aware that half the church was now following the preacher's lead and staring at her. Her rubber bloomers were

driving her to distraction now and she furtively tried to ease her position just as he paused. To her horror, a loud rubbery creak rang out in the sudden silence. There was a nervous girlish titter from somewhere to Amelia's left, and then the distinctive sound of a sharp slap and gasp of pain.

'There is a rod in pickle for the arrogant,' the Reverend repeated in stentorian tones, once the commotion had ceased, 'and I think we may safely predict that it will not be steeping there for much longer!'

A knowing chuckle rippled around the church. Amelia stared miserably at her silk-sheathed knees and tried not to think about where the taut rubber was chafing.

The walk back from church was no more cheering. Amelia and Clara, together with all the Hope Hall maids, walked back solemn-faced and subdued. Lord and Lady Alex, Jamie and Mrs Pritchard, on the other hand, were positively animated and jolly. They swapped witticisms and pleasantries, and affected puzzlement when Amelia did not join the general jollity.

The rubber drawers were vexing her now and the corset's grip was equally unrelenting. But the discomfort occasioned by her underclothing was but part of the reason for Amelia's misery.

She was dreading the famous Sunday Service. All Amelia's recent experience had not inured her to public humiliation, and she knew that many of the Whippery seats were bound to be filled that afternoon. Also, she was truly frightened of the birch. She had only ever had it once before, and that had been a light switching at school. Light or not, she remembered the experience with terror. The thought of a more severe birching made her feel faint.

'What - what is the birch like, Amelia?' Clara asked with frightened eyes, as they waited in the nursery parlour to be summoned.

The cousins had been left with the nursery-maid after a cheerless luncheon of bread and water shared with a subdued and ashen-faced Betsy. Jamie had left the girls to their crust repast and gone down to the dining room for cold pheasant and claret.

'What is it like?' Betsy looked as if she was about to cry. 'Two words for a proper birching, girl. Just two words: red hell.' She put a knuckle in her mouth and started chewing it.

'What are you worried about, anyway?' Amelia demanded of her cousin crossly. 'You did not even get a black mark in the book!'

'Jamie - Master Jamie, said he would mark me down so that I got a dozen anyway.' Clara's voice had died almost to a whisper. 'On general pr-pr-principles. He said that I ought to know...'

'A lot that little beast knows about principles,' Amelia hissed. Both Betsy and Clara stiffened as she spoke and she suddenly felt afraid. What if these sycophantic creatures reported what she had said? she thought, appalled. Could she trust them? No, of course not. Betsy disliked her and loved nothing more than to see her betters thrashed. And Clara? She seemed to think that Jamie was some sort of demi-god!

So Amelia held her tongue and tried not to listen as Betsy expounded on the terrors of the birch.

'Next to the tawse, taken on the hand, I think the birch is the worse. A heavy cane, see, after a dozen or so good hard strokes, it dulls the nerves a little. The birch, though, that is a surface-scourer. It doesn't bruise, you see. There is no weight to it and the nerves never get stunned and numbed. But, oh, how it scours your skin! There does not seem to be a peak of pain after the first dozen, or the second. It just—' her voice had become very quiet, no more than a hoarse little whisper '—it just gets worse and worse and worse.'

The glum trio was interrupted at that point by the arrival of Mrs Pritchard. The housekeeper regarded the three of them with smug satisfaction.

'Right, Amelia and Clara, come with me. Betsy, time to put on your flogging smock. Then you can join us in the Rod Room. Quick as you can. Come along you two, there is a little job for you to do.'

Soon Amelia and Clara found themselves following Mrs Pritchard down the long corridor, now familiar to them from their visits to the barber's. Amelia felt the churning knot in her stomach grow tighter with every step. Her legs seemed to have grown inordinately heavy. It was almost as if there was a force, some malevolent radiation, pushing her back. She was compelled to walk forward to her fate, but a growing sense of dread made it ever more difficult to progress along that doleful passage. Mrs Pritchard seemed to have no such problems, however. She fairly skipped along.

'Not like the old days, but with you two and the new kitchen-maid it will be a decent Sunday Service for a change. The last few weeks, there has barely been a brace of bottoms to be blistered.' The woman's lips curled contemptuously; she clearly felt that the very idea of such thin pickings was an insult to the traditions of the house. 'Some may call me old-fashioned, but I say that there should always be at least a half a dozen ready, all nice and shivery, for the rod!'

Amelia had assumed that they would march right up to the Whippery, but Mrs Pritchard paused halfway down the frieze-lined corridor. Selecting a key from her collection, she unlocked a dark oaken door and threw it open.

Amelia felt her knees weaken. So this was where Betsy had brought the birches they had cut on their return to Hope Hall. There was the pile of twigs, their leaves curled and shrivelled now, stacked up to one side. It was not that that made her heart hammer in her breast, however.

The Rod Room was big, no mean ante-chamber but a long hall lit by a row of windows set high in the far wall. First Amelia's attention was drawn to the canes.

There were dozens of them, arranged on racks hanging from the walls. No, she realised as she noticed the half barrels stuffed with rods and the coils of uncut rattan hanging from hooks, more like hundreds. The room smelt odd, of linseed mixed with green wood and something that might have been the tang of vinegar. Something told Amelia that, from that moment on, this pungent mixture would always represent the true smell of fear.

'Now girls, this should have been done already, so you had better get busy. Take those branches—' Mrs Pritchard indicated the pile of recently cut birch '—and start stripping off the leaves. If you have not done sufficient on my return, you may rest assured that you will have a black mark entered in the big book.' The housekeeper favoured them with a cold smile. 'Yes, there is still time, just!' She indicated some small three-legged stools. 'Sit down there and get on with your task.' She looked around the grim chamber with evident satisfaction, then took a deep breath, as if drinking in the gloomy atmosphere, and turned on her heel.

Amelia did not want any more marks in the big book. She had been sent to inscribe the black cross by her name on the previous day. The journey, alone down the long corridor, had seemed even worse than in Mrs Pritchard's irksome company. Somehow, she had done as she had been told, pausing at the entries, looking at the marks inscribed by the various maids. It had been some small crumb of comfort to see that other girls, and Betsy in particular, had black crosses stalking their names. Some comfort, but not, alas, enough.

The Honourable Amelia Colinbrooke was thoroughly frightened now. The whole day might have been designed to force her to dwell on her impending fate. How much would it hurt? She tried to remember the birching at school as she stripped the leaves away. Then she tried not to remember; to think about something else, a task nigh impossible in that place.

'What an awful lot of canes,' Clara said in a small voice. 'What do you think are in all those barrels, Amelia?'

Amelia glared at her cousin. Clara was sitting next to her on one of the little stools, bent over the birch branch she was stripping of its leaves. They sat in a pool of light from one of the high windows, the better to see their work. The sunbeams made Clara's golden curls glitter and made her cream smock glow angelically. The girl's face was angelic too, innocent and apprehensive, as she turned questioningly towards her cousin.

'How should I know?' Amelia snapped. 'Nothing good in this damned place, I would warrant.' She had wondered about the rows of big barrels herself. If it was wine or beer, the vinegary smell did not bode well for the palatability of the contents. She shrugged and picked up another leafy bough to strip.

The cousins had not finished their task when Amelia heard a commotion at the door, for they had cut a good load of birch branches on that sunny afternoon. She looked down anxiously at the prepared twigs which lay denuded at her feet, and wondered if it would be adjudged enough. Fortunately Mrs Pritchard seemed satisfied, more concerned with issuing fresh orders than inspecting the cousins' work. For the maids had arrived with her and Mrs Pritchard lost no time in giving them their instructions.

'Kitty, Lucy, Betsy, you will show these new girls how to prepare their rods before braiding your own. Emma, as you have not yet been to the groves, you will take some

87

of the young ladies' switches. I am sure they will not begrudge you a few twigs! Make haste, girls, for I shall be back in half an hour to take you through.'

Amelia looked up from her withy in time to see the

housekeeper's black receding back as she swept out of the room. She turned her attention to the new arrivals and her eyes widened in surprise. In place of their usual uniforms, the maids were wearing short white smocks, similar to her own.

'What are those garments?' she asked, without disguising her astonishment.

'What a question, coming from such a fashionable young lady!' Kitty, the blonde maid, retorted sharply.

'She only asked.' The brunette girl, Lucy, seemed less hostile. 'These,' she fingered the hem of her little gown, the hint of a blush on her pretty cheek, 'these are our flogging frocks. Have you never seen them before?'

Amelia shook her head and Lucy smiled wanly in reply.

'Emma,' she instructed, 'come over here.'

The small girl blushed much more obviously, but did as she was bid. Amelia stared. The smock was clearly fine cotton, rather than silk, and it was a little longer than the cousins' garments, falling to about halfway down the girl's slender thighs. She also wore black silk stockings, gartered just above the knee, and a band of bare flesh was thus left visible, despite the longer hemline. If the other maids were used to this exposure, Emma clearly was not, and she hung her head and fingered the hem of the garment distractedly.

'They are very practical, you see.' Lucy favoured Amelia with a bleak little smile. 'Turn round, Emma.'

The kitchen-maid did as she was told and Amelia watched intently. The flogging frock opened at the back and was secured by three pink ribbons, one at the neckline, one in the middle and one along the hem. Each of these had been secured with pretty bows. Lucy pulled the bottom ribbon and undid the bow, then did the same to the middle tie.

'Bend over, girl,' she ordered. Emma glanced around anxiously, but obeyed, and Amelia understood how clever the little frocks were. Secured at the back now only by the top ribbon, the garment fell away to either side as the girl bent over.

Emma wore no drawers. The welts had gone from her chubby little bottom, and it was proffered invitingly by her posture. Despite her situation, Amelia could not help but smile at so inviting a sight. As the flogging smock had fallen away, it had revealed a tight little waspie of black satin and lace. Lucy patted the straining laces of the stays ruefully.

'And this is a flogging corset. Short, you see.' She indicated the expanse of bare flesh which the girl's clothes and posture had exposed, from the small of her back to just above the knee. 'So as to allow the greatest target area.' She gave Emma's bottom a sharp slap and the girl squeaked in response. 'All right, we had better get you done up, and get on with the task in hand.'

Preparing a birch rod, Amelia had thought, was a simple matter. One lashes the bases of several limbs together with cord to form a handle and then, if necessary, secures the twigs in the middle of the rod to prevent too much splaying. At least, that was how Amelia had learnt at finishing school.

'No, no - it won't do. You must make a neater job than that, or you will get another dozen, if not two!'

Lucy sighed in exasperation. Kitty had deigned to instruct Clara and Betsy had taken little Emma in hand, but it was Amelia who was having the greatest difficulty.

'For heaven's sake, what does it matter?' she said crossly. 'It won't hurt a jot more or less if the handle is braided prettily.'

Lucy untied the pale blue ribbon from the handle of the rod.

'The patterns are traditional,' she said patiently, as if explaining to an obstinate child. 'It is the Hope Hall way.'

'Oh, let her do it her way!' put in Kitty sourly. 'I'd like to see her catch an extra couple of dozen for poor rod preparation. That will soon teach madam some respect for tradition. It really is not that difficult, Amelia. Clara seems to have picked it up right away.'

Amelia shot the pair a furious glance, thinking how much she detested blondes, before trying to braid the ribbon in the prescribed pattern once again.

'We had better get our own rods out,' Betsy mumbled. The nursery-maid had been very quiet since entering the room - very quiet and distinctly pale. Amelia watched as Betsy, Kitty and Lucy walked over to the row of barrels. Removing the tops of the casks, the maids each removed half a dozen dripping birch rods, laying them in long white enamel trays. These they brought back to the little ring of stools. Using cloths to dry the ends, they set busily to work, braiding ribbons about the handles.

Amelia watched aghast. There was something worse about these dark damp withies, that had been steeping silently for who knew how long, in their barrels of vinegar and brine. Something appallingly incongruous about the pretty ribbons in their bright colours against the dark, forbidding red of the birch twigs. The maids' fingers worked nimbly, braiding and plaiting with skill that could only have come from much doleful practice in that oppressive chamber. The very thought of it made Amelia shiver. She bit her lip and tried to braid her own handle again.

'Here you go, girl, a little treat for you.'

Blossom bent, put her lips to Dick's hand, and took the piece of carrot. She stood and chewed, eyeing the stable-lad cautiously. It had been an odd day, the first since her arrival that Lord Alex had not run her through the park. The first day she had not, yet, been flogged unmercifully. It had been a quiet morning. She had heard the church bells ringing and it stirred a memory, but it did not seem to have anything to do with her. She had been left long, undisturbed, to lie in her stall. It was late when Dick had come for her.

Blossom had trembled when she saw the long whip in his hand and an equally long rope bridle coiled there, too.

'Easy, girl. Just a bit of gentle exercise, my beauty,' he had soothed. The lad had slipped the bridle over her and led her into the meadow beyond the lake. Here he had let out the rope and made her run in circles, flicking her from time to time with the long lunge whip. It had stung, when he snapped it across her bottom or her back, but it had been a sharp, not unpleasant pain. He had been true to his word, too. To begin with, her thighs had shrieked as she ran off the effect of the hard training from the previous days, but he had not run her hard. Around and around she had cantered, naked, first clockwise then anti-clockwise. The bees had buzzed, the sky larks sang as they rose, and the lunge whip had snapped in the midday sun.

After half an hour, he had called a halt. Blossom had gasped as Dick sponged her down by the courtyard pump. She steeled herself for the inevitable curry-comb, but the inevitable had inexplicably not come. Instead he took her back to her stall and gave her carrots, his rough hand stroking and patting her naked body as she chewed.

'That's it. Good girl, good girl, Blossom, easy girl, that's it, get down there now.'

Dick pushed her down onto the straw and she caught a glimpse of his hand unbuttoning his flies. He made her face the back wall of the stall, kneeling on all fours. Blossom bit her lip as she felt his fingers probing, exploring the wetness of her sex.

'Well, well, seems like this mare is in season.' There was amusement in the boy's voice but it did not trouble Blossom. It was as if, treated as something less than human, she no longer felt a human sense of shame. She closed her eyes as she felt his cock slide into her. Soon, she was moaning with pleasure as he took her in the cool of the stable-block. The moan became a groan as his hand reached round and began to massage her clitoris. Soon both Blossom and Dick were crying out as they reached their climax together.

'I'm going to have to rub you down again,' Dick said ruefully as he stroked her perspiring back. Blossom followed her groom back out to the pump and let him sponge the cool water over her again. Then he let her drink and took her back.

'I had better be going, girl.'

For some reason she did not want to be left alone in the empty stable. Blossom did not dare speak, but she stepped towards him and looked at him with wide, pleading eyes. Dick gave her a grin.

'Oh, no, you stay here, sweetheart. Believe me, you do not want to come with me!'

Sadly, she watched him leave. Alone, she listened for sounds of people in the courtyard. There was nothing, nothing but the noises of the horses in their stalls. No gruff laughter, no squeals of pain, no sound of hobnailed boots or high-heeled shoes clattering on the cobbles. Where was everyone? she wondered as she sat back in the straw and let her fingers rest between her legs. Part of her liked the peace. Part of her wondered what was happening to Emma, what she was missing, stuck there in the stables all alone.

'Six!' Amelia was aghast. 'Surely they won't need six?'

'Don't worry,' Lucy said, though the apprehension on her own face was plain now. 'I've never seen six used on one girl. They like to have plenty of spare rods made up and to hand... just in case.'

Amelia was not entirely reassured, but there was little option but to take the six freshly prepared rods and place them in the tray that Lucy had brought over to her. To her horror, she read her own name inscribed in the white enamel.

'When - when did this come?' she asked. The name 'Amelia' had been written in fine copperplate handwriting, in black against the white of the enamel. Something about it sent a shiver down her spine, perhaps because it seemed a terribly permanent sort of object.

'Oh,' Kitty said brightly, as she watched Clara put her own rods in a similar tray bearing the blonde girl's name. 'They came last month. They have to order them weeks in advance. Emma will have to make do with a plain one, for the time being.'

Amelia felt her ears burn with indignation. Proof positive that her humiliation had been long-planned. Why this should upset her so, she did not know, but she felt a renewed sense of outrage burning in her breast. The pretty ribbons around the handles of the birch rods, the delicate nosegays decorating the switches, her name in the enamel tray: all these details seemed especially terrible to her.

'I hope you are all ready.'

Mrs Pritchard's voice startled her; she had been so bound up in her furious contemplation of the rods that she had not heard the woman enter.

'Now girls, in your places - Amelia then Clara, Emma at the end. Pick up your trays now and follow me.'

No funeral procession was ever more solemn than the file of girls who followed Mrs Pritchard along the corridor to their appointment with pain. The big enamel tray weighed heavily in Amelia's hands, but not so heavy as the feeling in the pit of her stomach. Footsteps from seven pairs of high heels clacked crisply on the parquet, echoing mournfully around the cheerless corridor.

The big book and its lectern were gone from the end of the corridor. Amelia noted its absence with a little pang of terror. Then she turned, took a deep breath, and followed the housekeeper into the Whippery.

Lord Alex, Lady Alicia, Jamie, the grooms, and several people whom Amelia did not know were seated on the benches facing the little stage. The buzz of conversation ceased abruptly as the girls made their entrance. The worthies, who were gathered to witness justice done, turned towards the miscreants and stared.

Mrs Pritchard indicated to Amelia where to place her tray. She put it at one end of the edge of the stage, with her name facing the audience. The housekeeper indicated the wooden stage-side seat known as the Miscreants' Bench, and Amelia went and sat in her place. Clara placed her tray of rods next to her cousin's, and joined Amelia, beside her on the bench. Kitty followed suit, then Lucy, then Betsy. Blinking nervously, little Emma brought up the rear.

Amelia stared at the floor. She did not want to look at the equipment on the stage, nor the stock of waiting birch rods, and she dared not raise her eyes to the audience. The conversation had begun again, however, and she could not close her ears.

'My, don't they look glum!' Lady Alicia's voice brimmed with merriment. 'Six such solemn little souls, all awaiting their desserts.'

'A damned pretty little parade, though, what!' Lord Alex put in. 'Six on the bench is a bit more like a Sunday Service than we have had of late.'

'The Revered Dawes expressed an interest in bringing over his little class, once it begins in September,' Jamie drawled. The very enunciation of that name sent a cold shiver down Amelia's spine.

'Did he now? Capital idea. Half a dozen, is it?' Lord Alex demanded.

'Yes, six, I believe.'

'By God, then we might get a round dozen of bums in need of birching. What would you say to that, Mrs Pritchard? Like the old days, what?'

'It would certainly be a pleasure to see more of these facilities put to use, sir,' the housekeeper replied.

'Well, I expect we had better get on with the job.'

Amelia felt her heart lurch at these words, for while she wished fervently for the ordeal to be over, that did not mean she felt ready for it to begin. Taking a deep breath, she forced herself to raise her head and look up.

The lectern had been set up in front of the centre of the seats, facing the stage, and the big book had been set up on this. Lord Alex stood in front of it, waiting for silence, his usually languid expression serious and grave.

'It has long been the tradition,' he intoned in sepulchral tones, 'for the sins of the wicked to be paid off on the Sabbath day, in this place.' He swept a hand towards the girls waiting on the bench. 'The miscreants await their fate in the appointed place.' He gestured towards the stage. 'The instruments of their correction and instruction have been prepared according to established custom.' He turned to the book before him. 'It is time to deal with their several crimes. Emma Swift.'

He turned from the book to the kitchen-maid. Although she was at the other end of the bench, Amelia heard a frightened little gasp. The tension in the air was terrible now. It almost felt as if the air was too thick with fear to breathe. Lord Alex turned back solemnly to the big book. Then his eyes widened with astonishment. He rubbed his chin in puzzlement and then turned to the other members of the audience with a rueful grin.

'Ladies and gentlemen,' he said. 'Something remarkable seems to have occurred. This new kitchen-maid, Emma Swift, arrived earlier this week, yet it seems that no black marks have been entered against her name.'

There was a rumble of astonishment amongst the audience. Mrs Pritchard glared at the girl and gave a disappointed hiss. Lady Alicia clapped her hands together delightedly and laughed aloud at this absurdity.

'But, Alex,' she said brightly, 'if the girl has no marks in the big book, she surely must have been either good, or already punished for her sins. Surely she must be released from the bench?'

'No new girl is that good!' Mrs Pritchard said furiously. 'It must be an - an oversight. Simply a mistake! Look at the little trollop. If ever there was a girl who needed to be thrashed—'

'Yes, quite, but,' Lord Alex said with an amused smile as he regarded the seething housekeeper with evident amusement, 'you must own, Mrs Pritchard, the oversight is ours and not the maid's. Now, everyone knows you as a stickler for tradition. If there are no black marks in the big book, what does custom dictate?'

Mrs Pritchard's mouth set in a thin line. She looked at Emma and then back at Lord Alex and gave a defeated sigh.

'The girl must be released,' she said.

'My dear!' Lady Alicia beckoned Emma and patted the upholstered bench beside her. 'Come over here to watch the show, and sit with me.'

Uncertainly, Emma left her place on the Miscreants' Bench and trotted over to sit beside her mistress. Lady Alicia immediately put one arm around her shoulders and with her other hand patted the girl's knee.

'You will get a good view from her, my pretty little darling,' Lady Alicia said. 'You will be able to watch that which will certainly be coming your way next week!'

This observation seemed to calm Mrs Pritchard, for she finally stopped glowering at the girl, like a grizzled cat regarding escaped prey.

Lord Alex, who had seemed hugely amused by the whole unprecedented procedure, turned back to the book with a wry smile. 'Well, after that, one wonders if this outbreak of obedience has proved catching. Perhaps our treasured nursery-maid has been behaving herself, too?'

The laughter that Emma's escape had provoked had lightened the oppressive atmosphere in the chamber for a moment. Amelia felt the ambience curdle again as miscreants and audience awaited in tense, anticipatory silence.

'Alas, no.' Lord Alex sighed a sigh of palpably hypocritical regret. 'Betsy Billings has three black marks against her name. Mrs Pritchard, we have newcomers to Sunday Service today. What does tradition demand in way of reparation?'

The housekeeper drew herself up to her full height, her chest swelling proudly. She seemed to Amelia like some great black looming crow. 'Hope Hall tradition demands a minimum of one dozen strokes of the birch for every cross. The imposition of further penalties is customary, though not mandatory, after two.'

'Well, well.' Lord Alex turned his gaze on Betsy. 'Betsy Billings, stand out, girl.'

The nursery-maid stood, and walked to stand facing Lord Alex and the company. Between her judge and the little stage a sort of portable dock had been placed, consisting of a small platform and a rail. Betsy stepped onto this and gripped the rail until her knuckles whitened. Her usually ruddy complexion had turned pale.

'Customary but not mandatory. Well, Betsy, what do you say to that? Will three dozen do you, do you think, or should we make it four?'

There was an awful, heart-stopping silence. For a few moments, Amelia wondered if Betsy had completely lost the power of speech.

'Please, sir.' The maid's voice was a desperate supplicatory whisper. 'Have mercy. Please have mercy on me, sir...'

'Give her four, Alex. That fat arse of hers will take it easily!' Lady Alicia put in helpfully.

Alicia noticed that the Marchioness's hand had travelled up Emma's leg, and was now gripping the girl's bare thigh above the stocking-top.

'It is true, my Lord. The girl can take a good count. She is sturdy and can take a real thrashing without harm.' Mrs Pritchard interjected.

'No, I think that three will do it,' Lord Alex said at last. Amelia observed Betsy's shoulders sag in relief. 'But three marks is a poor show.' The shoulders tensed again as he went on. 'There are some fine nettles in the deer park,' Lord Alex remarked, as if remembering something else. 'You can trot along and fetch some after your thrashing, girl, and I'll urtify those lovely titties for you, my dear!'

The thought of nettles applied to Betsy's breasts sent a cold shiver through Amelia, but she did not have long to dwell upon the image.

'Pick out three rods, Betsy, and go up to the block.'

The nursery-maid obeyed. She picked three birch rods from her enamel tray and mounted the stage, taking up position before the ominous apparatus at the centre of the platform.

'Do we have a volunteer to administer the sentence?'

There was a silence so profound that, for a long moment, one might have heard a feather fall. Amelia watched Betsy as she bit her bottom lip and stared hopelessly at the floor.

'Aye, I'll whip the chit!' A male voice broke the spell at last, and Mr Blackstock lumbered up onto the stage.

There was a sort of ledge on one side of the block and, in obedience to a gesture from the groom, Betsy placed the three rods there. Clearly, she was used to this procedure, for she clambered onto the block without further instruction.

Fashioned of some ancient black wood, the birching block consisted of a sort of triangle in section, with a ridge positioned at the top. Her thighs were braced against one side of the triangle, which was close to vertical. Her upper body followed the gentler slope which descended on the far side of the ridge. There was a shelf for Betsy's knees, and a handle the far side for her hands. There were also straps, heavy leather straps that Amelia thought looked worn with use and age.

Mr Blackstock first undid the lower two bows of Betsy's flogging-frock. The garment instantly fell back on either side, exposing her buttocks and thighs. A broad leather strap was buckled about her corseted waist, securing it to the more gradual backslope of the block. Wrist-straps followed, then thigh-bands, just above the knee. It was clear to Amelia that Betsy could not now move the target area more than an inch or two. The convulsive clenching and quivering of the nursery-maid's bottom, suggested that Betsy knew how helpless she was, too.

Although the day had clouded over, the windows and glass cupola of the Whippery lit the scene on the stage extremely well. The audience watched in reverential silence as Mr Blackstock picked up the first birch rod.

'Lay on, Mr Blackstock,' Lord Alex exhorted. 'She can take it, I assure you!' He took a seat next to Lady Alicia and gestured for the groom to begin.

THE SUNDAY SERVICE

The birch rod that Betsy had prepared was still wet from its steeping, and the big groom tapped it against the side of the block a few times, scattering droplets of the pickling fluid on the floor. The whispery sound of twigs impacting on the wood sent a *frisson* of fear coursing through Amelia's belly. The rubber bloomers seemed even tighter, as she sat there, and it took a real effort of will not to fiddle with them, to try to make herself more comfortable. Somehow she resisted the temptation. It would be futile. She had learned that much. No quick and furtive fingering could assuage that itch, any more than it would relieve her need. Instead she bit her lip hard, to provide a distraction, and concentrated on the compelling little drama being played out on the stage.

Mr Blackstock rolled up his shirt-sleeve, revealing a forearm almost as big as Clara's thigh, but a great deal hairier and tanned a deep brown. His biceps were still covered by his sleeve, but the bulge in this material looked ominous for Betsy. For all her own fear, Amelia could not help a smile of sheer vindictive pleasure coming to her lips. The groom looked the man to put the nursery-maid in her place all right, she thought, excitedly.

'Are you ready to receive correction, madam?'

The groom's tone was not sarcastic, and Amelia concluded that it must be a part of the ceremony, another archaic ritual of the hall. There was a pause.

'Y-yes, sir,' Betsy sobbed at last and, almost before she finished speaking, the birch rod came down and lashed across her bottom-cheeks.

Amelia's stomach clenched in sympathy again. The twigs made a nasty, diffuse sound, halfway between a hiss and a crackle, as they kissed the nursery-maid's bare bottom. Betsy remained silent; the only sign that the birch had achieved its purpose was an increase in the convulsive clenching of those great white rounds.

Mr Blackstock took a half-step back, adjusting his stance now that he had found the range of the rod. He raised his powerful arm again.

The birch twigs whistled as they cut through the air and hissed into the girl's bare behind again. This time the sound of impact was a little louder, harsher, fiercer. Betsy gave a low, strangulated moan in response.

'She felt that one, I suspect.'

Amelia glanced over at the speaker. Lady Alicia was leaning forward intently, her dark eyes so bright that they seemed to be glistening. Emma was no longer on the seat beside her but was now kneeling on the floor with a frightened expression on her face, Lady Alicia's hand gripping the nape of the delicate girl's neck.

Another sickening whistle brought Amelia's attention back to the birching-block. By the time she had turned, the stroke had been delivered, but Betsy's magnificent bottom-cheeks were still quivering from the impact. The creamy flesh of her buttocks was laced with an angry tracery of welts now, and the nursery-maid was groaning with pain and tossing her head from side to side. She had taken off her shoes before mounting the block, and Amelia watched with horrified fascination as her stockinged toes curled and uncurled convulsively. Amelia could only see one of the maid's hands, where she gripped the bar on the far side of the block, but she could see that Betsy grasped this so hard that her knuckles were white.

The fourth stroke was delivered with gusto, hissing into the helpless maid's thighs. She howled now. The fortitude that Betsy had displayed for the first strokes had seemingly fled. She could move but little in her bonds, but that little she did. The leather straps creaked in protest as she struggled vainly against their grip.

Mr Blackstock unleashed another blistering stroke. He whipped her thighs again, provoking another howl. There was a disapproving murmur from the audience.

'For heaven's sake, be quiet, Betsy,' Jamie said sharply. 'One would think you had never embraced the block before.'

'It's just a lot of silly girlish nonsense,' opined Lord Alex. 'The chit has hardly even been tickled, as of yet - eh, Blackstock?'

The groom turned to face the audience, a wide grin on his face. He gripped the handle of the birch rod in one hand and felt the middle of the twigs.

'Quite right, my lord. This rod has hardly splintered yet.' He turned back to his victim and patted her bottom roughly, provoking a new gasp of pain. 'Mind, I mean to tickle this fat trollop all right, before I'm through.'

This comment provoked some merriment amongst the audience, and Amelia found herself suppressing a smile. There was no doubt that the thoroughness and severity of the whipping boded ill for her, and this filled her with dread. On the other hand, it did delight her ill-used pride to see the insolent nursery-maid so thoroughly reminded of her place.

The birch rod sang through the air again, this time in a slightly higher note, as if the twigs hissed a little faster to meet their trembling target. Betsy's whole body froze for an instant, as if she were completely paralysed with pain. Then she shrieked in agony.

Another stroke was delivered, and then another was unleashed. Little broken bits of twig were flying now, as the birch rod was gradually shattered against soft flesh, stroke by stroke. Betsy shrieked and struggled futilely against the straps.

'The first dozen is complete!' Lord Alex called the tally as the twelfth stroke cracked across Betsy's bottom, sending most of the remaining twigs flying off in all directions.

'Ooh, it h-h-hurts!' the nursery-maid howled.

Amelia blinked at the girl's bottom. Her buttocks and thighs glowed an angry red. The tracery of individual weals from the birch twigs was still visible around the edges of the punished area. More centrally, the hundreds of tiny stripes had merged into one great furious red glow. Amelia could not help biting her knuckle anxiously. The maid had only gone a dozen and it looked as if her bottom were ablaze!

Mr Blackstock tossed the shattered remains of the rod to the floor and took up the second birch. He waited for a few moments, allowing Betsy to regain some semblance of self-control. The girl stopped howling at last, although a ragged sobbing was still audible.

'Carry on, Mr Blackstock, whenever you are ready.'

The groom bowed towards Lord Alex. Amelia caught a half-smile on the man's lips before he turned and brought the birch hissing down again.

The birching continued with a slow, unhurried rhythm. Betsy shrieked anew with every stroke, but no one seemed to take the least notice of her cries. Amelia watched in horrified fascination. The tingling in her loins was unbearable now. She bit her lip again, trying to think about something else. Half-turning in increasing distraction, she found herself looking towards her Aunt Alicia. There was something odd about the scene.

What was odd might otherwise have been obvious enough, but Amelia was in a most distracted state of mind. The feel of the rubber and the hiss of the descending birch seemed to fill her mind, reducing everything else to a mere jumble of arbitrary colours and random tones.

She took a deep breath and shook her head. Then she realised what was wrong with the scene; little Emma had disappeared. No, not disappeared, exactly. Amelia's eyes widened as she noticed the bulge beneath Lady Alicia's full skirts. Glancing down, she saw the maid's slender calves and ankles emerging from beneath the marchioness's hems. Looking up again, she saw the dreamy look in Lady Alicia's eyes. Then those eyes came into focus and locked onto Amelia's own.

There was another sickening hiss as another stroke was unleashed. Amelia, still staring into her aunt's eyes, felt a pang of terror in her heart as Lady Alicia broke into a broad and wicked smile.

Betsy howled in agony once again.

Blossom moved fretfully in her little stall. She had slowly fingered herself to a climax, squirming like an eel among the straw. Then she had dozed for a while before languidly stroking herself to ecstasy again. The naked girl kept expecting somebody to come, but no one did. The minutes had turned into hours and she was still alone.

The fact was that she was bored. They might treat her like a pony. She might even sometimes react like a dumb animal as the grooms rubbed her down or Lord Alex whipped her through the park. But, equine as she might feel when they stroked and punished her, she lacked a horse's capacity for patient inaction. In the end, she was still a girl, with a girl's sense of curiosity.

Once again, she had been left untethered in the stall. From where she sat, on the straw-covered floor, she could see the open stable door. It was a real effort of will to step outside of the stall. One step, two steps into the large space where the tack was kept. Blossom's heart was pounding in her breast at the effrontery of her actions.

She was completely naked, something she was becoming accustomed to. It was not so much the lack of clothes that made her feel odd, even disorientated, as she walked, taking a few more tentative steps over to the wall where the tack was hung. Blossom reached out to touch a leather bridle. Her finger ran along the shaft of a metal bit. Hardly knowing what she was doing, she found herself bending towards it, taking the cold steel between her lips. No, she realised as a little thrill ran through her body; it was the lack of harness, of any restraint, that made her feel so peculiar.

Letting the bit fall from her mouth, she looked at the open door again. She could smell the leather from the tack beside her, richly pungent and strangely reassuring. For some reason, she felt safer here, next to the bridles and harness straps. The door, by contrast, seemed terrifying; the gateway to a world that was limitless and without any comforting bounds. But for all that it was dreadful, her curiosity pushed her. Blossom stroked one of the leather straps for reassurance one last time, and took a step towards the open door.

Amelia watched in awe. Betsy had the biggest, firmest, most protuberant set of buttocks she had ever seen, yet even so she did not see how the girl's bottom had withstood the onslaught of Mr Blackstock's merciless birch. The second rod had gone down the splintered road of the first, and there were precious few twigs surviving on the third to shatter against Betsy's sore behind as the final stroke whistled down.

The nursery-maid still shrieked with pain at every fresh atrocious stroke, but now her yells were hoarse and much less loud. Clearly, she was well on the way to losing that voice which had given such sterling testimony to her sufferings. The glowing redness of her rear had grown ever more furiously deep, yet somehow the skin had withstood the blistering kiss of the birch twigs without blood being drawn. Amelia found this astonishing. However, she reasoned, that as the young woman's hide received such healthful treatments on so regular a basis, the slut's skin must have become tougher than it looked.

It was clear that the maid had felt her correction, nonetheless, because when her bonds were finally released she jumped up like a startled rabbit, grasping her bottom and jumping from foot to foot. Betsy's breasts were free beneath the thin cotton of her flogging-frock, and the sight of her huge titties jiggling about as she danced her little dance of pain provoked much merriment amongst the company.

The nursery-maid was allowed a few minutes to compose herself. Now that her face was in view, Amelia saw it was almost as scarlet as her well-scourged bottom, and her cheeks were slick with the tracks of many tears. The sight gave Amelia a deep sense of satisfaction. The next time that that low-born bitch was pert to her, Amelia thought, she would remember this little scene!

Betsy's ordeal, it seemed, was yet far from over. Once she had recovered a measure of composure she was made to kneel, still sobbing and gasping for breath as fresh tears coursed down her cheeks, and gather up the shattered stumps of the three broken birch rods. These she handed to Mr Blackstock, who held them before him. A hush descended on the Whippery.

'Has the miscreant anything that she wishes to say?' Lord Alex's stentorian tones echoed around the chamber's glass dome.

'Uh... ah... Oh, th-ha, haaoow.' Betsy clenched her fists and took a deep determined breath. 'Uh... th-thank you... Ooh, thank you... Ooh, for correcting my, my, f-f-faults, s-s-sir,' she sobbed.

'Kiss the means of your chastisement, girl,' the groom growled. Betsy leant forward and pressed her quivering lips to the three broken birch rods, one after the other.

'All right,' Lord Alex said when it was done, 'let Mrs Pritchard examine you now.'

The nursery-maid turned big brown eyes towards her master in mute appeal, but must have known that this was futile, for she said nothing. Instead she dropped her eyes and got to her feet. Wincing as she walked, she stepped down from the stage and made her way to the side where the housekeeper was waiting. She bent over without being instructed, placing her hands flat on the stage and giving the audience a fine view of her scarlet bottom-cheeks. Mrs Pritchard examined the punished area thoroughly, pinching and probing the sore-looking flesh to an accompaniment of a slew of squeaks.

'The skin does not appear to have been broken,' Mrs Pritchard announced at last, in tones that suggested that this was a matter of great personal regret. 'However, it is best to be on the safe side!' She took a handful of something white from a bowl set on the edge of the stage. Amelia had seen it when she put her tray of birches down. Suddenly she realised what the bowl contained.

Betsy gave a breathless, almost suffocated sounding squeak of agony as Mrs Pritchard rubbed the substance vigorously into her rear. Amelia licked her lips, wishing as she did so that her mouth was not so dry.

'Rock salt,' she said, almost silently, to herself. No wonder Betsy was making such strange noises. She hardly dared to think how much that rock salt rubbed into such a well-whipped bottom would sting. Amelia was very glad she had the hard bench to sit on at that moment. If she had been made to stand, she thought she might have fallen in a swoon.

'Mr Blackstock, would you send one of your boys with Betsy to fetch some nettles to complete her correction?' Lord Alex asked genially.

'Of course, your lordship. Davy, go with the girl. Make sure she picks a good bouquet of nice fresh leaves. Oh, and whatever the temptation,' the big groom paused, 'don't dilly-dally too much on the way!'

This instruction caused some amusement among the audience, and even an anxious snicker or two from the Miscreants' Bench. As soon as the stable-boy and the nursery-maid had left, a serious hush fell on the Whippery again.

'Now then, stand out, Lucy Frampton,' the Marquis said as he turned to the big book once more. His voice was serious, even sombre, but there was a distinct twinkle in his eyes. 'Two black marks, Lucy. It will have to be two dozen, I am afraid.'

The maid stood in front of the Marquis of Hatherby, her brown ringlets bobbing slightly as she bowed her head.

'Have we anyone prepared to thrash some discipline into this wicked girl?' Lord Alex asked. Once again there was a pause, broken in the end by Lady Alicia's rich voice.

'I suppose one has to do one's duty.'

Amelia looked over at her aunt. Emma had emerged from beneath her ladyship's skirts, and was kneeling by her side once more. The kitchen-maid looked a little dishevelled. Her hair was awry and she was licking something from her lips and chin. Lady Alicia was beaming at the trembling figure of Lucy, who seemed awfully isolated before the lectern, in the little dock.

'Yes,' Lady Alicia went on, 'I will essay to beat some better manners into the minx!'

Blossom's mouth was dry. The fact that she could see the pump in the middle of the courtyard did not help, but the reason she felt so parched was not lack of water, but anxiety. She had made it, heart pounding, right across the stable-block. Now she stood in the entrance looking out. It was as if there was an invisible barrier preventing her from stepping into the courtyard. Every time she had been out, since her arrival, she had been bridled, if not in harness. Before that, in the reformatory she had been a prisoner behind iron bars. Prior to Hatherby reformatory, she had spent long weeks in irons. Blossom put her hand to her throat. Sometimes, the fact that she no longer had an iron band about her neck still felt a little strange.

The fact was that the last time she had been in the open air, yet not secured by iron, rope or leather bonds, seemed years away. Perhaps it had been no more than weeks, but it felt as if that free life had belonged to another girl, another world, another time and place. Now the sensation was strange, and deeply disturbing. The boundlessness of the sky and the world beyond the courtyard filled her with a deep sense of unease.

There was no one to be seen. Everyone, grooms, maids, the lords and ladies of the hall, seemed to have disappeared. Part of Blossom wanted to see someone; part of her was terrified of being found, wandering unbidden from her stall. She would get a belting at the very least if she was discovered. Blossom knew it in her bones.

There was no one to be seen. She could make a break for it. Her long legs were growing stronger by the day. She could make a run for Hatherby, or for the train. What would she do for clothes? Perhaps she could find some. In her heart she knew it was impossible. Anyone she asked for help would surely turn her in. That was the way it seemed to be in this strange part of the country. Once you were marked as the property of the Marquis, that seemed to be how everyone treated you. She would be captured and brought back and whipped unmercifully. Blossom shivered at the very thought.

From her vantage point she could see much of the back of Hope Hall. The stable-block faced the main body of the house, making two sides of the square. The other two were incomplete, one being partly formed by the back part of the east wing. From the groom's conversation when the blushing cousins had been taken past through the courtyard on their leashes, Blossom knew that that was where, somewhere, the nursery was housed.

Opposite the east wing was the tower she had glimpsed on her arrival, ivy-encrusted and ancient-looking, with gargoyles and crumbling battlements on its top. For some reason the sight made her shiver, though the day was warm enough despite her nakedness. Partly it was the appearance of the Old Tower, she supposed. Its ancient gothic lines might have been designed to fill the heart with dread. More, it was the way the grooms talked about it.

Dick often teased Davy with references to the place.

'You wait, Davy boy - her ladyship will have you in the dungeon over there, if you don't watch it!' the red-haired boy had joked. Davy had told him to shut it, but Blossom suspected that the lad was as curious as she, for she had overheard him ask

Mr Blackstock later about the place.

'So what is that place, then? It looks like a castle.'

'It is - at least, it was. The west wing, also called the Old Tower, so-called cause it's very, very old. In the old days that was Hatherby Castle, the Marquises built the rest of the hall onto it, over the years. Not lived in now. It's too ancient and gloomy. Still,' the groom had grinned at the stable-boy and winked, 'it is made use of, every now and then.'

Blossom shivered again, remembering his tone, as she noticed that the tower's windows all seemed to be very small and barred. Her mouth seemed even drier. She looked over at the pump; the water in the trough glinted invitingly. Remembering how cold and sweet the pump water was, she was tempted to take the chance. She looked around again. There really did not seem to be anyone around. Blossom wiped her palms against her thighs, for they had become very moist. She could not do it. She could not make herself step outside. With a last regretful glance towards the water pump, Blossom turned and trotted back towards her little stall.

If only it were her, Amelia thought bitterly, if only it were her there, instead of Uncle Alex, raising his birch rod for one final blistering stroke. Clara had only been sentenced to one dozen, but Lord Alexander had certainly made them count. Clara's pert little bottom was now a furious red and the girl was crying out in pain most plaintively. Jealousy and fear of her own fast-approaching fate vied in her breast for supremacy. Amelia had a wonderful view from her place on the bench. She was almost three-quarters on from Clara's lovely bottom, ideally placed to watch the whipping proceed. Opposite her, was the low wooden Penitents' Bench on the far side of the stage. Lucy and Kitty knelt on these, facing the wall. The well-whipped bottoms of the penitents were stuck out in a truly doleful display.

Lord Alex made his last stroke count, lashing Clara hard across the upper thighs. The blonde girl let out a heart-rending squeal. Lord Alex ignored her cries of pain and regarded the broken birch rod. Clara's bottom had not wreaked the destruction on it that Betsy's big behind had visited on the rods in Mr Blackstock's hand, but nonetheless it was obvious that the birch had been well used.

There was a pounding in Amelia's temples as she watched her uncle unstrap her cousin. She watched the sobbing Clara get down onto her knees and kiss the proffered birch, as Lord Alex looked down fondly at his well-whipped ward.

'Go over and see Mrs Pritchard now, Clara,' he said, patting the golden locks of her bowed head fondly, 'then present that pretty little bum of yours to the company.'

Wincing, and still sniffling a good deal, Clara made haste to obey her uncle's instruction. After some squealing and desperate squirming, as the rock salt was applied to her abraded flesh, she hobbled to the Penitents' Bench. Clara took her position, kneeling on the bench and facing the wall, next to Kitty. Three thoroughly birched bottoms were now presented, most fetchingly, on display. It was a sight that Amelia would have paid good money to see, on another day.

Lord Alex made his way back to the lectern. 'The Honourable Miss Amelia Colinbrooke,' he said, his voice taking on a sterner, much more serious tone. Every one looked at her. She rose reluctantly and made her way to the little dock, where she stood. Amelia was frightened, it was true, yet a surge of anger coursed through her veins. The nursery was bad enough; the canings and the rubber pantaloons and sheets and all the rest. But this was intolerable. There were grooms here, grinning at her, and stable-boys. Amelia's whole body thrummed with indignation. Somehow, however, gripping the rail of the dock determinedly, she managed to hold her peace.

'Two marks,' Lord Alex said in a voice dripping with mock sorrow. He looked up at Amelia and smiled. 'Two dozen strokes, and to that count I shall add another six for general pertness. Stand out, Amelia. It is time to atone.'

For a second or two Amelia very nearly balked. Two and one half dozen: how would she ever endure such a count? She looked around wildly, seeking an avenue of escape. Instead, she saw Mr Blackstock and the remaining stable-lad. They stood by the doors, clearly positioned there to forestall any such attempt. The expression in their faces, part eager, part amused, left Amelia in no doubt that they would relish a struggle with their semi-naked female better.

Amelia took a deep breath, realising she was trapped. She silently swore bloody revenge.

On trembling legs she walked to the stage and approached the awful block. So many birches had been broken that bits of twig were strewn all around, and these crunched sickeningly beneath her soles.

'Take your boots off!' instructed Mrs Pritchard, still stationed by the salt at the edge of the stage.

'Do we have anyone prepared to administer correction to this girl?' Lord Alex's voice rang out. The pounding in Amelia's ear increased. Jamie had flogged Kitty, Lady Alicia had taken the birch to Lucy's lovely bottom. Who would step forward to administer her own thrashing? Desperately she prayed it would not be the powerfully armed Mr Blackstock again.

There was a commotion at the door. Betsy came in, eyes streaming with tears, holding a bouquet of stinging nettles. The stable-boy who had accompanied her followed. Then a figure entered that made Amelia feel suddenly weak at the knees.

'I would be glad to offer my services,' the Reverend Dawes said dryly, giving Amelia a polite bow before turning to Lord Alex. 'There is, I see, as I remarked earlier today, a rod in pickle for the wicked, and it would be a veritable pleasure to employ it on this impudent little chit!'

'So glad you could make it, Reverend! You arrive in the very nick of time.' Lord Alex exclaimed jovially.

'I had some business with those maids of mine, after church was over. Then when I was walking through the park I met these young people engaged in their urticarious pursuits—' the Reverend inclined his head towards the still-sniffling Betsy and her escort '—and thought I would accompany them back. It took a little longer than I anticipated, I am afraid.' He looked disdainfully at Betsy, who cowered under his ferocious glare. 'This young lady was reluctant to pick the nettles, for some reason, without gloves.'

'So you delayed our guest, Betsy?' Lady Alicia sighed. 'I might have known. I swear, girl, I do not know what has got into you of late!'

'Spare the rod and spoil the maid!' the Reverend said, shaking his head regretfully. 'That girl needs plenty of stick, and laid on with a will, if you will permit the observations of a visitor.'

Amelia had been left with only one hope after the unexpected arrival of the Reverend Dawes: that she might at least get her ordeal over with just as soon as soon could be. Even that impoverished aspiration, however, was soon dashed.

Having taken off her boots, she stood waiting by the block disconsolately. The Reverend Dawes vaulted, surprisingly athletically, onto the stage, and was at her side in an instant. Amelia tried not to quail as his hand reached for the hem of her smock, but could not prevent herself from flinching in fear.

'Stand still, girl, and keep your legs apart!' Mrs Pritchard snapped from her position at the stage side.

Amelia felt her cheeks burn as the Reverend Dawes slowly pulled up the hem of her garment, until her rubber bloomers were fully revealed for all to see.

'Still having problems, I see, Amelia,' the Reverend said pleasantly. Amelia was too mortified to reply. She kept her eyes fixed on the twig-strewn floor and did her very best to fight back the tears that threatened to burst forth.

'Best peel them off now.'

To her horror, the Reverend gave her a friendly pat, just on her mons. It was an appalling liberty, but no one else seemed to be concerned. Biting her bottom lip hard to stop it quivering, Amelia put her hands in the waistband of the bloomers and began to pull the wretched things down. This was no easy task. The rubber knickers were so tight that, in places, her perspiration had acted as a seal. As well as the sheer grip of the latex itself, it was now like trying to pull off a suction cup. Worst of all, her struggles with the noisily squeaking rubber provoked a great deal of amusement among her audience.

'Come along, Amelia. Get those knickers off!' her aunt cat-called as she struggled with the rubber. Finally, with a last loud rubbery 'plop' the airtight seal was broken. Then it was just a matter of pulling the still-taut latex down her legs, trying to ignore the fact that she was exposing herself to stable-boys and grooms.

She knew what she had to do, and put her knees on the ledge of the block, as the other girls had before her. Feeling the ridge of the block's solid upturned wedge below her belly, she reached forward with a sigh and grasped the bar. She felt her smock pushed back until the soft silk fell about her shoulders. Now her hindquarters were completely bare. Amelia gave a grunt as the Reverend secured the belt, tight around her waist, affixing her firmly to the block. The little waspie was already very tight and her position made her all the more aware of it, yet he put so much pressure on the strap that she felt her belly constricted even further by its grip. Wrist and thigh straps followed, and soon she was helpless. It felt as if she were embracing the odious, heavy wooden block, almost as if she were melded to the thing.

Her legs had been strapped some way apart and, she knew, her sex must be exposed between her legs to all the company. Amelia closed her eyes and, that it might soon be over, prayed that her ordeal would soon begin.

'If you do not mind, I will deal with this one first, Reverend,' the voice of Lord Alex cut in.

'Of course. We are in no hurry, are we, Amelia?'

Amelia's blushing cheeks burned with a new intensity as she felt the Reverend Dawes pat her naked bottom, but there was nothing she could say.

She was strapped down facing the side of the Whippery that housed the Penitents' Bench; thus she faced the row of three previously birched bottoms as Lucy, Kitty and Clara knelt, sobbing quietly, on display. To see what was happening she had to turn her head, for Betsy was standing forlornly in the dock, still holding her irksome burden of stinging nettles.

Lord Alex had withdrawn a pair of fine grey pigskin gloves from his jacket pocket and was pulling these on with a studious air. 'I expect you would like to put those down, eh, Betsy?' he said pleasantly.

'Oh, yes sir. Oh, they really st-st-sting.'

'Mm, yes, it is the time of year, of course,' the marquis said sympathetically.

'June,' Lady Alicia said languidly. 'I always think they sting the most in June.'

'Fresh growth.' The Reverend Dawes's voice came from behind Amelia. 'Plenty of urticarious irritant in the stings. No use whatsoever after October, as the fluid dries away.'

Interesting as this conversation might have been to botanists, Betsy seemed not to be appreciating it greatly. Instead she hopped from foot to foot, tears streaming down her cheeks. The buxom maid held the nettles in both hands, which were outstretched, as if she wished to keep the things as far from her vulnerable body as ever she could manage.

'Very well, give them here.' Lord Alex took the bunch of nettles from Betsy and placed them on the lectern, in the middle of the big book. Betsy did not seem to be in any less distress, continuing to hop from foot to foot; first she blew into her hands as if they were hot, then placed them under her armpits and jumped around some more.

'For heaven's sake, stop fidgeting, Betsy!' Jamie called out.

'Quite right,' Lord Alex said, selecting a long and verdant nettle from the bunch. 'Stand still, stop blubbing, and lift your frock.'

His Lordship's sharp tone immediately did the trick. Betsy stopped hopping and grasped the hem of her flogging frock. There was a murmur of appreciation from the audience as she pulled the garment up, until the material was bunched below her chin. The maid stood, relatively still, blinking apprehensively at her master and at the green spray of leaves he waved in his hand.

It was not hard to understand the appreciative comments and low whistles. Amelia had seen Betsy's astonishing figure before, yet even she stared in wonderment. The whipping-corset had cinched Betsy's waist to something approaching narrowness, and this emphasised her magnificent bosom all the more. Betsy held her frock above her breasts. Her eyes were wide and her bottom lip was quivering uncontrollably. The sight was so compelling that Amelia almost forgot about her own peril for a moment.

'Come here, girl.' Lord Alex spoke quietly, his voice almost gentle, but there was no mistaking it as an order.

Betsy's eyes seemed to get even wider, but she took a hesitant step forward. Then another. Amelia saw the girl swallow hard. Then she took another unwilling step. Lord Alex reached out with his free left hand and grasped her right breast, squeezing gently.

'Your titties are magnificent, Betsy.'

There was a pause. He cocked an enquiring eye.

'Th-thank you, sir.' Betsy said at last. The leather-clad hand continued to fondle and squeeze with brusque professionalism, as if Lord Alex were appraising a piece of horseflesh.

'The question is,' Lord Alex continued languidly, 'are they also sensitive?'

Again he seemed to await a reply.

'Y-yes, sir.' Betsy swallowed again, staring at the nettle as if hypnotised by its sway. 'They are v-v-very s-sensitive.'

'Oh, good.' Lord Alex murmured. Without releasing his grip on her right breast, he brought up his other hand and brushed the breast gently with the nettle. Betsy's face contorted with pain. Amelia watched her hands clench and unclench as the girl turned and grimaced. Somehow the maid managed to stand there as Lord Alex stroked the soft globe studiously. He ran the nettle over the top part, circled the nipple languidly and then gently dusted the tender underside.

Betsy shook her head from side to side. Grunts and groans of pain escaped from between her tightly clenched teeth. Once Lord Alex had thoroughly dealt with the right breast, he turned his attention to the left.

'Ooh... argh... ooh!' Betsy was quivering violently as the nettle did its work around her left nipple. Both the girl's nipples were standing out like wine corks now. Amelia looked lower. Betsy's shaven mons was clearly swollen, and the glistening moisture running down her inner thighs was almost as copious as the hot tears on her cheek. The sight reminded Amelia of the urgent, awful need growing in her own loins. There was nothing she could do about the feeling, so she tried her best to push the thought away.

Betsy's breasts were stippled with hundreds of tiny little white spots. Amelia's own breasts hurt just from looking at them. She could not imagine how on earth the maid managed to hold her place. But she did so, somehow. Lord Alex cast the used nettle aside and walked back to the lectern. Betsy kept her eyes screwed tight shut and her fists clenched as she held up the frock. She blew and hissed and slowly bent double in pain, before straightening and then bending again.

'All right, you wicked girl, go and take your place on the bench,' Lord Alex ordered.

Still hissing, Betsy managed to prise open her eyes. She hobbled, still holding up the garment, to the Penitents' Bench. Amelia supposed her breasts were now so tender that even the weight of cotton might seem unbearable on them.

'Poor girl,' Lady Alicia said slyly. 'After that stinging nettle, I do not think she wishes to leave the dock!'

This witticism provoked much chuckling from the audience. Betsy knelt beside Lucy on the bench and quivered there. The marks of her birching were still lurid on her great behind. Her ordeal was not over, however. Lord Alex took the nettle bunch from the lectern and strode over to the bench.

Betsy must have heard his tread because she gave a little whimper and her trembling became even more pronounced. Lord Alex thoughtfully plucked a leaf from one of the nettles.

'Something to keep your mind on your manners, minx!' he said cheerfully, and pushed the nettle leaf into the top of her stocking, against the inside of her thigh.

'Ooh!' Betsy gave a pained groan. Lord Alex's gloved finger probed higher, between her legs, and she gave a subtly different moan. Then he placed a second leaf in her other stocking.

Amelia watched, appalled, as he walked down the little line, plucking leaves and placing them in the stocking-tops of all the kneeling girls. Lucy whimpered. Kitty gave a breathless little gasp. Clara gave a series of pained sobs. Lord Alex placed the rest of the nettles on the bench beside the blonde girl. Then he turned around, caught

Amelia in his gaze, and winked. 'Do carry on, Reverend,' he said with a smile.

Something cold and slithery entered Amelia's soul. It was happening. From the corner of her eye she saw him take the birch rod from its place on the side of the block. In front of her were the four well-birched bottoms, each one quivering as the nettles did their work. They might as well have not existed. All Amelia cared about was the dreadful presence behind. She tried to swallow, but had run out of spittle. Amelia set her teeth and closed her eyes.

The sound of it, the whispering hiss as the birch cut through the air, reached her ears just before the rod arrived at her bottom. Her stomach had just started its involuntary lurch when the pain cut in. Amelia imagined fireworks. A hundred pinpricks of scalding white light. She had sworn to herself that she would not cry out, and she kept her teeth clenched tight and somehow managed it. It was hard, though. So very hard. It was like no pain she had ever felt before.

The blaze in her bottom reached a peak, levelled into something like a plateau, then started to recede. The whispering hiss froze her soul again.

She would not cry out! She would not scream! She would not give him that satisfaction! Amelia clenched her fists harder, digging her nails deep into her palms. She shook her head until her auburn curls danced about her ears. It was so hard not to scream. The birch just hurt so much. It was true that the impact was much lighter than the tawse or cane, but it stung so terribly.

As Lucy had warned her, the pain grew worse and worse with every passing stroke. No numbing of the nerves compensated for ever more sore and welted bottom-flesh. She felt as if she had been scalded, as if the punishing birch was a torch of scourging fire.

At five a hiss escaped her gritted teeth. At six, a wicked cut across her tender thighs, she yelped.

When the seventh searing stroke seemed to skin her underbum, Amelia shrieked.

From then on she was lost in a red mist of agony. The strokes were hardly distinguishable as discrete lashes any more. They were the crests of waves in a scalding sea of pain. Someone was screaming, a girl, perhaps, somewhere. Someone was fighting, uselessly, against tough leather restraints. All Amelia knew was that she was lost, engulfed completely by insanely, impossibly intense pain.

She was aware, in a way, of the first rod being cast aside. Some vestigial fragment of functioning intelligence noted that the Reverend had taken up the second birch, and told her that this was something to be feared. Most of her mind was too overloaded by the stinging of her bottom and thighs, to even know what fear was any more.

The second dozen was administered pitilessly. Amelia was hoarse but she still shrieked as the strokes came down and down again. Her wrists were rubbed raw as she fought the bonds, but this was a discomfort too small to register in a mind completely overloaded and overwhelmed with pain. Slowly, the agony began to ebb. Little by little she became aware of who and where she was. Her bottom still throbbed atrociously, but at least the pain had subsided to the point where she could register other things. It must have stopped. The red waves had stopped crashing on the shore. There was just a long, slow, searing blaze of heat.

Amelia stopped screaming. She was gasping now, desperate for air. Her disoriented mind tried to make sense of it. The Reverend Dawes tossed the second shattered birch rod on the floor.

'Two dozen,' the man behind her called.

Sense was returning to her mind in fragments. It must be over; she had survived somehow. Oh, thank God for that, Amelia thought. The blaze in her behind continued to subside. The decrease in intensity had slowed, though, and she still could not seem to catch her breath. Amelia let her head drop with exhaustion. The Revered Dawes was beside her now; she sensed his presence and it made her tense. He must be coming to undo her wrist-straps, she hoped desperately. No, he seemed to be picking something up.

What? Amelia thought wildly. Surely not another rod? She had had two dozen strokes, had she not? Somehow she had survived them. But now her bottom was as tender as a—

'Ow!'

Something told her it was just his hand, and that it was no more than a gentle pat. Her bottom-cheeks were so sore it felt more like a blow-torch had been passed across it.

'Ready, Amelia?' The Reverend's voice rang in her ears, teasing, mocking, belittling her once again. 'Don't tell me you have forgotten about your final six, my dear?'

The wicked whispering hiss cut through the air again.

TENDER IN THE NIGHT

'Ooh... ooh... ooh...' Clara whispered as Jamie spread the cooling ointment over her delicious little bottom. The slender girl wore nothing but her corset and her stockings, and he found the sight bewitching, draped as she was over his knee.

'Hush now,' he told her, though his voice was fond. He gave the still-welted bottom a pat, and Clara gasped and squirmed a little on his lap. The rubbing of her hip and belly against his aching erection threatened to provoke an eruption at any moment.

After the afternoon's activities Jamie had brought Clara back up to the nursery. After the Sunday Service, as was customary, the denizens of Hope Hall had severally gone off for a rest before supper was served. Each member of the company had chosen his or her companion from the ranks of those who trembled on the Penitents' Bench. Then each chosen girl had been chivvied off to assist her betters in taking their ease.

It puzzled Jamie a little that he had chosen Clara. He had noted the smile on Lady Alicia's face when he had made haste to bag the slender young blonde. He understood that smile. Why would he pick the chit who quivered under his rod every day of the week? Why not choose Lucy or Kitty for a pleasant afternoon of change?

He gave the bottom on his lap another, harder, slap, as if cross with Clara for having such an entrancing effect on him. The girl gave a whimpering cry of pain as his palm cracked against the sore skin of her so recently birched bottom.

'Get up,' he ordered gruffly, 'and get that corset off.'

Clara scrambled to obey, struggling with the fastenings on the front of her corset until he gestured her to step forward and helped unhook the thing. Betsy had laced it preposterously tight, she realised as he grunted with effort. The nursery-maid saw the waspies as a way to vex the cousins, and the minx would use them mercilessly if he allowed her to. Which, of course, he would.

Clara stood uncertainly, naked now except for her white silk stockings, an arm's length away. She regarded him solemnly. Her slender hands were held obediently at her sides, though she could not prevent her fingers fluttering. Unlike her cousin Amelia, Clara had soon learnt not to cover herself when made to stand naked in his presence like this. Only the beginnings of a blush betrayed her shyness, and the fact that she continued to find this exposure a real ordeal.

Jamie dropped his gaze to her shaven quim. It was so pretty that he felt the urge to kiss it, and his cock twitched eagerly at the sight. 'Feet wider apart,' he ordered thickly.

Clara complied. Her pussy-lips were neat, the inner labia hidden by her swollen mons. It had been more than two days since the barber's last visit, but he would hardly have known. Her pubic hair had been fine and blonde, and the only hint of stubble was the suggestion of gold dust in the region, glinting when she moved and caught the light. Or was that something else that glistened there?

'Come here,' he grunted.

Clara took a tentative step forward, bringing her more easily into his reach. He reached forward, grasping her left leg above the knee and gave a squeeze. Jamie enjoyed the feeling of flesh beneath the silk, but his need was too great now to dally very long. He heard her moan, and noted the trembling in her leg as his finger traced its languid way up her inner thigh.

'Legs further apart,' he said gruffly. 'I do not want to have to tell you that again.'

Clara obeyed with alacrity, adjusting her position so that her feet were now a good two feet apart. His fingers resumed their upward journey. As they rose, the soft warm flesh of her inner thighs was increasingly slick and wet to his touch.

'You really are a little tart, aren't you, Clara?' His fingers teased her sex-lips and she gave a loud moan. Jamie kept his gaze on her distracted face. Clara had closed her eyes and was biting her lip. Jamie slid his index finger deep inside her. 'Such a pretty little pussy,' he said as he probed, enjoying the way she moaned and writhed in response. 'It needs something, though...' Jamie used his thumb to stroke the outside of her swollen flesh as his index finger continued to explore her slit. 'A silver ring, perhaps two, through these lips. Something I could use to chain you to my bed, or padlock to ensure your chastity.'

Clara's writhing and moaning was getting ever more distracted. His heart thrilled to watch the shy girl succumb to his touch with such helpless abandon. It was a game he could have played for hours, another day. This afternoon, his own desire was barely more in check than that of his companion. He considered making her suck him, torturing her by taking his pleasure while denying her the chance to assuage her own obviously desperate need. Jamie smiled at the thought, but he wanted something else at that moment.

He withdrew his finger, which glistened with her juices, and stood up. Bending over, he pushed forward, scooping Clara over his shoulder in one move. The girl gave a little startled gasp as he carried her away. Jamie was no weakling and Clara was so slender that he carried her with ease into his bedroom. He tossed her casually into the centre of his bed, and hurriedly stripped off his clothes.

It took but a moment, then he turned, his erection arching skyward. Clara was lying where he had thrown her, waiting, her eyes regarding him with their usual solemnity. Jamie gave an animal growl and leapt at her. Clara squealed and clutched the counterpane, but did not attempt to get out of his way.

Then he was upon her, covering her body with his hands, biting her perfect breasts and invading her rosebud lips with his tongue. For a few frantic moments he felt and kissed and bit every tender morsel of her body as Clara cried out distractedly in response. Then he was inside her. Clara was tight and Jamie was not lightly endowed, but she was so ready that he went in with a few well-lubricated thrusts.

'Yes, oh yes, yes, master... oh yes sir,' Clara called out as she bucked beneath him, more frantic by the second. For all that her frame was slight, her thrashing was so violent that Jamie had to hold on to her waist with all his strength. The sight of her lovely face in ecstasy turned his own simmering juices up to boiling point. They came together, Clara crying out like a wounded bird as Jamie grunted obscenities.

'Sir, master... Can I tell you something?'

They lay entwined together on the bed, both bodies lightly misted with perspiration. Jamie's cock, though no longer hard, was still inside her. He did not want to withdraw it, for the feeling was so pleasant and comforting. Her vaginal muscles held him in a firm caressing grip.

'You may call me Jamie, if you like, just while we are alone like this.'

Clara snuggled into him, rubbing her little nose into the hollow where his shoulder met his chest. Jamie squeezed her tight.

'I just wanted to say, sir... Jamie.' Her pretty face was looking up at him seriously. Her eyes were so blue and wide and trusting that a man could fall right into them and drown, he thought.

'I - I love you.' Clara blushed and buried her face in his chest. Jamie squeezed her again, reassuringly. The girl looked up at him again, even more irresistible than before. 'I just wanted to tell you,' she said seriously, 'I just wanted to make sure you knew that I... that I belong to you.'

Betsy winced, letting out an audible cry as Lord Alex took a firm grip of her nipples between his thumbs and forefinger.

'Still a little tender, are they, my dear?'

'Ooh... yes, sir,' she managed.

The nursery-maid was kneeling on the carpet of Lord Alex's private study. Apart from her stockings, she was entirely naked. Lord Alex, in stark contrast, was in full dinner-dress. He might have seemed the picture of refined respectability, had he not just unbuttoned his fly and taken out a stiff and very eager-looking cock.

Betsy licked her lips, as if mesmerised by it. Lord Alex had gruffly ordered her to shuffle closer. It had seemed to Betsy that Lord Alex must intend her to fellate him, and she had leant forward, lips opening, until she was disabused of that idea.

When the Marquis grabbed her nipples, she knew differently. The knowledge of what he planned sent a quiver through her loins. Though the first stinging of the nettles had subsided, the skin of her breasts still throbbed. It most certainly was not the night she would have chosen for this particular little game. With a resigned sigh she realised that, no doubt, that was exactly why Lord Alex *had* picked it.

Not that she had much to say about the matter. Her master opened his legs and tugged at her tender nipples, forcing her to squeeze even closer, wincing as he brusquely pulled the tender nubs of flesh. He eased her in close to his belly, and his rearing cock. Then, when she could move no nearer, he pulled the nipples back in, catching his manhood tight within the sumptuous embrace of her cleavage.

Betsy gasped as the nettle-flayed flesh of her inner breasts was pressed against an erection hard as a hornbeam.

'Be quiet, you silly girl. Now then, I want you to raise your hands and press in on the sides of your titties. That's it. Now, now, no need to make such a face or start blubbing again.'

It was diabolically clever and, because her breasts were still throbbing from the nettles, distinctly uncomfortable. Lord Alex pulled her nipples upward and inward, tugging the swollen buds hard in his strong fingers, tweaking them for his amusement. Betsy pushed her own breasts in together, trapping his cock in a tight envelope of warm flesh. Lord Alex grinned down at her from above, cigar clamped between his teeth, and began to pump enthusiastically.

He thrust up and down, frigging himself furiously against her soft flesh, as Betsy gave a series of increasingly startled cries. Her breasts were so big, and Lord Alex had hoisted them up so high, that she saw little of his cleavage-engulfed erection, even when she looked down in alarm. However, as his pumping became ever more frantic, at the apex of each thrust, the ruby cock-head started to emerge, surging out of her cleavage, perilously close to her quivering chin.

The pain in her nipples was excruciating now. His lordship seemed to be twisting as well as hauling in his excitement. Betsy, who had been gritting her teeth desperately, found herself compelled to open her mouth and give a cry of pain.

She had not realised that his climax was so close. The hot stream of silky fluid spurted at exactly that moment into Betsy's mouth. She choked and spluttered in alarm before she recovered enough composure to swallow. As Lord Alex finished spending, she licked her lips furtively, like some great cat stealing a jug of cream, hoping against hope that he had been too distracted to notice.

The Marquis released her nipples and pain flooded into them as the blood returned.

'All right,' Alex growled, 'clean me up, now.'

Betsy leant forward and cautiously licked the dribbles of semen from his rapidly deflating cock-head, swallowing the slightly bitter emanations with a well-drilled show of dutiful enthusiasm. For a moment, she thought she had gotten away with it.

'Stand up, now.'

Betsy did as she was bidden, quivering as he laid a hand upon her still-raw bottom. She was soon more aware of his right, however, which reached around, explored her folds, and slid two fingers deep inside her moist slit. The nursery-maid moaned as she was fingered. Fellating Lord Alex, and having her nipples kneaded so pitilessly, had all but brought her to the brink.

Lord Alex moved his left hand from her bottom to her waist and used it to steer her onto his lap. Betsy tried to sit still but the fingers were driving her to and beyond distraction.

'Turn a little towards me. I want to bite your breasts.'

The order was straightforward if somewhat brutal. Betsy did as she had been told, half turning and leaning towards him until he caught one of her nipples between his teeth. He teased the swollen strawberry of flesh, nipping and sucking it in turn while his fingers continued with their work. Betsy could not stop herself from squirming in response. She could not stop herself from closing her eyes in ecstasy. Her body responded to his brusque toying, even as she winced at the pain.

'Not a good start to the week,' Lord Alex said during a break from her nipple. 'You are wriggling like an eel. Worse, you lost some of my spending, Betsy: the evidence is all over your chin. When we are finished here, you had better go and put yourself a black mark in the big book. It will be the birch for you again next week, I am afraid.'

As he spoke, he worked his fingers even deeper, letting her grind her clitoris against the firm heel of his hand. The mention of the birch brought back all the seething agony of the afternoon's three dozen strokes, in a blinding flash of overwhelming memory. Betsy gave a high, abandoned scream, and came.

'Well, girl, do you want it or don't you?' The Reverend Dawes sat at his ease in the smoking room. He smiled in amusement at Amelia as she struggled with herself.

Really, she ought to tell him to go hang, Amelia thought, but she knew that would be unwise. Even so, he was giving her a choice, and her pride told her to disdain his office. Her bottom, on the other hand, still felt incredibly hot, and the ointment in his hand looked so very cooling.

'No, thank you... sir,' she forced herself to say at last. Amelia had no intention of putting herself willingly over that man's knee. Once his fingers started smoothing soothing ointment... No, best not to think about what might happen after that. Amelia stood, awaiting the Reverend's response. Her chin, though held up proudly, was trembling traitorously. Amelia clenched her fists in frustration as she tried to keep it still.

'As you wish, girl.' There was amusement in his manner but not the least hint of disappointment. Did she wish him to be disappointed? Of course not - what could she be thinking? No, it was just surprise, for she was sure that the Reverend Dawes was just itching to paw her body. The memory of him looking at her, that first day, came back to her. Given half a chance, he would take monstrous liberties: abuse her, ravish her, do whatever awful things men like him liked to do to pure and innocent girls like her. Those things she could not seem to stop imagining in bed...

'Well, then.' He put the tin of ointment back into his pocket in a way that seemed worryingly final. His index finger beckoned. 'Come here, my dear.'

If only she had been permitted some more clothes, she thought. It was hateful to have to be alone with the man, dressed so inadequately once again. The corset, stockings and smock did nothing to hide her form from his steady and amused gaze. Unable to stop the blush spreading, not daring to defy him, Amelia stepped closer. Her palms were perspiring at her sides now. Funny, how one's hands and... other bits became so moist, whilst one's mouth went dry.

'Now, now, be quiet.' The hand on her sore bottom evoked a moan which she seemed powerless to prevent, though whether it was a cry of fear of pain, or a release of unbearable tension, Amelia could not have said. The patting hand sent sharp shards of pain coursing through her as he stimulated the still-abraded skin, but then Amelia was also extremely frightened of the man.

'Actually Amelia, I admire your fortitude.'

The hand smacked again and Amelia bit her bottom lip as pain jolted through her in response. It was not hard, no more than a little pat, but on her poor birch-blistered bottom, it was sore enough.

'Most girls take the ointment, when it is offered. I suppose you are confident you can escape further chastisement until the after-effects of the birching fades. Good, very good - for I take it that that means you have resolved to behave yourself.'

Amelia's stomach gave a sudden sickening lurch. She had not even considered this appalling prospect. What if the Reverend Dawes decided to cane her now, for some peccadillo? What if Jamie took the tawse to her on some outrageous trumped-up offence as soon as she returned to the nursery? Suddenly, her sore bottom felt even more horribly vulnerable. Amelia swayed as she felt her knees go weak.

'Get on your knees, child.'

Wondering wildly what he had in mind, Amelia scrambled to obey. She was seriously frightened now, half-expecting her tormentor to find an excuse to thrash her throbbing bottom right away.

Amelia knelt on that hard wooden floor of bitter memory, facing the Reverend Dawes. He had picked up his brandy glass in his right hand, but fondled the bulge in his black serge trousers openly with his left. Amelia felt the blood rush even faster to her cheeks and hurriedly dropped her gaze.

The Reverend leant forward and reached over, using his fingers to tip up her chin until she had to look into his eyes.

'You are a very pretty girl, Amelia,' he said at last.

Here it comes, she thought: he's going to make me suck his thing, or some other such appalling indecency.

'I should like to have you. I bet you bugger like an angel,' he growled.

Amelia, caught between terror for her tender bottom, outraged indignation, and a strange excitement surging in her loins, said nothing. She blinked and tried unsuccessfully to stop her bottom lip from trembling.

'But you don't want me to, do you, Amelia?'

There was an awful, portentous, pause. Amelia felt the blood pounding in her temples and for a moment found it difficult to breathe.

'No. No, sir,' she said at last, somehow managing to blink defiantly back into his terrible gaze.

To her surprise and tremendous relief, the Reverend Dawes, smiled. 'Very well. I never yet took a girl against her will. But I warn you, Amelia,' he winked at her, 'if you change your mind, you are going to have to beg me for it!'

He stood, adjusting his trousers as if he were a little uncomfortable about the crotch.

'Well, I must be off,' he said with a chuckle, 'I do not want you to relieve me. I have maids at home who will literally leap at the opportunity. I will send someone to escort you up to the nursery, my girl.' He bent and patted Amelia's cheek fondly. 'I shall see you in church next week, if not before, miss. I trust that until then you will be good.'

With that, he left. Amelia still knelt on the parquet floor, astonished and bewildered by this turn of events. She could hardly believe that she had escaped unscathed. Ruefully, she stroked her tender bottom and the backs of her thighs. The rubber sheets would be even more vexing tonight, she thought. She stood up, wincing, and wished that the Reverend had left his ointment tin. She wondered how long it would take for the effect of the birching to fade.

There was a rattle at the door and Amelia froze.

Mrs Pritchard entered, regarding the semi-naked girl with disdain. 'Are you ready to go back up? Finished with you, has he?' the housekeeper smirked.

Amelia did not care. She had had the courage and moral fortitude to refuse him. Beg him to abuse her? Hell would freeze over and corporal correction cease in Hatherby before Amelia Colinbrooke would do any such thing. He had had a shock, Amelia assured herself, trying not to smile. She was ready for her ordeal with the sheets, and she would not think about the Reverend Dawes at all tonight. She was resolved upon the matter.

'Yes, Mrs Pritchard,' Amelia said, head held high. 'I am ready.'

Rather than lead the way, Mrs Pritchard came over to her with a smile that Amelia did not much like. The housekeeper pulled up the hem of Amelia's smock, though this was scarcely necessary.

'Oh, no. Not quite, missy! The Reverend asked me most particularly to make sure—' she produced from behind her back a pair of the hateful rubber bloomers '—that you put a pair of your favourite pantaloons on.'

Amelia's heart almost stopped. Not only had her bottom been birched almost raw, she was sure that it was swollen. Terror seized her as she thought about the prospect.

Mrs Pritchard's eyes twinkled maliciously. 'Come along now, madam, we had better get a move on. I have the feeling that this is going to take some time.'

Runners and Riders

That summer was a hot one in Hatherby. Slowly it unfurled, drifting by in a seemingly endless succession of dreamy days and languid nights, punctuated by the sound of rod on resilient flesh, the clink of chains, of girlish shrieks of pain and cries of pleasure.

Amelia never ceased to chafe under the relentless nursery discipline but, as time and the distressingly frequent floggings went by, she did grow more and more adept at disguising her displeasure. Clara continued far more content, and no one who encountered her failed to remark upon her sweet air of exquisite submission.

And the maids? The maids did what maids had always done within those ancient walls. They were worked and they were whipped and sometimes they were pleasured. Little Emma Swift was trained in the immemorial iron regimen of Hope Hall, taught to dance to the tune of birch and cane and leather.

The greatest change as the weeks rolled on was to be found in the stables. Blossom bloomed with the summer flowers. Not that she found her training easy, for it was nothing of the kind. Many nights she whimpered in her stall, back and bottom welted from her master's whip. Many days her legs shrieked with pain as she was forced to canter up Holly Hill, hauling Lord Alex in his sulky to the top for the sixth successive time.

But weals faded and her thighs waxed ever stronger. Blossom's big body slowly became sleek and powerful on her diet of raw fodder, and regime of relentless exercise. Her times around the course grew faster, and Lord Alex petted her more and flogged her less diligently as time went on.

At night, before stalling her, Dick would scrub her down at the pump as she stood placidly. With time, Blossom even learnt to stand still while he used the curry-comb. Her skin turned golden as she ran under the sun and, with Dick's attentions and her diet, soon it shone with health.

She found that she was, if not exactly happy, strangely content. She wept when she was whipped or when Dick held her steady for Mr Blackstock's punishing strap. Blossom felt desolate when her master scolded her or when the grooms were cross. But then, when they stroked and praised her, she was suffused by a warm glow. Life was simple. Safe. All she had to do was run and pull. Run and pull, eat and sleep, be silent and obey.

Nor did she mind the hands of the groom and stable-boys when they came to her stall at night. They stroked her body, fondling her thighs and breasts fervently as she became sleek and beautiful with the passing weeks. She sucked them willingly when they wanted, and let them mount her bottom-hole or sex without demur, for they touched her with increasing reverence and affection. Blossom felt herself more adored than abused and anyway, the long days in harness under the whip stirred up urgent needs that were all her own. When, for some reason, no one came to take her, she would lie in the straw of her stall and press her hands between her legs until her cries disturbed the swallows nesting beneath the stable eaves.

Best of all, on a warm evening, Dick would often take her to the meadow behind the ornamental lake at the front of the great house. Here he would set her free to run naked through the long soft meadow grass. After a hard day in bit and bridle, hauling a well-built man in a heavy cart, she would feel so free that it almost seemed like she was flying, as her long legs galloped through the grass.

Occasionally, the stable-lad would saddle one of the ponies and chase her, whip in hand, through the field. But this was play rather than work; the stinging strokes he aimed at her bottom were not hard ones, and she would laugh and dart away as his mount struggled to keep pace.

July came and went and August wore on. Then, as the end of August approached, so a hum of anticipation began to grow around Hope Hall. The maids were worked harder but vexed less for, as

every year, there was much to do in preparation for the day of the Silver Cup and the Hatherby fete.

September came at last, and with it the first crisp scent of frost in the air of the darkening nights. For a few days the weather clouded, and chill rain provoked much muttering and many furrowed brows.

'There will not be much of a picnic for this year's Silver Cup if this keeps up.' Jamie stared gloomily out of the nursery window at the driving rain. 'Lord Alex says he cannot even exercise Blossom, it is so cold and wet.' He turned to Clara and Amelia. The cousins were bent over, knickers about their knees, trembling as they struggled to keep their legs straight and their fingertips on the floor.

'Oh well,' the young man said languidly as Betsy handed him a stiff-tailed leather tawse, 'I expect we shall find a way of keeping you girls warm.'

Then, in the week before the great day, the weather began to change. Wednesday dawned, still cool, but bright with but a few fugitive clouds lingering in the sky.

'Giddup there!'

Blossom no longer flinched as she heard the cracking of the whip perilously close to her bottom. Instead she put her head down, grasped the shafts of the sulky tightly, and ran. There was still water in pools on the driveway and she splashed through these as she gathered speed, her long legs almost effortlessly eating up the path.

Blossom knew the day was coming, for she had overheard enough to gather that she was going to be raced. The stable-boys talked of whippings for the losers. She would have smiled if the bit had allowed it. All summer she had been trained, and now she was as strong and sleek as any thoroughbred. The path turned and the big rise known as Holly Hill came into view. Blossom felt the extra weight as pressure in her legs as the slope grew steeper, then felt her thigh muscles deal with the extra load. Still breathing steadily, she powered up the hill that once had nearly killed her, even at a trot.

Let them come, she thought exultantly. After the long days confined in the stables, she ran with extra energy and joy. Let them come, let them just try to race me. I will beat them all.

The weather continued to improve. Thursday was almost clear and warm until the evening. Friday was warmer still. By now, Hope Hall was gripped by a frenzy of preparatory activity.

'Not there, on the table, you silly girl!' Kitty waited until the red-haired girl placed the baskets of nectarines on the table. As her short reformatory skirt rode up, Kitty gave the girl a sharp crack with the cane across the backs of her shapely legs.

'Ooh!' The girl's manacles and leg-irons jingled as she leapt up in pain.

'Now,' Kitty said with a grin on her full lips, 'off you run back to the kitchen garden and fetch another load.'

She watched the reformatory girl hurry off as quickly as she might without tripping on her leg-irons. The house was full of manacled young women, hurrying hither and thither on all sorts of tasks. As usual, Hatherby Reformatory had lent two score of its most comely convicts to help with the preparations for the great event. Thus the maids found themselves temporarily promoted, issued canes and told to supervise the felons as they fetched and carried, scrubbed, polished, and peeled.

The house, in short, had entered its annual state of glorious uproar, and Kitty devoutly wished that it could be like this all year round.

Itching to lace another pert behind, she looked out of the back door. There were some fruit baskets abandoned in the courtyard and two of the girls in Kitty's team of helpers were being hauled off to the stables by Mr Blackstock, who had a fist around each one's upper arms.

Kitty pouted crossly at the sight, but she knew that she dare not protest against this blatant filching of her workforce, even though she suspected that the girls would be good for little by the time she got them back.

The maid was still staring impotently at the stables when the jingling of reformatory manacles made her turn. A small, pretty brunette and a buxom blonde were trotting across the courtyard towards her with big baskets of blackberries in either hand.

Kitty looked into the anxious eyes of both of them in turn, and swished her cane meaningfully through the air. The stealing of Maude and Anne by the stable was forgotten.

'Right, put those down and touch your toes!' the blonde maid ordered. 'I'll teach you lazy reformatory sluts to take so long!'

'Well, girls, all ready for the big day? Betsy, I want these minxes scrubbed and in their best smocks. Amelia, Clara, before your baths you can polish your leashes, cuffs and collars. Everyone from Hatherby, and miles around, will be here today.'

Amelia polished her brown leather collar in sullen silence. Next to her, Clara worked away with that air of serene acceptance that made Amelia want to box the blonde girl's silly ears. Almost everyone in Hatherby had already seen Amelia naked or half-naked, but the knowledge of what was coming still gave her a tight knot in her stomach, and a lump in her throat that felt just like a stuck plum-stone.

'That's it, good girl. Just relax, my beauty,' Mr Blackstock spoke quietly as his strong hands worked. He had made a sort of couch out of hay bales and covered this with a horse blanket. Blossom had been made to lay on this, at first on her back, as she watched him warming the oil in his hands.

For such a big, rough-seeming man, his hands were cunning. He massaged her with dedicated concentration, stroking and probing her entire body before making her turn. Blossom felt herself transported as he worked the kinks and tensions out of her now lean and muscular back.

There was a crack, the sound of leather on flesh and a pained female cry, from one of the stalls. Blossom knew that Dick was in there with the reformatory girl called Anne.

'Stop that!' Mr Blackstock called out. 'You're unsettling the filly. Wait until Blossom is prepared until you have yourself more fun with that chit.'

The grooms had kept the two girls that they had corralled the previous day and, from the way that Dick was proceeding, the reformatory would do well to get their charges back after the cup. Blossom felt a little jealous, for she had grown accustomed to Dick's solicitous attention, but she was too excited herself to dwell upon the matter. In any event, Mr Blackstock's clever hands soon stroked away any such concerns.

'For heaven's sake, Emma,' Cook exclaimed, 'not like that. You ought to know yourself, that such paltry little pats have no effect on reformatory girls.'

Emma blushed at the reference to her own origins. Timidly she turned back to the girl who was bending over the sink. The kitchen-maid had been put in temporary charge of the scullery, and given two of the conscripted felons to help with the mountains of washing up. It was not a responsibility she relished in the least.

Daisy was a laconic young woman whose work rate slowed almost to a stop if she were left unsupervised. Emma gripped the wooden spoon and looked at the girl's exposed bottom. The grey shirt hem had been tucked into her belt and below the waist she was naked, except for woollen stockings. It was a firm bottom, with pale skin only marred in a couple of spots by not quite faded welts. Emma's own last effort had scarcely raised a blush.

The kitchen-maid took a deep breath and brought the spoon down on the bottom with a sharp crack. Daisy gave a wriggle and a slightly sarcastic-sounding gasp.

Cook gave an exasperated sigh. 'I would do it myself, but I have half a dozen of these slatterns to supervise. Now listen to me, Emma. You can put yourself a black mark in the big book for unwarranted leniency, when you get a moment. If you do not punish this girl properly, you will get two more. Do I make myself perfectly clear?'

She had. Emma wiped her perspiring palm on her apron before gripping the wooden spoon's handle again. Bitter memories of the birch and visions of herself strapped to the block, overwhelmed the little maid. There was nothing for it. She had to do it, hard.

This time she put her weight behind the stroke. The bottom-cheek flattened and then bounced. Emma did not give Cook time to criticise but struck again, letting her arm uncurl from the shoulder to the wrist. There was a retort like a pistol shot. Daisy gave a hiss of pure pain and dipped her knees convulsively.

'Straighten up, girl!' Emma heard herself order.

'Now, that's better, Emma,' Cook said, sounding a little surprised.

A strange joy coursed through the kitchen-maid as she tapped the wooden spoon thoughtfully in her palm. She watched the spoon-shaped patch bloom red on Daisy's bottom, which had begun to twitch.

'Ah, ooh, please, miss—' there was new respect in Daisy's voice, maybe even fear '—can I go back to work? I will be quicker, honest...'

'No, Daisy.' Emma sounded astonishingly firm in her own ears. 'Not just yet!' She raised the wooden spoon for the next stroke. A strange excitement gripped her. She would teach the lazy trollop to take advantage of her gentle nature. A couple of dozen sharp ones ought to do the trick.

'Oof, please Betsy, it's too tight.'

'Nonsense, Miss Amelia. Today is a special day and you girls must look your best.'

Betsy had her knee in Amelia's back, and she hauled on the laces of the corset with tremendous strength and an almost indecent enthusiasm. Amelia gripped the rail that had been set up for this, and other purposes, and groaned again. She felt as if she were being constricted around the waist by a python. Clara, already corseted, stood nearby, blinking at her. The blonde girl had been laced so tightly that Amelia thought she must be able to encircle her cousin's waist between her hands. The thought made her feel dizzy. There was a last grunt of effort from behind her, and a final terrible tightening about her waist.

'There! That shows off your figure lovely. The folk at the picnic will not be able to keep their eyes off you.'

Amelia clenched her fists in impotent fury. Creaking from her own impressive corseting, Betsy knelt to roll white silk stockings onto Amelia's shapely legs. Acutely conscious of the constriction of her stays, and the nakedness of her shaven sex so near Betsy's full lips, Amelia looked at the waiting Clara and felt her pulse quicken at the sight. Clara's stockings had already been fastened to the suspender-straps descending from her corset, and her sex was prettily framed. If only she might have a moment to herself, Amelia thought, her fingers twitching with the desire to assuage the itching in her loins. However, she dare not touch herself now, so she reluctantly tore her gaze away again.

As she did so, she heard the door open behind her.

'Is that as tight as you can get them, Betsy?' Jamie's voice asked languidly. 'Oh well, I suppose that will have to do. The usual knickers for Clara. Rubber bloomers for Amelia.'

Amelia turned, blushing furiously. The torture of the rubber pantaloons had been less frequent of late. She was so appalled that she almost got herself into real trouble, but somehow managed to turn her protest into a plea. 'Please, sir. Must I wear those things today?'

'Of course you must, Amelia. After all, everyone who is anyone will be there. Unless you would prefer something else?'

Amelia felt herself go pale at the implied threat. There was an awful silence that she dared not break, for fear of precipitating a fate even worse than she could imagine. Instead, she pleaded mutely, with her gaze. Jamie's own eyes laughed back at her and the fist in her stomach clenched even tighter.

'No, I think we will just have the rubber bloomers, Betsy.' He turned to go and Amelia was engulfed by a wave of relief. Jamie stopped at the door and turned back. 'Oh, but I do want them both in back-boards. Our girls must exhibit good posture and deportment on the day of the Silver Cup.'

'I must say, you have done a splendid job!' Lord Alex boomed.

It was true that the sulky and every piece of tack gleamed from long hours of polishing and that Blossom herself had been curried and combed and oiled to sleek perfection. Mr Blackstock acknowledged the compliment.

'Dick did a lot of work,' he said gruffly, 'and it is easy to make a rig look good when the filly is a fine fit thoroughbred like this.'

The groom was holding Blossom by the bridle and he patted her cheek affectionately. She felt a surge of pleasure at the compliment. The words of approbation made her feel proud and happy.

'Think we'll win?'

'No doubt about it, your Lordship. The Reverend always gets the best from his mounts, and his Rose is a sturdy wench, but he has nothing to match these—' he gave Blossom's thigh a hearty slap '—thoroughbred legs.'

'What about other entries?'

Blossom felt the sulky move as Lord Alex got into it.

'Well, Justice Ormorund has not a prayer, as usual. I have seen his pony out on the downs, a big buxom girl called Belinda. Strong, but not fast enough to give Blossom a run. Then there is Mrs Treadwell. She's been training one of her girls, so they say.'

'Not sure it's cricket, women riders in the Silver Cup. After all, Fanny Treadwell is a slip of a thing. She must weigh half of what I do.'

'Aye and a quarter of what the Justice's poor mount has to pull! But I would not worry about the lady, sir. After all, it's her first year on the course.'

'Well, I'm taking no chances. That blackguard Jack Campion has bet me a hundred guineas against the filly that I'll not win. I wonder if he knows something about Fanny that we don't? At any event, I'm going to take Blossom for a trot, just to the meadow and back to make sure she is well warmed-up.'

Blossom felt him take up the reins and listened for her master's voice. She knew she was as ready to run as she would ever be. The reins flicked on her bared shoulders and she gripped the shafts and pulled.

"Against the filly", she thought as she moved off. What had her master meant by that?

'Giddup!' Lord Alex called as she pulled the little sulky over the cobbles of the courtyard towards the drive. 'Good girl, we'll show them, Blossom. That's it, girl—' the whip cracked, echoing around the court '—giddup!'

'Jamie, they look delightful. Amelia dear, today is a happy day. No need to look so glum!'

Seated next to a small table upon which gleamed an impressive silver cup, Lady Alicia looked splendidly imperious in purple silk with a matching parasol. She was the still centre of a bustle of busy maids, as the nursery party arrived at the front of the house. There was something about Lady Alicia's air of languid elegance, her amused eyes and relaxed confidence, which made Amelia's blood boil. Even after all these months of bitter bondage, her aunt's amused disdain was almost too much too endure.

The cousins looked ridiculous. Apart from the usual shaming costumes, they both had back-boards buckled to their corsets beneath their silken smocks. These monstrous devices prevented any slouching at all. The girls' hands had been attached to a steel ring set in the top of the board, where it emerged from the neckline of the smock. A chain pinioned their wrist cuffs to this anchor, set so short that their arms were pulled up high behind their uncomfortably rigid backs. Amelia's arms ached terribly already, and the afternoon had barely begun.

An extra-wide collar that forced her to keep her head up and a long leash completed the ensemble. Amelia could not even look down to see how much of her distractingly tight rubber bloomers were showing beneath the smock. This is torture, she thought bitterly, as the cousins were told to kneel on the blanket laid by Lady Alicia's feet.

The centre of the picnic site was a little plateau of lawn, just in front of the house. Below it the lawns sloped down to the ornamental lake, in front of which passed a winding gravel drive.

'Is Alex getting ready?' Jamie sat down next to Lady Alicia in one of the wicker chairs that had been set out just on the grassy plateau's lip.

'Yes. Look!' She pointed her parasol at a little flurry of activity on the drive before the lake. 'They are setting up the starting line already...'

'Your Ladyship, what a lovely day for racing, *n'est-ce pas?*'

'Mademoiselle Isobel, you look lovely. Everyone seems to be late today. Take this seat by me. Your girls can sit on one of these blankets.'

'I saw Mrs Ormorund's carriage in the courtyard, so I do not think she will be very long. Ah, here she is!'

Amelia shifted her weight surreptitiously. The back-board and the wicked position of her arms was causing some distress, but she did not want to be accused of fidgeting. Once the race began, she thought, the company's attention would be on other things and then...

'Do stop fidgeting, Amelia!' Jamie said sharply.

'Ah, the pretty cousins.' Mademoiselle Isobel's voice was excited and gay. 'You still have trouble with Amelia, monsieur?'

'Amelia is a very wicked, wilful girl,' Jamie said regretfully.

'I suspect that the devil himself would have trouble with that little minx,' Lady Alicia put in.

Amelia's face burnt. The collar prevented her from lowering her head so she stared at the starting line of the race, straight in front of her.

Mrs Ormorund arrived, then Hermione and Antonia Lockheart. Spinster sisters, ever active in the Townswomen's Guild, these ladies ran the genteel tearooms in Hatherby. Such grander folk took the wicker seats, their maids and shop-girls kneeling at their feet. A gaggle of gardeners, grooms and estate-workers took up position to the right. The reason was not hard to discern, for there it was that the reformatory girls sat in their neat rows, under the eagle eyes of their wardresses.

The tradespeople of the district brought their own blankets and spread them out on the grassy sun-bathed slopes. To Amelia's horror the little barber, Mr Catchpole, sat just below her with his wife. Worse, he turned and said something to the little woman, who looked at Amelia and giggled. Amelia cursed the tightness and semi-transparency of the rubber knickers, and wished most fervently that she was allowed to close her legs.

As more and more people arrived, it seemed as if Lady Alicia was the calm centre of a small cyclone of convivial sociability. Her friends grouped around her, more distant acquaintances pitching their blankets further from the elegant epicentre of the hubbub. This only heightened Amelia's ordeal. Kneeling at her aunt's feet, Amelia felt dozens of amused eyes on her, the sheer shame worse than the constriction of rubber or discomfort of the back-board. Her words to Clara that first day came back to her, bitter and unbidden. 'Yes,' she had said, innocent and unknowing, 'I expect that there will be lots of fetes.'

Blossom broke into a gentle trot as the gentle incline down to the lake made the sulky and Lord Alex seem the lightest of loads. He did not pull her up, seeming to sense that she was not tiring herself but just warming up her long legs as she loped down the drive. The slope steepened and the path dog-legged several times as it ran down to the lakeside. There were several other carts on the lawn below the house. Several naked pony-girls stood sweating between the shafts. The sight of them came as something as a shock to Blossom. It was not that she had thought of herself as a real pony, exactly, but she had almost forgotten that she must look like a nearly-naked girl. The sight of the others brought this fact home to her with a real jolt.

'Ready to be beaten again, Justice?' Lord Alex called out.

A corpulent and florid-faced fellow waved dismissively. His pony was a big buxom girl with fine blonde hair. Blossom glanced down at her legs, which looked powerful, though neither so long nor so sleekly exercised as her own. Her pale face was a little red already, and pale blue eyes blinked, seemingly anxious, although the bit between the girl's teeth made her expression hard to read.

'We will give you a run, this year,' Justice Ormorund said jovially. 'Won't we, Belinda, girl?' He gave the girl a crack across the tops of her big thighs with the whip he held in his right hand. Pain furrowed the girl's pale brow, and she might have started forward but for the fact that he held her reins tight. Blossom watched Belinda's breasts wobble as the girl jiggled around in a dance of pain, constrained by her jingling harness. Then she felt herself urged on.

'Women in the Silver Cup. Damned impertinence, to say nothing of the matter of weight,' Lord Alex boomed.

A small, attractive woman in her early forties grinned back unabashed. 'Don't be a poor sport, Alex. You men are just afraid that I will beat you.'

'Oh, you may beat me, Fanny,' the Marquis said jovially, 'but I am damned if I will let you win the cup.'

The woman's mount, a sturdy-looking girl with brown hair in a ponytail, suddenly stepped forward and the little woman gave a slightly startled grunt. She hauled back on the reins and somehow got the girl to stop.

'You stupid mare, Connie!'

Blossom's stomach tensed in sympathy at the unmistakable hiss of riding-whip cutting through the air. Mrs Treadwell gave her pony three sharp cuts, struggling to hold the girl back with the reins. Blossom looked on, astonished. Pony and rider were no better attuned than she had been with Lord Alex in her first few days. She knew she had nothing to fear from that quarter. Which was just as well.

Lord Alex guided her across the sward towards the watching crowd. Just before the slope began to climb in earnest towards the hall, some carpenters were finishing an odd structure. It was something like a football goal, with two uprights and a crossbar. Into this had been fixed a series of eyebolts. The workers were threading chains through these.

'This is the whipping-frame, girl.' Lord Alex's voice was in her ear and the workers paused, distracted. Blossom felt the men's eyes on her all but naked body. 'This is where the losers are brought to be flogged after the race. Not that you need worry, if you do what you are capable of.'

'I would not count any chickens yet, Alex, nor polish any silverware.'

Blossom glanced sideways, grateful that Lord Alex no longer ran her with blinkers. The red-haired girl next to her was doing the same, giving her a cool appraising sideways stare. She was not as tall as Blossom, and her legs were not so long nor so well muscled, but she looked strong and fit. More than that, something determined in her eye made Blossom feel that this was her real rival.

'Ha, you have had it too long, Richard!' Lord Alex snorted. 'Your girl is good, but she does not have my Blossom's legs.'

As the other girl looked at her legs, Blossom was gratified to see something that looked very much like fear enter her eyes.

'Look at the whipping-frame, Rose. Remember girl, I shall thrash you without mercy if you fail me,' the Reverend said quietly to his mount.

The girl looked away from Blossom at last, and up at the frame. Blossom saw her close her eyes, just for a second. Then the Reverend Dawes pulled his pony away. Lord Alex flicked the reins and Blossom moved off.

'Almost ready to start, your Lordship.' A tall thin man in a stationmaster's uniform looked at his fob watch.

'Very good, Mr Hollis.'

Lord Alex guided her towards the other carts, which were gathering before a rope which was strung out across the path. Blossom trotted across to the far right of the field. The first corner of the course turned to the left, and so this was not the most favoured starting position. However, Blossom knew that Lord Alex was more worried about fouling wheels with less skilled riders, than being ahead for the first bend in a long and arduous course.

Everything was going splendidly. No one disputed their safe position on the right. The sun was shining, she could hear the hubbub of the watching crowd above them on the lawns. Best of all she knew, in her heart, that she could beat the rest of the field.

'What is the hold up, Mr Hollis?' Lord Alex bellowed, so loudly that Blossom saw Connie, to her immediate left, flinch, and heard her mistress curse as she struggled to hold the skittish girl in place.

'Just one rider to come, your Lordship.'

'What? Who? Who the devil else is taking part?'

'Ah, here he comes, your Lordship! Now we can get off.'

Blossom sensed as much as heard the stir around her, as riders and mounts craned to see the newcomer. To curses from Lord Alex, the newcomers eased into position on her right. Blossom stared, astonished. Level with her was a woman like no other she had ever seen. The girl was black, with sleek ebony skin, and elaborately braided hair. Her breasts were big, and jutted forward with an almost pneumatic vigour, counterbalanced by an extraordinarily well-developed bottom. It was not these endowments that compelled Blossom's attention, however, but her thighs. The girl was not so tall as Blossom, nor her legs so long, but her thighs were splendidly muscled and looked ominously fit.

'I do hope you were not going to start without me,' an amused male voice drawled.

There was a rueful chuckle from behind her. 'I might have known that you had something up your sleeve when you bet so much against me. Well, I'll be damned if I let you win today. Prepare to say goodbye to a hundred guineas, Jack!'

The stir produced at the starting line by the new arrivals was mirrored amongst the audience of picnickers on the slopes above.

'I say, is that Jack Campion?' Lady Alicia said. 'You know, I do believe it is. But who is that magnificent girl between his shafts? I swear those titties jut out further than our Betsy's do.'

Lady Alicia put her field-glasses to her eyes, but the scene below was near enough that the amazing figure of Jack's pony-girl was evident to the naked eye. Jack Campion raised his Panama in the direction of Lady Alicia, who burst into a peal of delighted laughter.

'Oh my, that man is such a devil. If he wins with that exotic creature, Alex will not be fit to speak to for a week. He has bet Blossom against a hundred of Jack's guineas, you know. That husband of mine never seems to learn that it does not pay to gamble with our Jack!'

'But he has not lost yet, *cherie*,' Mademoiselle Isobel put in, 'and everyone says that Blossom is the fastest filly that was ever entered for the cup.'

'Hm,' Lady Alicia said, passing the glasses to her friend. 'I suspect that "everyone" has not seen Jack's girl run. He must have been keeping her hidden in the lodge, and exercising her in secret. Now why, do you suppose, would the sly old dog do that?'

The back-board, and her wrenched-back arms, were causing Amelia serious discomfort now. She shifted surreptitiously to try to ease the strain. Unfortunately, she moved her legs an iota too much in the process, and the action produced a moist and rubbery squeak.

'Amelia, do stop fidgeting, or I shall ask Lady Alicia to spank you,' Jamie said sharply.

Amelia felt her aunt, who must have leant forward, take a handful of her hair and wrench her head back until she could see Lady Alicia, upside down, smiling wickedly at her.

'I think I shall have to thrash you later, anyway, Amelia.' She produced the little paddle with the holes which she had used on Clara to such evident effect. Maintaining her grip, she patted the whimpering girl's cheek with the paddle. It felt hard and cold and unspeakably mean.

'*Cherie*, they are taking positions.' Isobel's voice brought merciful relief, as Lady Alicia released her hold and Amelia resumed her position, blinking back a tear.

'The course is clearly marked. Up Holly Hill, through the rhododendrons, around the back of the stable-block—'

Blossom shook her head impatiently. She had run the course scores of times and needed no reminders. Glancing sideways, she met the gaze of the black girl to her right. It was hard to tell, with the bit and bridle harness, but she thought that the young woman smiled.

Mr Hollis, the stationmaster, was clearly relishing his chance for importance, and he took his time in detailing the course.

'The course goes around the walled garden, and down the slope in front of the house, back to here. Two full circuits complete the race.' He had been addressing the riders up to this point, but now he put his hands in his waistcoat pockets and assumed a satisfied smirk. 'You should all know by now that all losing ponies will receive a thorough flogging,' he inclined his head towards the frame that had been set up, 'in the traditional way.'

To her left, Connie whimpered. Blossom took a deep breath and put her head down ready. Mr Hollis gave the signal and a rope was raised across the course. Moving forward until her breasts brushed against it, Blossom willed the signal to be given, and the race to begin.

The stationmaster gave a sharp blast of his whistle. The rope was raised high to a roar from the crowd. Blossom powered forward, a tugging of her bridle forcing her to incline to the right. She wanted to run. She wanted to stretch her long, perfectly trained legs and leave the field behind, but Lord Alex kept her reins tight and held her back.

She followed Mrs Treadwell's trim back as Jack's black girl kept pace to her right. They made their way along the shore of the ornamental lake, a short but easy first stage that was nearly level. For all her eagerness to gallop, Blossom understood why she was being held back. Holly Hill loomed in front of them and, as the human ponies reached its sharp incline, the pace slowed dramatically.

The Reverend Dawes had taken the lead and the sound of leather on flesh, up ahead, demonstrated his determination to maintain a cracking pace. It was the next sulky that almost caused disaster. In front of them, Connie swerved violently, almost tipping Mrs Treadwell from her cart. The reason was immediately plain to see. Belinda had hauled Justice Ormorund's great bulk at a canter along the lakeside, but as soon as she had hit the steep slope their progress had slowed, almost to a walk.

Blossom felt her bit pulled to the left and she turned quickly, overtaking the semi-stranded sulky with consummate ease. Jack and his pony-girl had done the same, but to the right. Mrs Treadwell was trying to control Connie, who had bolted right off the path and onto the grass slopes.

Soon she was shoulder to shoulder with the black girl once again, the two of them slowly gaining on the Reverend and his mount.

'Giddup!' There was a crack as the Reverend Dawes belaboured his pony's bare bottom with his thin black crop. 'Go on, girl, you can do it. Giddup! Giddup! Giddup!'

The flogging produced a spurt of speed and the sulky in front began to pull away. Blossom wanted to increase her speed but the tight rein held her back.

'Steady, Princess! Whoa, girl, easy, *whoa!*'

It seemed that she was not the only pony-girl who was being held back. The two kept pace with each other as the slope levelled off. Through the gloomy lanes at the back of the house, they ran. Here the path was lined with glossy-foliaged rhododendrons and camellias. There was a maze of paths here, but the wrong turnings had been ribboned off. Princess moved into the lead as they came in sight of the back of the stable-block. Blossom was running well and knew that she had strength in reserve, yet still Lord Alex held her back.

'Oh, please, let me go.' Emma did not dare push the man's hand off her stockinged thigh but tried to back away, without dropping her tray of drinks.

'Don't be shy, sweetheart.' The man, one of the gardeners, she thought, leered at her. He licked his lips like a hungry wolf eyeing a lamb. 'I shan't eat you,' he said, as if reading her mind, 'exactly.'

Emma took a deep breath and spun away. This time he allowed her to escape. Teetering on the unaccustomed heels, she tottered through the groups of picnicking people.

'I'll catch you later, then!' the man called after her.

Some of Mademoiselle Isobel's shop-girls grinned up at her as she passed, horribly aware of the brevity of her little skirt.

'Looks like someone has a date,' a red-haired minx chortled as she tottered by.

It was Emma's first time in the uniform that the maids called a "tutu", and it was her first time in such perilous heels. Silver Cup day was not the easiest occasion to practise. In fact, it was proving to be a true baptism of lust. The crowd of men and women were getting increasingly excited, and the sight of the little maid in her revealing costume commanded much more attention than Emma would have liked. It had not been too bad while the race was still in sight. Now the sulkies had passed out of view, the revellers were looking for alternative amusement.

'What a sweet little bon-bon, Alicia,' Mademoiselle Isobel cooed as she reached her goal at last. 'Where have you been hiding this one, eh?'

'Oh, she is our kitchen-maid. You must have seen her at church. We got her from the reformatory in May. A pretty little chit; she squeals most amusingly under the birch. Perhaps later we should see if we can make the baggage squeak!'

Emma blushed as she bent to serve the drinks, feeling the women's eyes upon her. The glasses rattled on the tray as she felt Jamie's hand on her bare thigh above the stocking-top. He pinched the tender flesh of her inner thighs, hard, as Lady Alicia took a drink with an amused smile. The little maid could not stop a moan escaping as his fingers probed the frills of her knickers until finding some buttock to pinch. She had nurtured hopes of a respite, once she had reached her goal, but this was almost as bad as being held up by those rough men.

'Doesn't like the cane either, do you, pet?' Jamie asked. His fingers had trapped some bottom-flesh, preventing her from stepping over to offer Mademoiselle Isobel a drink.

'Well, girl?' Lady Alicia looked at her with malicious amusement. 'Don't you bother

123

to answer your betters any more?'

'No, sir, madam, I - I mean, yes, sir, madam... I—' Emma did not know which question she was supposed to answer and mumbled, red-faced and in complete confusion.

'It seems she cannot decide,' Jamie said, releasing her bottom at last.

Emma winced and tottered over to Mademoiselle Isobel, who took a glass from the tray with a broad smile.

'Then we must help her to remember, *n'est-ce pas?*'

'But naturally. All right, Emma, offer Mrs Ormorund and the others drinks, then cut along to the rod room and fetch a nice whippy cane.'

Blossom was perspiring freely now, and her breathing was very heavy, but the months of training had paid off, and she was still feeling strong. They had run down the Reverend Dawes and his mount, in the long stretch of the course that looped behind the walled garden. First Princess had taken up the lead, and then Jack Campion had reined her in to allow Blossom to overtake. At first she was surprised, then she realised what was happening. Lord Alex and Jack had decided to work together to reel in the Reverend and his Rose. They wanted the latter part of the course free for their own personal duel. If one had made a break, the other would have followed, helter-skelter, but they were content, for now, to pace each other, and run down the cart in front.

This was not difficult. Blossom was the pacemaker as they emerged on the high ground above the lake. The drive wound down back to the starting point and she could see the Reverend and his girl in front. They were going downhill, yet the girl was stumbling. Blossom would have smiled if not for the bit. He had ridden her too hard, she realised; the pony-girl's breath was broken. No amount of fear or pain would get the rector up Holly Hill in front.

She could have overtaken on the way down. They had practised this, and many times she had hurtled down the slope at a perilous rate. To Blossom's surprise, Lord Alex reined her back, forcing her to keep to a safe controlled pace.

There was a roar from the crowd as each sulky came into view. At the bottom of the slope the driveway widened and Blossom heard, then saw, Princess pull up level on her right side. This time she was not reined back and she knew the pace making for each other was over.

They caught their quarry a little higher up Holly Hill than the place where they had overtaken Justice Ormorund. Rose was a fair-skinned girl and Blossom caught sight of a mass of livid welts on her pale bottom as she passed. The hill had stopped her almost as short as it had arrested Belinda on the last ascent, and they surged by.

Belinda and the Justice were still not much higher up. He had pulled her off the path to allow the frontrunners to lap him. Blossom heard some oaths and agonised whinnies as she passed, but it hardly registered, for now the race was well and truly on.

Blossom's wind was not broken, but she was gasping as she cantered up the hill. This time around she was really feeling Lord Alex's weight. It occurred to her for the first time that Jack was a much smaller man than her master, and a much lighter one, no doubt. Whether because of the relative weight of the drivers, or due to the comparative strength of their mounts, one thing became clear as they ground up the slope: little by little, Princess was, inexorably, pulling away.

There was a crack and a sharp sting in her flanks. The first time that her master had used his whip. Blossom put her head down and hauled with all her might. To no avail for, when she glanced up again, their rivals were several yards in front.

The slap was so sudden it took Amelia by surprise.

'You see? Such a wicked, wilful child,' Lady Alicia sighed. 'Now keep still, you dreadful fidget.'

They had watched the stragglers for a few minutes, the company laughing as Belinda struggled fruitlessly to haul her burden for a second time up the hill. The sound of riding crop on girlish bottom echoed across the lawns, but it was all too obviously failing to have the required effect. Eventually Lady Alicia had bored of the prospect.

Amelia and Clara had been made to turn, kneeling up and facing Lady Alicia and Mademoiselle Isobel respectively. The object of these ladies' scrutiny was their nipples.

'They do stand out so, against the silk; why, they might almost as well be bare.'

Amelia tried to bite back a groan as Lady Alicia's crimson talons pinched the objects of her interest. She heard Clara give a pained whimper beside her.

'These are stiff and pretty, but not nearly so protuberant as her cousin's,' Mademoiselle Isobel said gaily. Clara gasped with pain as the corsetier tweaked.

'No, but then not many girls have nips like our Amelia's, do they dear? They are like claret corks, once they get engorged. My maid, Kitty, has nipples like loganberries, but I think Amelia's are even longer. Perfect for clamping. I say, that gives me a splendid idea.'

Amelia moaned as Lady Alicia's nails dug into the sensitive flesh through the gossamer silk. Lady Alicia pinioned the nipples between the nails of her forefingers and thumbs, and then she rolled. Amelia grunted as they were twisted through almost one hundred and eighty degrees. Tears sprang to her eyes and her fingers flexed helplessly behind her back, in their bonds, as Lady Alicia held this excruciating position for a few long seconds. Just as she thought she must explode with pain, the Marchioness untwisted them and relief flooded through Amelia. It was a sadly short-lived sensation, for her aunt promptly wrenched the engorged flesh, just as far, the other way around.

'Ooh, please, Aunt - I, ah, ooh.'

'For heaven's sake, be quiet, girl. You know, flimsy as this thing is, I do believe that this would be more fun on the bare.'

Lady Alicia released her hawk-like grip and Amelia gasped. Her aunt pulled up the hem of her smock, lifting it to Amelia's appalled mouth. Half of Hatherby was watching. She could hear the laughter from behind her and from either side. The discomfort of the back-board and her bondage, the constriction of the rubber bloomers, which were sticky now in places: all these things paled into insignificance besides her choking sense of shame.

There was no choice, however. Amelia knew she was helpless in her bondage and appallingly vulnerable to Lady Alicia's capricious cruelty. She took the silk in her mouth and held it there, trying to forget the fact that her breasts were now publicly exposed.

'You see.' Lady Alicia beamed down and patted her cheek, which was still burning from the slap. 'You can be good if you try, Amelia.'

The Marchioness of Hatherby flexed her fingers thoughtfully. Amelia stared, as if mesmerised, by her long blood-red nails. Clara gave a startled gasp of pain beside her, and she heard Mademoiselle Isobel give a delighted little laugh. Then Lady Alicia once again took hold of Amelia's already throbbing nipples between crimson talons, and Amelia heard herself shriek with pain.

Pain was shooting through her thighs now, and Blossom was gasping for air as she hauled the sulky up the last part of the hill. There was a sickening whistle and a flame of agony, even more intense than that in her muscles, blazed across her bottom.

'Go on, Blossom, giddup! You can do it, girl!'

She blinked away tears as she hauled the little cart around the clump of holly that marked the crest of Holly Hill. Her arms ached, her lungs were bursting, and her thigh muscles were shrieking from the strain, but Blossom was far from beaten yet.

Taking a great lungful of air, she settled into a lope through the rhododendron maze. Lord Alex was showing his anxiety by giving her frequent lashes with the whip, but she had to get her breath back so she did not run full pelt. Blossom understood what had happened on the hill. Princess had been the stronger. She had not been able to match the strength in the black girl's powerful thighs, certainly not when hauling a greater load. Now they were on the flat, things were different. Blossom's legs were longer and she was very fast. If she did not succumb to panic, there was a way that she could still win.

Moving swiftly through the rhododendrons, she began to feel better. She was still blowing like a steam train, but her lungs did not hurt as much as they had. They passed the stable-block and the familiar sight made her quicken her pace. What if she were to lose? Blossom thought, fighting back the panic. What would happen to her then?

Princess had passed out of sight by the top of the hill, and Blossom ran through the rhododendron groves alone. She caught sight of a carriage as they set off around the walled garden and her heart surged with excitement. Then she realised it was only Connie and Mrs Treadwell, still struggling to complete their first lap. Connie was bathed in sweat, her broad back and bottom welted now. Mrs Treadwell reined her mount over to the side to let them thunder past.

Panic was truly setting in now. Surely they should have caught up with the other cart by now? Then, as they rounded the last corner of the garden wall, she saw them up ahead. Lord Alex must have seen his rival, too, for the lashes fell like a boiling rain across her back and bottom. Not that Blossom needed the encouragement. There was no more thought of reserving strength, the final slope was far too close. Blossom just put her head down and ran.

'That's it girl! We're gaining on them! Come on, Blossom, giddup, girl! We can take them on the slope!'

For all the pain in every screaming muscle, Blossom felt a sense of exultation seize her. Every time she glanced up the target was closer. Now it was only a matter of yards ahead. Blossom knew how difficult it was to run down the slope full tilt. No one else had had the chance to practise it like she had. Her master was right; they would take the other sulky on the slope.

With perhaps five yards of lead, Princess hauled her cart over the lip of the long downhill slope. She was so close now that Blossom could see the beads of perspiration gleaming in the sunlight on the girl's dark skin. Gulping what air she could, she followed as fast as possible, meaning to overtake her rival as soon as Princess slowed.

The black girl did not slow. There was a roar from the crowd as the two carts emerged into view, but Blossom was barely aware of it. Her eyes widened as she watched Jack Campion's pony-girl hurtle down the slope. Surely they would upend at the first bend. Blossom sprang after them, long legs eating up the ground now that gravity had removed the weight of her load.

The other cart did not go over, not at the first bend, nor the second: incredibly it did not slow. It was as if Princess knew that switchback descent as well as Blossom did herself. The prodigiously endowed pony-girl fairly galloped down the slope, slowing just enough to navigate the turns before her powerful thighs sprinted on again. Not only could Blossom not catch her, it was all that she could do to keep up without tipping over her own cart at this phenomenal rate.

The final lakeside stretch was a formality. Blossom's legs no longer had the strength to make up several yards of lead. In fact, her powerful, perfectly conditioned thigh-muscles, felt about to buckle beneath her. Lord Alex must have realised that the game was up, too, for he scarcely bothered to whip her bottom as she staggered, gasping for breath, along the shore.

Blossom did not see Princess canter through the ribbon held up by the stable-lads. She heard the roar from the watching crowd, though, and that told her that Jack had won his bet, as she staggered, head down, over the last few yards of the course.

THE TUNE OF BIRCH AND LEATHER

'Amelia! Amelia! Pay attention to your aunt.' Jamie's voice cut into Amelia's reverie.

Like everyone else in the crowd, she had watched the final stages of the race with rapt attention. So exciting had been the final descent that she had even forgot the discomfort of the back-board, and the maddening rubbing of taut rubber over her clitoris, and the throbbing of her tortured nipples, for a moment. The two front runners had hurtled down the slope, careening around the corners in the winding drive so precipitously that it seemed they must overturn. Jack Campion's girl had held her lead somehow, her breasts bouncing as she hurtled down the hill, her dark sweat-soaked skin gleaming in the September sun.

No more than a few paces behind had hurtled Blossom. The tall girl's breasts had jiggled as she ran in great loping strides. It seemed she must catch the shorter girl. But Amelia could see that Blossom's gait was ragged now, her long legs less steady. Amelia felt a surge of secret satisfaction, knowing that Lord Alex was going to lose.

A great cheer rang out as Jack's mount breasted the ribbon. Blossom limped in a few yards behind.

'Oh, heavens,' Lady Alicia said in a voice that sounded secretly delighted, 'Alex has lost his fabulous thoroughbred filly!'

'How did he take the slope so fast?' wondered Jamie.

'The sly dog must have been practising,' Lady Alicia said, 'it is the only way. He must have found a similar slope somewhere.'

At that point the cracking of a crop on flesh drew the company's attention. Rose pulled into view, hauling the Reverend Dawes. The buxom redhead limped down the slope, the welts on her back and bottom visible even from a distance. Amelia watched the Reverend whip her mercilessly as she stumbled on. Great heavens, she thought as she watched, appalled, that man really is a brute.

Somehow Rose managed to stagger the final furlong, only to sink to her knees as she crossed the line. Then there was a wait. The hubbub of conversation in the crowd resumed, though Amelia kept watching as the pony-girls were unharnessed and sponged down by the stable-boys. The sight made her shiver. How terrible it must be, she thought, to be treated like an animal that way. The awful compelling sight of the naked girls provoked a more insistent tingling in her loins, and she shifted carefully, trying not to make her bloomers squeak.

After several long minutes, Connie appeared, pulling Mrs Treadwell's sulky down the slope. She seemed less exhausted than Rose had been, but she descended slowly and cautiously. Clearly neither rider nor mount felt confident. Wondering how far back Justice Ormorund had fallen, Amelia looked over to her left, to Holly Hill. The Justice was trotting Belinda dejectedly down the incline. It seemed he had abandoned the attempt to complete the course altogether. He arrived at the finish line the wrong way, at the same time as Mrs Treadwell and her girl.

'It is customary to give the ponies some minutes to recover,' Lady Alicia said as she looked into Amelia's eyes, 'before presenting the Silver Cup and... what not. We usually like to provide some amusement for the company. Stand up, please, my dear.'

Amelia's mouth went dry as she saw her aunt produce the evil little paddle, and slap it into her palm with a sickening crack.

'Jamie, dear, would you mind peeling those rubber bloomers off?'

For a moment Amelia very nearly bolted. It was insane. Pinioned in her back-board bondage, where was there to go? What on earth could she do? It was not the fear of the nasty thing in Lady Alicia's hand, though that was real. It was the shame. Amelia heard a score of conversations trail away, and knew with sickening certainty that the eyes of half of Hatherby were now firmly fixed on her latex-encased rear.

Somehow she managed not to bolt. The thought of whooping stable-boys chasing her across the lawns helped to keep her in her place. She closed her eyes and bit her lip as Jamie took a firm grip of the waist of her rubber pantaloons and began to tug, producing a positive cacophony of rubbery creaks and squeaks.

'I say, what a peculiar noise!'

'One might think those things were glued to her, they seem to grip so tight.'

'It's the wet - it makes a vacuum. The slut has been producing fluids all afternoon, and now her drawers are stuck!'

Amelia fought tears of pure humiliation as the laughter and ribald comments came thick and fast. She was almost relieved when Jamie finally got the damned things off, for all that comment now turned to another source of shame.

'By God, that is a juicy-looking little pussy! I'd love to see if it's as tight as it looks!'

'Ah, your little motte is so pretty shaved, *cherie!*'

'The trollop is not looking so haughty today, eh?'

'I do hope her Ladyship fairly skins that bottom for the proud little bitch.'

'All right now, darling,' Lady Alicia's rich tones cut through the general raillery. 'Come and put yourself over my knee.'

Amelia went almost eagerly. Eager, she was at least, to get the ordeal over with and to regain some shred of modesty. Her aunt helped her, as she could not use her arms for balance, to lower herself over the Marchioness's silk-skirted lap. The smock rode up in the process and she was horribly aware that her bottom was now naked for the amusement of the company. If she had not been, the comments would have soon let her know.

'By God, what a beauty!'

'Sweet as a peach. That bum looks to be a really tender treat!'

Amelia felt a hand gently stroke her naked buttocks.

'*Mais oui*, her skin is still as smooth as that of a baby.'

Amelia endured Mademoiselle Isobel's fondling, and tried to close her ears to the comments of the crowd. Despite the depth of her humiliation, her clitoris still throbbed urgently. She shifted on her aunt's lap, seeking to press the tingling nub against something more substantial than skirt silk, but to no avail.

'Your bottom will be the toast of Hatherby tonight, Amelia,' Aunt Alicia said fondly.

Amelia hung her head in utter shame.

The first stroke of the paddle put her humiliation in sudden and very sharp perspective. It felt as if her skin was on fire.

Crack! Crack! Crack!

Lady Alicia brought the paddle down in quick succession. Amelia was engulfed in an atrocious wave of pain.

Crack! Crack! Crack!

Amelia had witnessed the effects on Clara and had known that the little paddle with its drill-holes would be bad. Part of her, though, had thought her cousin feeble to have cried so bitterly and wriggled so much under its strokes.

Now she knew better.

The pain was extraordinary. Like the birch, it scalded the surface of her tender skin without dulling the nerves.

'Ow! Ooh! *Ouch!*' she yelped and groaned and gasped as the strokes rained down on her unprotected rear.

'Stop that silly kicking, Amelia, or you will get more strokes.'

By the end, Amelia was half-delirious from the pain. Consciousness came back but slowly, in fragments of awareness that there was something else in the world, apart from excruciating pain.

'Good show! She felt that, I'll warrant!'

'By God, that bum looks like a skinned tomato.'

Amelia blew and gasped and sucked in needed air. The paddling had stopped, she realised slowly. The pain must be subsiding, though that was difficult to comprehend; her poor bottom and thighs were still in a state of scorching agony.

'There now.'

A pat, or was it a smack? Her bottom was now so tender it was impossible to tell; it made her squeal helplessly again.

'Tsk, tsk, Amelia. No need to make such a fuss. Get down and stop snivelling, girl.

The losing ponies are about to meet their fate.'

Whimpering pitifully, Amelia was made to stand between her aunt and Jamie. This position placed her excruciatingly tender bottom easily within the reach of both her tormentors. She gasped as Jamie grasped her right buttock and squeezed.

'Good Lord, Amelia,' he said, 'it feels as if you have been sitting on a stove.'

Amelia could not prevent the tears from coursing down her cheeks. Worse, she could feel another moistness trickling down her inner thighs from her naked quim. The slight breeze made the fluid feel cold, and horribly obvious, on her skin.

There was at least one small mercy, she told herself as a pinch from Aunt Alicia on her left thigh made her wince. Few of the Hatherby *hoi polloi* were watching her now. Almost all eyes were fixed on a position between the crowd and the finishing line; the place where the carpenters had erected the wooden frame.

If the whipping had been inflicted straight after the race, Blossom thought as she eyed the frame nervously, she would have barely felt it. The agony of her over-taxed muscles would have rendered her all but impervious to more pain. As it was, the results of the flogging she had received from Lord Alex's crop, which had barely registered as a mild stinging at the time, grew more galling by the minute. As she slowly recovered, the dread began to grow.

'Sorry, girl,' Lord Alex patted her cheek as she stood quivering in the sunshine by the lake. 'You ran your heart out, but they beat us on that hill.' He glanced at the whipping-frame regretfully. 'Can't get you out of it, though. You see, it is the tradition.' He leant forward and kissed her tenderly on the cheek, between the bridle straps. 'Afterwards, you will belong to Jack,' he said, his voice a little thick with emotion. Then he shrugged and turned to walk away.

Dick was looking upset, too. He had unbuckled her harness. The sense of relief as the leather straps came off reminded her of her first training days. The bridle and bit were pulled off, too, giving her lips the sweet sensation of release. He poured some badly needed water into her open mouth before leading her off to be sponged down.

Davy was already sponging Princess. The girl stood impassively as the lad rubbed the wet sponge over her magnificent physique. Blossom blinked, as she realised that the girl was steaming. Then she gasped as the cold water cooled her own well-flogged flanks. The sensation was delicious and she tried to lose herself in it, wondering if she was steaming with perspiration, too.

'Well, now.' An amused voice brought her back with a start. 'Let's have a little look at what I've won.'

The man was considerably shorter than Blossom. He looked up at her, his gold tooth flashing wickedly as he grinned. Blossom moaned as he seized both of her nipples and worried them between strong forefingers and thumbs.

'Lovely titties,' he grunted. 'Fabulously long legs.' He dropped one hand to feel between her thighs. 'Hm, the filly's responsive, too.'

Dick continued to sponge her down as Jack Campion appraised his newly won girl-flesh with professional expertise. Powerless to stop her body responding to his knowing hands, Blossom gave a low moan. She sensed that Dick was bitterly disappointed; upset that he was going to lose her from the stables. The thought provoked a pang of sadness, almost homesickness in her breast.

'I'll get two thousand guineas for this filly in the girl-markets of Fejr,' Jack said conversationally to Dick. 'I'll race her first, on the flat, so they can see her run. Those sheiks will pay a fortune for a white pony-girl as fast as this beauty.'

Blossom struggled to make sense of his words as Dick led her off to the frame. What could he mean, "the girl-markets of Fejr"? Something knotty in her stomach told her that she would find out one day soon. She had more immediate concerns, however. Her wrists and ankles were being buckled into leather bands. Looking to the side, she saw a frightened-looking Connie undergoing the same process. The welts on the girl's back were fading but still visible on her pale skin. To the other side, Belinda was having her ankles fastened into place. Beyond her, Rose was already being spread-eagled in the frame.

Each girl had her wrists fixed, wide apart, to eyebolts in the crossbeam of the frame. Next their ankles were pinioned. Connie's right ankle was fixed to the right-hand upright post. Her legs were spread wide and her left ankle fixed to Blossom's right. Strong hands hauled Blossom's painfully stiff legs open, and her left ankle was padlocked to Belinda's right. Finally the process was completed, with Rose's left leg being affixed to the left upright post.

Blossom felt appallingly exposed. She was completely naked, but could scarcely move an inch to protect herself. To move her legs at all she had to fight the girls to either side, and after a few panicked moments, the futility of this dawned and they stopped struggling, lapsing into a state of tautly stretched, terrifyingly vulnerable, equilibrium.

The girls had been chained on the frame so that they faced the ornamental lake, their backs to the crowd on the rise. Some of the stable-lads and gardener's boys had lingered by the finishing line, and now stood grinning at the naked girls and fingering themselves. Blossom was used to being seen naked, yet this position, with her legs chained so wide apart, made her feel peculiarly exposed. However, the leering youths were a minor distraction. What made her flinch, and the girls on either side of her whimper with fear, was imagining what was happening behind.

They did not need a lot of imagination. All too soon, the losing riders trooped around to the front of the frame, chasing off the lascivious stable-lads and their friends: Lord Alex looking peevish, the Reverend Dawes whose countenance was stern, and Mrs Treadwell, seemingly tiny next to the great figure of Justice Ormorund. Each of the four carried a carriage whip.

'Now, girls,' Lord Alex said, 'as you may have guessed, you are going to be whipped. The losing fillies in the Silver Cup have been flogged since the days of the twelfth Marquis and, believe me, tradition will be fully honoured here today.'

Belinda gave a little wail of fear beside her.

'Oh, do be quiet, girl,' Lord Alex said, as Justice Ormorund glared at his losing filly.

'The procedure is as follows. The first whip, myself in this case as I came second, will give each losing mount a stroke. Next, the second driver,' he nodded at the Reverend Dawes, 'will whip down the line, and so forth. When each of us has given one stroke, I start again, this time giving each girl two lashes in turn. This procedure is followed until the final round, in which the drivers will inflict a stroke for every entry in the race. Very well, let us begin.'

The drivers turned and trooped around the frame. Blossom was in a panic now. She knew how much those carriage whips could sting. Desperately, she tried to calculate the number of strokes. A mumbling to her right told her that she was not the only one.

'Five and four is nine and three is twelve, and two is...'

There was an evil whistling sound and a crack of whipcord snapping against tender flesh. Rose gave a startled cry of pain.

There was a languid scattered round of applause, the sort of polite sound that might have greeted a boundary at a county cricket match.

Connie's calculations seemed to have been upset by these distractions because she gave a frightened squeak and tried again. 'Is twelve and...'

Another whistle, another crack, another outbreak of clapping. Belinda hissed. Almost paralysed with fear, Blossom awaited the next stroke. There was the whistle again and her back was scored with a sizzling line of fire.

She was still gritting her teeth and trying not to cry out when she heard the next stroke of the whip lace Connie's back. Again there came that round of clapping from the picnickers, as the buxom girl beside her gasped with pain.

It was bizarre, strung out there in the afternoon sun, each seething stroke of the whip drawing its response from the spectators. It was the snap of leather on soft flesh, rather than crack of leather against willow, that provoked each round of leisurely applause. Yet the genteel parkland scene seemed oddly familiar to her, almost comforting, as if these were the sights and sounds of some lost dream of home. Another searing stroke, this time cutting across her naked buttocks, put all such musings right out of her mind.

The Reverend Dawes! She might have guessed that his stroke would be vicious. By the time the pain had started to subside, the next wave of strokes was hissing down the line. Belinda's leg jerked convulsively as Mrs Treadwell's lash laced the girl's shoulders, and Blossom was struggling against the yanking of her leg when a blistering stroke impacted on her back.

'Hoooo...!' It was not the worst stroke, but the Reverend's brutal lash seemed to have loosened the moorings of her self-control. Chains rattled as she fought fruitlessly against her bonds. Then Connie was crying out in pain beside her, too.

The fourth stroke came with horrible inevitability. The worst thing about being in a line, like this, was that she heard the strokes approaching on the backs of the other girls. The sound concentrated the mind on what was coming. Justice Ormorund's whip caught her hard across the thighs. Blossom shook her head furiously and made a hissing noise.

'Oh, God, oh, no, I can't bear it...' Connie babbled to one side. On the other Belinda was breathing brokenly and sobbing.

Hiss... crack! Hiss... crack!

Rose let out a heart-rending shriek. There was no room for any doubt about what was coming to her. Belinda was trying to kick again, as the whip whistled and cracked across her back. Then Blossom felt Lord Alex's whip sear across her own skin. One blistering stroke striped her from right shoulder to left side; a second later, its twin bisected it, leaving a red-hot wire of pain from her left shoulder to her right side. Tears sprang to her eyes as she clenched her fists impotently. She was so tautly stretched in the frame that there was little she could do in response to the atrocious pain, but jiggle furiously on the spot within her bonds.

After that the strokes started to blur. The agony seemed to be a constant blaze, the new whip-strokes providing extra pulses of intensity, like a constant fiery glow pulsing to white heat, rhythmically as some diabolic bellows pumped away. The clapping was a distant, disconnected thing now. Blossom no longer knew what it was, although she was dimly aware of the sound. Some searing whip-strokes made her open her eyes in surprise, but the tranquil lake view meant nothing to her. The shrieks of her companions in this purgatory, the whistle of the whip, the crack of cord on buttock and back, the desperate rattling as the girls fought against their bonds, most of all the swirling crimson pain that engulfed her, these were the only sensations that had any sort of meaning. As the whip lashes fell, again and again, ever more frequently, Blossom felt her mind swept away by a boiling tide of pain.

'Listen to them roar! I told you it would be better to win, eh, girl?' Jack Campion fondly pinched the cheek of his pony-girl.

As the whipping had progressed, Amelia had watched him stroll up the slope, leading Princess by a simple rope halter. Though her hands were free, the naked girl made no effort to hide her extraordinarily well-developed charms. She followed her master placidly, ignoring the ribald shouts of picnickers as she past. Amelia did not know where to look. The black girl fascinated her: those magnificent breasts gently bobbing as she trotted up the lawn, such wonderfully muscular thighs, the nest of luxuriant black pubic curls.

But even as the winner approached, the whipping of the losers compelled attention. Amelia's own blistered bottom twitched in sympathy at the sound of every stinging lash. The hissing carriage-whips left long welts on the backs and bottoms of the naked girls stretched out on the frame. The weals rose like brands, heart-stoppingly vivid, especially on the pale flesh of fair-skinned Belinda and red-haired Rose.

As the drivers took their turn to progress down the line, delivering three strokes to each victim on this pass, it did not escape Amelia's attention which of the whips produced the most piteous cries. The Reverend Dawes stood rock-steady in front of Rose and lashed the naked girl three times in quick succession, producing startled squeals. Then he stepped smartly to the side and raised his whip again. Three pistol shot retorts rang out across the park, and Belinda howled in turn.

'The Reverend Dawes is showing his usual enthusiasm.' Jack Campion had reached Lady Alicia's party now, and took up the winner's seat. Amelia found herself kneeling, her face but inches from Princess's superbly muscled thighs.

Another three cracks rang out and Blossom gave full-throated witness to her pain. Amelia looked down to see the tall girl's muscular tanned back writhing helplessly as she fought against her bonds. Welts criss-crossed the whole of her back now, and laced the girl's firm bottom and the top half of her thighs. The sight made Amelia shiver, but she could not look away.

'Richard is invariably enthusiastic when it comes to whipping girls,' Lady Alicia said in a somewhat husky voice.

Connie squealed as she was lashed in turn, and then the Reverend stepped aside as Mrs Treadwell prepared to take his place.

The pain in Amelia's bottom had faded to a dull throb, but the discomfort of the corset and the back-board grew more vexatious with every passing minute. Fascinated as she was by the prospect of the whipping, she devoutly wished for the spectacle to be over, that she might begin to hope for release. She glanced at Clara, who was kneeling at Jamie's knee. The blonde girl seemed to be feeling the discomfort less, for there was an almost blissful expression on her face as Jamie absently stroked her golden curls.

Amelia's wish was not to be soon granted. The flogging of the losing fillies seemed to take forever. The sun glowed red as it began to set. She tried to ignore the aching of her shoulders and the insistent tingling that tormented her loins. The languid clapping of the crowd was now reserved for especially vicious strokes, or particularly skilful applications of the whip.

The long shadowed September sun; the ripples of applause; the simmering sense of barely suppressed arousal in the crowd; the sound of carriage-whip cracking against flesh. It seemed to Amelia that she was lost in some dream world, beyond time and place. That, perhaps, she was stuck, condemned to kneel forever, tight-laced and trussed to an unbending back-board, her bottom throbbing from the last beating, uncomfortably awaiting her next appointment with the rod.

Blossom cried out in pain and the crowd clapped a particularly wicked stroke of the whip. Amelia moaned softly. Would she ever escape this state of bondage? The girls in the whipping-frame struggled against their restraints, silhouetted by the crimson sun, dancing to the tune of leather against tender female flesh.

The tune of birch and leather, that was the music of Hope Hall.

EPILOGUE

Amelia awoke to the familiar figure of Betsy standing over her bed. As usual the clamminess of the rubber sheets and the chemical smell of latex assailed her nostrils, and she rose with alacrity. Only once she had escaped the sheets' latex embrace did she begin to wonder what new torments might lay in store that day.

'I've run a bath for you, miss. Your clothes are set out in the dressing room.'

Amelia was not certain, but it seemed as if the nursery-maid was being more respectful than usual. Perhaps the frolics following the Silver Cup had taught the girl some regard for her betters, Amelia thought as she followed the buxom girl into the bathroom.

The bathroom was beyond the parlour and she had to cross this, naked as she was, to gain her bath. As she passed through the room she glanced at the mantel clock. To her astonishment, she saw it was almost nine o'clock. Amelia almost stumbled, surprised that she had been allowed such luxury.

The bath was wonderful. It was deep and hot and provided with rose-scented oils. As usual, Amelia found the combination of sensuality and privacy irresistible. There had been no sign of Jamie in the parlour; with any luck he would still be sleeping off last night's debauch. Amelia's fingers stroked her inner thighs, and then gently circled her clitoris. The vision of the Reverend Dawes imposed itself, unbidden, in her mind. She saw him whipping his pony-girl again, his grey eyes devoid of pity. Then she found herself imagining herself imprisoned between the shafts of his sulky as he flogged her on.

Her climax took her by surprise. A sudden explosion of ecstasy ripped through her, making her cry out with its intensity.

'Good Lord, Amelia, you sound like a boiled cat.'

The blood rushed to her face in shame, even as she froze in fear at the sound of Jamie's voice behind her. How could she have been so foolish as to let him catch her once again?

'If you can stop frigging yourself for a moment,' he said in an amused voice, 'I suggest that you get dressed. We are breakfasting with Lord Alex and Lady Alicia this morning.'

To her great relief he left then, saying no more about catching her in the act of masturbation. Why was it she always seemed to think about that man? Amelia wondered as she towelled herself dry. The Reverend Dawes terrified her and she hated his arrogance and air of superiority, but terror seemed to have led to a sort of horrified fascination. It was awful, and she wished she could think of something else when she touched herself, but he seemed to have mesmerised her, somehow.

However, she had more immediate causes for anxiety. Her bottom still felt blistered from her Aunt Alicia's paddle. What new torments had been devised to vex the cousins?

In the dressing room, Betsy laced her into her little corset. The maid hauled tightly but, to Amelia's relief, did not lace her so viciously as she had the day before. Looking around anxiously, Amelia saw no sign of the dreaded back-board, either. What she did see filled her mind with questions.

'Drawers now, miss?' Betsy asked, almost respectfully, holding up a pair of new, white cotton drawers.

Amelia blinked at the things, astonished for a moment. They looked respectable and comfortable. Was she really to be free of the awful latex bloomers? She stepped into the drawers and Betsy tied the strings. Then the nursery-maid picked up the gown of emerald silk that had been laid out.

Amelia just stared at the elegant garment for a second. Then, as she put it on and allowed Betsy to fasten it, she found she had to swallow a lump in her throat. Do not be so silly, she chided herself as she blinked away tears of pure relief. After all, proper adult attire was no more than her due.

Once dressed she joined Jamie and Clara in the parlour. Amelia stared at her cousin in surprise. Clara wore a gown, every bit as proper as her own, of pale yellow satin. The cousins looked at one another for a moment with wide eyes.

'Splendid, splendid. I must say that you both look splendid,' Jamie said jovially. 'One would hardly recognise you, Amelia.' The uncouth young man gave her a leery wink.

For once, Amelia really did not care. As the little party made its way from the nursery to the breakfast room, Amelia's mind was full of desperate questions. Could this be the end of her long humiliation? Might she have seen the end of those awful clothes and Jamie's rule? She tried not to allow her hopes to flourish, knowing that this might be some cruel trick.

Yet when they arrived at the breakfast room, they were treated in the way she had expected on that first dreadful day. Lady Alicia greeted them fondly and urged them to take kidneys and mushrooms from the dishes laid out on the sideboard. Lord Alex greeted them affably from behind his paper, as if their appearance were the most normal thing in the world, and the months of humiliation in the nursery no more than a bad dream.

Amelia did not dare to ask, so she sipped her tea and breakfasted warily on toast and some fine sausages, awaiting some explanation of the change. Lady Alicia said nothing until all had eaten their fill, then she clapped her hands together for attention, and even Lord Alex put his paper down.

'Now, my dears, we have an important announcement. Jamie has proposed to Clara, and been accepted.'

Lord Alex gave a grunt of approbation, Clara blushed and even Jamie coloured a little. Amelia looked at her cousin with astonished outrage. The little slut: how could she? After all the outrages that swine had perpetrated...

'I know this summer has been hard on you two girls. You have had a taste of life on the receiving end, the better to fit you for your place. I know that nursery discipline has been vexatious to you - especially to you, Amelia, for you have great spirit. You will both be glad to know that it is over. The summer season ends traditionally with the Silver Cup.'

Any resentment Amelia might have felt at what she saw as Clara's betrayal vanished at this news. It was over, it was finally over, she thought exultantly. Relief that she would no longer be subject to Jamie's tutelage vied with eagerness to pay off a few scores. Betsy would be bending for her rod, to name but one, just as soon as she ever got the chance.

'The wedding will be in April,' Lady Alicia continued, smiling broadly. 'Clara will stay with us, in new and more salubrious accommodations until then.' The dark beauty turned her near-black eyes on Amelia. 'You, my dear, I suspect, would like to get away from here.'

There was truth in that. Amelia had accounts to pay, it was true, but it was hard to forget that most of Hatherby had seen her naked, humiliated, and in bondage. It might be altogether better to begin, elsewhere, anew.

'A change,' she said cautiously, 'might be... appropriate.'

'Splendid,' Lady Alicia clapped her hands together delightedly. 'Then it is settled. You see, Amelia, we have some marvellous news. One of the girls on the Reverend Dawes's little course has had to cancel, and guess what?'

Amelia did not need to guess. Her stomach had turned into a churning fist. She seemed to have lost the power of speech altogether. There was a thunderous pounding in her temples, as if all the huntsmen of Hades were galloping her down.

'That means that there is a place for you.'

'You see, m'dear,' Lord Alex put in with a mischievous grin, 'we don't feel you have really learnt your lesson yet.'

'I'm afraid that my best efforts have failed.' Jamie shook his head regretfully. 'You still need taking down a peg or three.'

'And if I know Richard Dawes,' Lady Alicia said with a steely smile, 'he is just the man to do it. Six months of really rigorous discipline at the Rectory ought to do the trick.'

Amelia felt the world spin around her. She looked in turn at the faces around the table. Lady Alicia smiled steadily at her, Lord Alex had returned to his paper, and Jamie and Clara were staring idiotically into one another's eyes.

Amelia opened her mouth to protest, but no words would come. Six months, under that man's rule! The prospect made her dizzy with fear. When she finally managed to speak it was a desperate, terrified question. 'Wh-wh-when?' she stuttered at last. Just as she got the word out, Lucy bustled in.

Lady Alicia looked at the maid enquiringly.

'The Reverend Dawes's coach, ma'am. It's arrived for Miss Amelia.'

The world spun around Amelia and she fainted dead away.

Thanks for reading!

Damsels in Distress

'Get on your knees.' He enforced the order by pressing on her shoulder, and then Rose watched as if hypnotised as he unbuttoned his fly, his fingers working mere inches from her face, and then the thing he withdrew made her belly churn with panic...

Here we have eleven tales of damsels in distress; tales inspired by the ageless allure of peril, pain and pleasure.

Chivalry is in short supply when captive Eleanor must serve Sir Peris's dark desires and those of his malevolent dwarf!

A sacrificial virgin is saved from birch-wielding Druids; but what fate do her Roman rescuers have in store for her...?

Victorian maids are flogged and debauched by cruel aristocratic employers, whilst a pretty widow is blackmailed by a sinister schoolboy...

And even modern times bring scant respite for our poor damsels in distress, as pretty girls are stripped and whipped for their perverted masters' pleasure.

Rectory of Correction

Bella reached out the cane and used the tip to lift Linnet's chin until their gazes met. 'I am going to spank you, little Linnet. I am going to spank you very hard, because - well, because I want to, and because I can. After that, these other two bitches will want to play some games with you, I expect, but they will have to wait their turns. Let her go, girls. Get up, Linnet, and take your blouse off. Then I would like you to come and put yourself over my knee...'

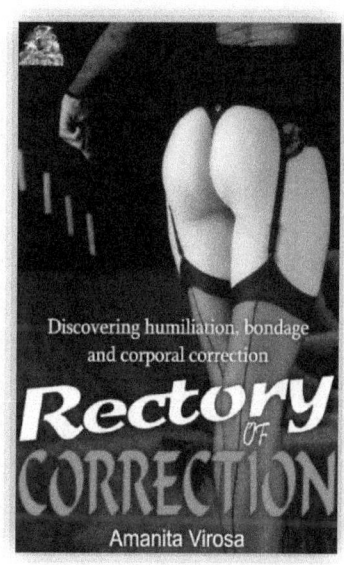

Escape from the humiliations of Hope Hall brings no respite for the lovely Amelia Colinbrooke. To her horror, Amelia is obliged to attend a special disciplinary course for wayward young ladies, devised by the Reverend Richard Dawes - the infamous 'chastising chaplain' of Hatherby, a man who brings a truly missionary zeal to the task of thrashing pretty, nubile girls.

Amelia and the other trembling trainees soon discover that bitter humiliation, excruciating bondage, and searing corporal correction, are not so much features of the Reverend's training programme, as their entire new way of life. Dawes takes a particular interest in Amelia.

Can Colinbrooke pride resist the rigour of his rod? Or will the whip finally break Amelia and her fair companions to absolute submission to the will of the diabolical Reverend Dawes...?